Lost Bells Farm

By

Gabriel Hernandez Ramón

New Generation Publishing

Dedication

In memory of my father

Ballad of the Little Square

My heart of silk
Is filled with lights,
with lost bells,
with lilies and Bees.
I will go very far
father than those hills,
father than the seas
Close to the stars,
to beg Christ the Lord
to give back the soul I
had when I was a child,
ripened with legends,
with a feathered cap
and a wooden sword.

Federico Garcia Lorca (1898 – 1936)

Prologue

My name is Sebastián Gonzalo Alvarez, and I have a tale to tell. A long time ago, when I was very young and living in Argentina, I did a stupid thing. I destroyed other people's lives, and I sent my own on a tangent which I could never have imagined. For the next twenty years, I used someone else's name. I hid from my past, and I lived a lie.

What do you do when the things you have done are irreversible? Do you stay and face the consequences, taking full responsibility for your actions? Do you subject yourself to the judgment and wrath of your community, your family, and society? Or do you run?

Me? I ran away. But you can't run forever, and you can never really hide. In the end, things catch up with you.

I won't start with what I did. I don't want you to judge me right from the beginning. I'll come to all that later. I'm going to begin near the end, in a hospital in Kabul, Afghanistan, after I was nearly killed in the fighting there. From there I'll work my way back to the beginning. I shall try to recall every thing as accurately as I can, and I promise to stick to the truth.

This is my story.

Chapter One

French Military Field Hospital, Kabul, 2004

My hair is unwashed and dirty, as are my hands and fingernails. Blood and dirt from the deep wound to my temple has dried solid, sealing the lids of my left eye shut. It's like mortar holding brickwork together. There's no chance of opening it. Both lids on that eye are badly bruised, and the whole area is swollen.

Outside, in the dark, it is snowing heavily. The army doctor examining me is a pretty officer. She looks to be in her early thirties. She tells me she's from Paris. Her blonde hair is tied back with a purple felt band.

I remember her hazel eyes, and the epaulettes on the shoulders of her desert-patterned combat uniform. I can't remember now if she has told me her name or not. I've just woken up. I'm confused and in pain.

She stands with her thighs pressed against the bed. I can feel them through the thin mattress.

"I'm going to get one of the nurses to help you open your injured eye in a couple of days. Okay?" she says. "But don't worry about it now. I'm sure it's fine. It will take a little coaxing open with some warm water and cotton wool, but anyway, I would like the swelling to come down first."

Turning away from her, I stare at the ceiling. Partly because of the pain I am in but also because I don't like the way she used the word *injured*.

"I'm not *injured*, Doctor. I have been wounded."

She tilts her head to one side like a puppy, a quizzical look drawn over her face in lines across her brow. I look back at her with my one good eye. "Injuries are accidental. These are *wounds*. Wounds are what someone else does to you. Someone did this to me on purpose. It wasn't an accident."

She sighs, because she's tired.

"Of course," she says. She reaches for a pencil torch in her trouser pocket and leans over me. I smell her breath, like summer hay, as she whispers softly, "I'm just going to have a look in your functioning eye. Look over my shoulder at the fan in the ceiling, please."

She shines a white lance of light into my right eye as I focus on the still blades of the fan. They remind me of the rotor-blades on the helicopter that picked me up from that deadly mountain pass and brought me here the day before. Moments later, she clicks off the torch. Then she pulls back the sheets so she can have a look at the dressing covering my left hip.

She replaces the sheets, then looks into my eye.

"Where are you from?" she asks.

"I'm from Patagonia."

"I remember reading about Patagonia when I was a child. I used to think it was a fairytale place." She slides her torch into the breast pocket of her uniform as I shift on the bed in an attempt at getting comfortable. The bed is too narrow and short for me. Trying to get comfortable in it would be difficult under normal circumstances, but I'm in a fair amount of pain from the wounds I sustained in the ambush yesterday near the Uzbin Valley. It's not only the width and length of the bed that is so uncomfortable. I feel like I'm too far off the ground to be safe, somehow.

"Sometimes I think that myself these days," I say.

"Why's that?"

"It seems so far away now. And anyway, so much has happened to me that it might as well not exist at all. But yes, it's a real place. It's part of southern Argentina, and I am from there."

This young doctor is the first person I have told in fourteen years that my homeland is Patagonia. Until now I have simply told anyone who was interested that I am from Argentina. If pressed, I will say that I'm from the capital, Buenos Aires, or Argentina's second city, Cordoba.

"Well, you are certainly a long way from home," says the doctor.

"Aren't we all?" I say.

"Yes, I suppose so."

She reaches over my head to the metal frame of the bed, a strand of blonde hair falling over her hazel eyes, whilst she unhooks a grey cylindrical pump with a plunger and places it in my right hand.

"I'm giving you morphine for your pain. Okay? You self-administer with this. It's on a timer so you can't overdose, but you can make yourself a bit more comfortable. Just push down here at the top with your thumb."

A tube leads from the bottom of the pump to a needle inserted into the basilic vein of my right arm. It's held in place with a piece of white tape.

"Can I have some now?" I ask. I'm embarrassed to be showing weakness in front of her. But it hurts.

"Of course," she smiles. "Just press down once, all the way until the plunger stops."

I press the plunger, and the machine it is attached to lets out two short electronic beeps in quick succession.

"That's right," she says. "Just like that"

I breathe out and sigh in anticipation of the comfort promised by the doctor and the drug.

"Do you have access to the casualty list?" I ask. I'm concerned about the fate of my colleague and friend, Martin Bruchard. The last time I saw him he was climbing into the back of a truck with his weapon in his hand, shortly before we left our compound. That was yesterday.

The doctor reaches out, stroking my close-cropped

hair lightly from back to front with her fingertips.

"A few men died yesterday. Some are still being worked on. I don't have a casualty list. I'm sorry. This whole war thing is sad, but you are going to be all right. You will be back in France very soon."

Feeling soothed by the doctor, I allow myself to settle. I will find out soon enough if my friend has survived. As I let my head sink into the pillow, she straightens my bedclothes and smiles again.

"You'll probably sleep until morning."

"Thank you, Doctor."

She leaves, and I try to relax. Perhaps it is because I'm hurt, maybe it is the morphine, or it could be because I only have less than a year's service to do in the Legion, but after the doctor has gone I have only one thing on my mind - and that is home. I am fully aware that because of the wrong turns I took so long ago, I really don't have a home. Nevertheless, as a platinum moon shines through the window of the ward in this troubled land, my mind travels back over the years and across the miles to another time and place.

The human mind is a wonderful thing. Not being constructed of physical material, thoughts have no mass or matter and therefore take no time to travel.

Within a nanosecond I am a continent and a lifetime away from Afghanistan and its wretched war. I'm back in Black River Province Argentina, the place where I was born and raised; the place where I spoke my own language amongst my countrymen every day.

The dreams I once had for my life were conceived there, without me ever thinking that they would be stillborn. It was there that I enjoyed the company of childhood friends, familiar surroundings, an older brother, a girlfriend and a family; reference points that both comforted and confirmed me, even though I never really appreciated them until they were well and truly gone.

The morphine wraps its arms around me and I surrender to its warm fug as the stars outside my window prick holes in the ink black sky. The needle pumping tranquillity into my body pierces the tattooed skin of my right forearm. The emblem, pricked into my twenty-one-year-old skin after serving in the first Gulf war of 1991, depicts the flaming grenade badge of the French Foreign Legion. Underneath that, four words inscribed in my skin forever:

Je ne regrette rien.

The tattoo tells a lie. It tells a lie, because whilst I genuinely regret nothing since joining the Foreign Legion, I cannot say the same about things before that. Before that, I regret a lot.

The morphine is doing its work. Instead of the shabby ceiling of the French military facility in Kabul, my mind's eye gazes up at a vivid blue horizon stretching over the Argentine Lake District and my far-away home.

Chapter Two

Rio Negro Province, Argentine Patagonia

We used to ride Criollo horses back then, my girlfriend Tania and I. Sure-footed, chestnut and dun-coloured, Criollos are descendants of the horses brought to the new world by Christopher Columbus in 1492.

The animals we rode belonged to Tania's father, Bruno. He bred Criollos on his ranch by a river in a wide valley, surrounded by spectacular mountain peaks.

Whenever Tania and I got the chance, we would saddle up and head into the Patagonian outback for a couple of days to camp and fish, perhaps shoot a partridge or a hare and cook it over the fire. We went to get away from town, our parents and the cops.

The world we attempted to lose ourselves in was one of extensive forests and deep blue lakes. Ancient beech trees, Arrayan pine, cypress and red willows stretched for miles, in forests cut through by swiftly flowing rivers rushing down from the mountains.

Riding Western-style, in deep leather saddles and with our reins held loosely, we would stuff our saddle bags with Spanish ham, cheese, fruit, canned fish, bread, and wine. Cantering deep into the back woods and wild lands, we found freedom and space. We went because it felt good and because we could.

We lived at the end of the world and it felt like it. Our town, San Carlos de Bariloche, lay in the eastern rain shadow of the mighty Andes, on the shores of Lake Nauhel Huapi.

First settled in the late 19th century by Swiss and German pioneers, many of Bariloche's buildings closely resemble those of Switzerland and Bavaria.

To the west of town, the almost impenetrable snow-covered Cordilleras scraped the sky 18,000 ft above the Argentine/Chilean frontier. To the east, the Patagonian desert stretched all the way to the freezing shores of the South Atlantic Ocean. To the north was the vast expanse of natural grasslands known as the pampas, and south, nothing but empty land and silent skies all the way to the end of the world.

I grew up on the edge of the town centre. I suppose you'd call it *suburbia*. My family and I shared a modest bungalow, three blocks back from the lake on the corners of Morales and Belgrano Street. There were my parents, me, and my older brother Raul.

The front lawn of our home ran down to the sidewalk, where a Post Box stood on the corner next to the grass. Our back yard was dominated by a 100 foot monkey puzzle tree.

During the summer it cast a cooling shadow over the barbecue area outside the patio doors, and in winter, thick mounds of marshmallow snow would cover its branches. Then it took on the appearance of a Himalayan Yeti, sneaking up on the house from behind.

When I was very young my parents would tease Raul and I about the "Yeti" in the garden. While we played in the snow as a family they would suddenly shout,

"Look out you two! The *Yeti's* coming to get you!" At once, Raul and I would pretend to panic, before scooping up Snowballs and throwing them at the 'Yeti'.

Then we would tear back to the safety of the house as our father roared and Mamma screamed behind us.

Once inside, my mother would make us 'Submarinos'; tall glasses of warm milk with a bar of melting dark chocolate sunk inside. While we stirred the chocolate round and round the glass as it slowly turned the milk a rich brown, Pappa would put extra logs on the fire to warm us up.

My father had a job with the local council and my mother worked part time in a florist's shop on San Martin, which was the main street running through town.

Every day until lunch time Mamma worked in the shop, preparing bouquets and organising the sprays of flowers in the window. In the afternoons she would shop for food, look after the house, and cook for us all.

Morales Street was just two blocks back from San Martin, so my mother would always walk to work. Every day she came home with fresh flowers for the house. Arum lilies were her favourite, although she liked roses too. Our house always had fresh flowers.

My parents had left rural Asturias on the Atlantic coast of Spain in the 1960s. Along with many other Spaniards, they were escaping the Franco regime of the time. Ironically, by 1976 they found themselves living under another military dictatorship in Argentina anyway. That was the year that the elected Government was ousted in a bloodless coup and replaced by a military junta.

By then Raul and I had been born, so I guess time and circumstance blocked my parents' way home. However, irrespective of events beyond their control throughout Latin America, they carried on with life as it was and concentrated on their work and family.

Chapter Three

When I was nine years old, everything in my life changed when my mother got sick and died. Then there were no more flowers in our house, and I began to get into trouble.

Bursting with energy and full of pain, I remember skipping school, breaking windows and stealing from shops. By the time I had entered my teenage years I was hanging out with all the wrong kids, and much to my father's disappointment I formed a gang. Trouble became my second name.

My girlfriend Tania and I met at school; we started going out with each other when we were fifteen. Her forefathers were Swiss and had arrived in Patagonia with the first settlers in the early 1800s. The exception was her Russian grandfather who had landed in Argentina as a merchant seaman following World War II.

After jumping ship he found work in Patagonia before settling down alongside some of the German Nazis he had fought back in Europe not so long before. I got to know him as he helped Tania and I groom the horses and clean out the stables at the Bauman's ranch. Through conflict, the old man had found peace.

"Never hold a grudge, boy," he would say whenever I asked him about the war. "Forgive and move on; live for tomorrow."

The Bauman ranch was a low-slung structure built of native Arrayan pine. It seemed to have grown from the land, like the white lantern trees that shaded it from the summer sun and protected it from the winter winds.

Each spring, Chilean swallows would arrive from Bolivia to nest under its low, wide eaves. Swooping and darting around the veranda in flashes of delicate blue, they would appear on the wing as the pristine blooming flowers of the lantern trees burst into a round of applause at their return.

Tania's mother Maria grew dog-roses around the front steps of the ranch house, and silver-beaked spectacle birds would knock drowsy butterflies from their tops to gorge on the insects inside.

Yellow Siskins flew from shrub to shrub around the unkempt lawn, whilst lavender and sage bushes grew here and there.

As well as breeding Criollos, Tania's father grew apples and plums on two hundred acres of land in the fertile valley; a land with soil so rich that for the previous hundred years of farming, the use of fertilisers had been completely unnecessary. Bruno Bauman was proud of his ranch, his horses, and his land.

"You could spit a pip out on the ground here, and I swear a damned tree would grow," he enjoyed telling anyone who would listen.

He also grew the raspberries that went into the jam that was sold in town to day-trippers from Chile. Coming over the border by the coach load they would enjoy the scenery of the Lake District, buying chocolate, ice cream, and waffles.

The endless skies of electric blue made the awe-struck tourists gasp as they gazed up at clouds of lace brushing the stratosphere, like angels in the grip of a jet stream that would have been invisible without them. The air, like the rivers we crossed and drank from, was refreshing and vitalising.

Unlike the tourists, Tania and I found Bariloche tedious. Our favourite thing back then was to get out of town on horseback. We would spend most of the day riding into the wilderness, before finding a place to camp next to a lake or river a couple of hours before dusk. This way, we could unpack our gear and start a fire before the fish began their evening feeding activities, hopefully biting onto one of my lures.

Whenever I got lucky, Tania would shout in delight, "Well done, Sebastián!"

Clapping her hands in the sunshine, she laughed as I pulled a fat wriggling trout from the glacial melt waters

I would directly clean the fish, stuff it with herbs and bacon, sprinkle it with salt and pepper, and put it into a pan over the flames. Once cut in two and on our plates, we would slice a lemon and drench the white flesh in the juice, knowing there wasn't a restaurant anywhere in the world that could offer us a better dish at any price.

Later, when the sun went down, Tania would butter the bread and pour wine into tin mugs, as we filled up on cheese and ham before eating apples under the stars. Most nights whilst camping, we would play cards and talk about how life would be when we were older.

Sometimes Tania managed to steal a bottle of her grandfather's homemade blueberry vodka, and we would toast ourselves by the glow of the fire as the horses drank from the river.

At midnight, I enjoyed telling Tania horror stories by the firelight. Laughing and squealing at the same time, she would beg me to stop. Afterwards she always held on to me tightly as we fell asleep.

We both smoked marijuana, but never on our camping trips. We were already high enough. Racing through vast forests pierced by shards of brilliant sunlight and trees hung with moss, pulling large trout from rushing rivers, or catching a glimpse of a mountain lion carrying her cubs along a dry river-bed, were thrills enough on their own.

I remember Tania often galloping alongside me, reaching out to touch my fingertips.

"Sebastián, I feel like I'm flying!" she would shout.

Laughing freely, I would shout back excitedly, "We *are* flying, Tania! We *are* flying!"

Back in town, it was a different matter. There we smoked pot and hung out with my gang. We never did anything too heavy, but we were no angels either. We entertained ourselves by joyriding in cars and selling and smoking marijuana.

Mostly, though, we spent our time hanging around and breaking the local bylaws relating to drinking in public. To the casual observer, we were troublesome 'local types'. Wearing heavy metal t-shirts and ripped jeans, we sneered at people in general.

Tania and I always laughed between ourselves about being seen as local types. We knew we behaved like that because we felt frustrated and trapped, but we had no intention of staying that way. We didn't even really like heavy metal.

Most of the kids in our gang lived on the poorer fringes of town, or in the ramshackle barrio a couple of kilometres out of Bariloche and out of sight of the tourists. They had Mapuche Indian blood in them and spoke a type of Creole that we emulated.

I say emulated, because of course Tania and I were both of direct European stock. Unlike most of our fellow malcontents in the gang, neither Tania or I could claim ancestral blood roots in Latin America, but we both felt a deep connection to the land of our birth and saw ourselves as proud Argentines.

One Saturday morning in 1987, when I was sixteen, the local Gendarmerie commandant, a man named Calvo, called at our house. I saw him through the living room window as he walked up the driveway to the front door. I couldn't help smiling as he failed to dodge the water sprinkler on the front lawn on his way past the flowerbeds.

The Argentine National Gendarmerie is the

paramilitary force charged with the defence of Argentina's borders and most aspects of its internal security. Commandant Calvo was a friend of my father's, and whilst I was sure I hadn't done anything to warrant a visit from him concerning matters of a criminal nature, I still felt paranoid as I answered the door.

"Afternoon, Commandant Calvo," I smiled nervously.

Standing in the doorway, Calvo smiled back as he brushed his hand over the newly damp patch on the shoulder of his uniform.

"Sebastián, why don't you come with me for a drive, eh?"

"Have I done something wrong, Commandant Calvo?"

"It's alright," said Calvo. "You're not in any trouble, I'd like to show you something, though; come on."

With my paranoia replaced by curiosity, I slipped on a pair of sneakers and followed Calvo back down the driveway to his patrol car.

Calvo knew my father through his connections with the local Round Table and the council. Consequently my brushes with the law had never ended too seriously and, despite a few nights in the cells, I was never actually charged with a crime.

Once in Calvo's car, the Commandant drove me fifteen kilometres out of town to Bariloche Airport. Once there we got out of the vehicle, passed straight through security, and walked out onto the Airfield. Calvo led me over to the Gendarmeries' helicopter parked on the helipad. I was totally thrilled by the aircraft. Just standing next to it was exciting.

"What do you think, Sebastián?" said Calvo as he lit a cigarette.

"It's amazing, Commandant Calvo; can I get in?"

"Sure…"

Calvo opened the chopper's door and allowed me to climb inside. As I explored the controls he walked around the aircraft, opened the other door and climbed in. Sitting beside me in the co-pilot's seat, Calvo took a drag on his cigarette, then turned to me.

"You know, Sebastián," he said, "there is only so much your father can do to stop you getting into real trouble with the local cops if you stick with that gang of yours." Letting go of the helicopter's joystick, I turned to the commandant.

"I know, Commandant Calvo," I said sheepishly.

Calvo flicked his cigarette out through the chopper's open window, then looked across the cockpit at me.

"What are you going to do with your life, Sebastián; don't you think its time to start making the right choices?" he said.

Looking down, I took the helicopter's joystick in my hand again.

"Do you think if I worked hard enough and stayed in school for two more years I could join the Gendarmeria and fly one of these, Commandant?"

"Of course, Sebastián; but you have to stay out of trouble," Calvo replied kindly. "Imagine it; you *could* actually fly one of these."

I looked out of the cockpit window to the snow-capped mountains beyond. At that moment, something about sitting in that cockpit holding the joystick in my hand felt right. I can't explain fully, but I felt something inside of me which I had never felt before. I guess it was potential.

A fantasy stirred inside me; the fantasy of freedom and flight, and in minutes it was alive. The thought of putting thousands of metres of fresh air between me and the world I lived in gave birth to a dream that I was determined to pursue. Calvo's voice invaded my fantasy.

"I'll make a deal with you, Sebastián," he said. "If you keep out of trouble and get good enough grades in school for the next two years, I'll happily give you a reference if you want to apply for the Gendarmeria Academy in Buenos Aires, when you're eighteen."

It was a deal. From that day on I never skipped school, got good grades, and tried as hard as I could to keep on the straight and narrow around town.

Chapter Four

Two years after my trip to the airport with Commandant Calvo, I had managed to get the required grades from school to be eligible for entry to the Gendarmeria as an officer candidate.

Then, with a little string pulling from my exasperated father and Commandant Calvo, at the age of eighteen I secured a place at the Escuela de Gendarmes in Buenos Aires.

Even though I was anti-establishment, I desperately wanted a career as a helicopter pilot and I saw the Gendarmerie as a way of achieving that goal.

The training for officer candidates in the Gendarmeria Nationale was a three-year programme. The policing aspects of the course were conducted at the force's own academy in Buenos Aires, whilst military elements took place at the National Military Academy at Campo de Mayo, outside the city.

On arrival in Buenos Aires, I very quickly realised that my attitude would have to change drastically if I was going to make the transition from angry rebel to someone mature and responsible enough to be trusted behind the controls of a government-owned aircraft.

Much to my surprise, this was not to be as difficult for me as one might have expected. The ranks of military and law enforcement organisations in all countries tend to be filled with men who have never really grown up. The opportunity to dress up in uniforms and use guns is just an extension of the games they played as children.

I took pride in keeping my weapon and uniforms in good condition. I had found something I enjoyed, and I was getting paid to do it. Relishing the feelings of identity and acceptance that came with being part of the Gendarmeria, I also worked hard on the academic elements of the course.

During leave periods from the Academy, I would return to San Carlos de Bariloche. Then Tania and I would eat dinner at a restaurant, lie in bed all morning, and go horse-riding in the woods.

"I miss you so much, Sebastián, when you are away," she would tell me. "I just can't wait until we can be together all the time."

My career choice had opened up a yawning chasm between myself and my old gang mates, not to mention between them and Tania. Now they would stare defiantly at me from across the street whenever I saw them around town. I responded with dignified indifference. I was a sell out; they knew it, and I knew it. Deep down, though, I was just surviving life like everyone else.

Opportunity had thrown me a lifeline, a chance to get away and become a pilot instead of a taxi driver or a supermarket manager. I took it, that's all.

Sometimes, when I was home on leave, Tania's mother would telephone to invite me over to their ranch for dinner.

"Sebastián, I've made peppered beef and pumpkin stew with peaches and sweet potatoes. Why don't you come over and eat with us?" she would say.

Sitting around the kitchen table with Tania's twin brother, Ignacio, in front of a roaring open fire, I enjoyed telling them about my training and experiences with the Gendarmerie, as large snowflakes fell gently like paper doilies outside the window.

During cold winter nights under warm blankets, and on spring mornings full of birdsong and hope, Tania and I made plans for our future. Being full of energy and youth, dreams of better tomorrows coursed through our systems like wild salmon rushing upstream, motivated by nothing other than instinct.

It was through Tania that I had my first experience of love. She was the same age as me, though much more advanced. I remember spending rainy Saturdays alone with her in the compact, single-roomed apartment over the stables at the Bauman ranch.

Dressed in a rugby shirt, panties, and socks, she taught me to drink vodka and blow smoke rings to the sounds of Bob Dylan and treacle-sweet jazz; both habits which she had picked up from her Russian grandfather.

One autumn afternoon in 1989, we lay cosily together in bed under an Alpaca skin blanket. Below us in the stables the horses snorted, restlessly stomping at the ground as a cold rain lashed against the apartment window.

Rolling over and yawning, Tania pressed her warm body against mine as she swept her hair away from her face and behind her ear.

"I want to get away from here some day, Sebastián," she said quietly. "There's a whole world outside this valley and I want to see it."

"Me too," I said. "I'm going to graduate from the Escuela de Gendarmes with good grades and become a pilot if I can. Everything's going to work out fine, you'll see."

The steady rhythm of the rain drumming against the window provided an easy accompaniment to the music of Joni Mitchell as Tania spoke dreamily of future possibilities. "We could go anywhere," she said. "Buenos Aires, Cordoba. Even Mendoza with the mountains close by would be fine, but I would love to live in Buenos Aires." Looking out of the window next to the bed, I stroked her hair.

"I'm thinking the same way. I don't want to end up like the others in town. There's more to me than that," I said.

Crossing her soft leg over mine, Tania kissed me gently on the mouth.

"I believe in you, Sebastián; you can do anything," she whispered, her silky words embracing me as the rain increased its relentless demands against the window pane.

What I loved about Tania was her ability to see, talk, and think beyond. She was beautiful and clever; a lot smarter than me. With a sharp and enquiring mind, she had taught herself to speak English fluently simply by watching American movies and listening to records.

I admired her capacity to rely on her brains and talents, not just her physical beauty, to give her a sense of completeness. I loved her very much and wanted nothing more than for us to spend the rest of our lives together.

The plan, like most plans made in the first flush of youth, was simple. I would graduate from the Academy as a sub-lieutenant; we would get married and have children. If I excelled in my studies and duties I would go to flight school and become a helicopter pilot with the force. Life would be good.

I had much to prove to her parents, and much to make up for with my own father. As my mother had died, I guess I had to do things for her too. After all, my father had always told me as a child how disappointed she would have been if I didn't make something of myself.

"Think of your poor mother, Sebastián, when you behave the way you do," he would often say. I could never find a way of telling him that my pain over her passing and the jagged gaping wound it left in me could never be healed by "succeeding" at anything.

Burying his own pain beneath his job with the local council and his activities with the Round Table, my father carried on as best he could; my brother Raul side-stepped his own hurt by focusing on and gaining his academic qualifications. He then immersed himself in his studies at university. Eventually, he graduated as a dentist.

By the time I had completed the first two years of the three-year course at the Academy, I was in a pretty stable place in my life. Tania discovered that she had become pregnant during one of my visits home in October 1989, and we quickly decided to get married in the summer of 1990.

We would tell our families of our news and of the baby when Tania was three months gone and the pregnancy firmly established. The future seemed promising. My father was treating me as an adult, and Tania's father was also coming around to the idea that perhaps I wasn't the wayward rogue that would surely drag his beloved daughter down into the gutter after all. Life was good, and things were looking up.

But that was before I did the things I did. You see, that was before I went and ruined it all and caused so much pain to so many people.

That was before I made the choices that led to the mistakes that I could never take back, and broke the hearts and dreams of the people that made up my world. Because the things I did meant I would never graduate and never train as a pilot.

Tania and I would never get married and build a home. Never again would we laugh over dinner, sip blueberry vodka by a campfire, or pass a sunday morning making love in the single bed of the tiny apartment above the stables on her father's ranch. The mistakes I made at the age of nineteen years old meant that I would not be around for Tania and our baby.

In fact I would run away, leave Patagonia, and never go back.

Chapter Five

Djibouti, East Africa, 2003

Sitting behind my desk late one afternoon at Camp Lemonier barracks, I fingered a white envelope with an Argentine stamp in the top right-hand corner. Beads of sweat trickled down my back, running between my shoulder blades. Nearly a decade and a half had passed since I had gone on the run.

It was the first letter I had received from home in thirteen years. It had been sent from Buenos Aires to the Legion Headquarters in Aubangne, just outside Marseilles. Someone had forwarded it to me where I was presently serving, with the Legion's 13th Demi Brigade on the horn of Africa, but not before correcting the address from Legionnaire Alvarez to Acting Adjutant Alvarez.

As the fan above my head stirred the thick heat around the room, I took a fighting knife from the desk drawer and cut the envelope open in one smooth action. Then I pulled out the letter that had last been touched by the hands of my brother, in the country I had run away from thirteen years earlier.

In words void of emotion, my brother informed me that our grandmother had died some months previously, and that in her will she had left her farmhouse in the northern Spanish Principality of Asturias to our father. I absorbed the information without any feelings. Besides, it was offered without any.

The letter went on to inform me that my brother had married, started a family, and was running a very successful dentistry practice in Buenos Aires. Our father had passed the farmhouse on to him. He also explained the he had no interest in the property, as he was deeply involved in his work and family.

He went on to say that he assumed I was still a serving soldier with the French Foreign Legion if I had managed not to "fuck that up as well", so I should either stay exactly where I was for as long as possible, or make good use of our grandparents' house in Europe. He also made it quite clear that there was a prison cell waiting for me at home. As if I needed telling.

Nothing Raul said had any effect on me. My sensitivities in that regard had been eroded long since. Bosnia saw to that, Iraq, and the jungle too; and all the rest of it, for that matter.

It was as if the horrors I had seen as a soldier of fortune for France had erased any potential I had for feeling sadness over past mistakes.

Raul rounded off by giving me the contact details of a lawyer in the Asturian capital, Oviedo. The lawyer would only need to see documentation in my brother's name to hand over the keys to the property.

Raul said that if I did ever decide to live at the farm, then I could probably do so without any chance of a connection being made between myself and the authorities at home. According to him, I had left a cold trail behind me years ago in Argentina, and no-one would be looking for me in Spain or anywhere else.

Putting the letter back in the envelope and opening the desk drawer, I dropped the envelope inside.

I walked over to the thin metal locker in the corner of my office, removed my khaki shirt, and replaced it with a clean fresh one. The pleats running down its back were crisply ironed and evenly spaced. The epaulettes adorning the shoulders stood out above the six medal ribbons lying in a line two over four above the left breast pocket. Between my ribbons and the epaulettes, I wore the metal jungle Commando Badge which I had earned eleven years previously in the green hell of the French Guyana rain forest.

Two braided lanyards hung from my left shoulder, their metal tips resting by my medal ribbons. Each lanyard signified the completion of five years' service with the Legion.

I tucked the shirt into my dark green trousers, and replaced the blue cummerbund around my waist. Turning to look in the full-length mirror by the door, I gave my black shoes a quick shine with the soft brush on the stand at its base.

I had a little business to attend to over at the guardroom by the main entrance to the barracks. I was expecting a delivery.

As I reached for the door handle, the phone on my desk rang. It was Corporal Stein in the guardroom, phoning to inform me that the lads from the kitchen had returned in the truck with the goats I had sent them to buy from the locals.

I was organising an Argentine-style barbecue the following day for a group of Djiboutian officials and officers of the local police and army. The fires in the compound were built and ready to go, the beers were chilling in the kitchen cold rooms, and now the meat had arrived. I wanted to go and have a look at them before they were given some water and a last meal.

Taking my black *kepi* from the wooden hook on the back of the door and placing it on my head, I walked out into the dry African heat and along the path to the tarmac road leading out of the base.

When I arrived at the main gate, I found the troops from the guardroom huddled by the back of the open tailgate of the truck. With their white kepis gleaming in the sun, they resembled a bunch of snowdrops as they chatted and smoked with the lads from the kitchen. At my approach, they smartened up and saluted.

"Right - stand back and let me have a look at the

goods!" I shouted.

Everyone stepped aside as I hauled myself up into the rear of the vehicle and grabbed the fidgety goats by their flanks. Standing astride each one and holding them by the horns, I checked to see that their eyes and noses were free of discharge or infection.

"Good goats!" I said.

Standing in the doorway of the guardroom, Corporal Stein held his nose.

"These guys were gone a long time; they must have pulled over on the way back and raped 'em all. They look traumatised!" he said. Everyone laughed, then laughed again when I said,

"Jealousy will get you nowhere, Corporal, but I will be sure to send you to buy the goats next time, if you promise to wear a condom."

Stein pulled a face.

"There probably aren't any left. This lot just used them all," he retorted in a futile attempt at saving face, before retreating into the shade of the guardroom. Jumping down from the back of the truck, I brushed the animal hairs from the insides of my trousers.

"Right, you lot, take them to the compound and make sure they have water. I'm going to kill them in the morning. Then you will put them over the heat like I'm going to show you." I left them with the animals and walked back to the accommodation block under a fierce sun.

No sooner had I walked into my room and begun to undress than my friend, Chief Sergeant Martin Bruchard, knocked and let himself in.

"Sebastián!" he beamed. "Are you going to get that bottle of Pernod out, and we'll have a quick drink to remind us of civilisation?" I laughed.

"Sure, Martin, but I'm tired. You know where everything is. Shut the door and do the honours. I need to relax."

Martin poured out two measures of Pernod from the bottle on top of my little fridge in the corner of the room. Then he handed me a glass and a carafe of cold water, and sat down. Kicking off my shoes, I sat back on my bed and propped myself up against the white wall with a pillow behind my back.

"Fuck, I want to get back to France, Martin. I'm sick of this place."

Martin took a sip of Pernod, and shrugged.

"Don't we get sick of everywhere they send us? That's what being in the Legion is all about, you know that. The jungle, Mururoa Atoll, here; then when you are in France too long, you crave a change and want some action. It's all about redemption, Sebastián; Redemption through suffering, my friend."

"I've suffered enough now. I want to get back to Nîmes, get around to Carole's place, and give her good seeing-to."

Carole was my girlfriend back in France. We had been seeing each other when time permitted for a year, and I was smitten with her.

"Sebastián, *I* want to get around to Carole's place and give her a good seeing-to as well! Anyway, you don't have long to wait now." We both laughed as he topped us both up with Pernod.

Martin lit a cigarette from a packet on my bedside table and offered me one. Our smoke rose in the heat before dipping and swirling as it was dispersed by the fan.

"Carole, Carole, Carole," I said slowly whilst watching the smoke in its airborne dance with its invisible partner. Martin winced.

"I'm off if you're going to get all soppy over her, mate. Did those goats arrive, by the way?"

"Yes, I'm killing them in the morning."

Martin downed his Pernod in one, then took a drag on his cigarette.

"Why don't you get the lads from the kitchen to do it? What's the point in having rank if you don't use it?"

"I'm doing it *because* I've got rank, that's why."

"And because you want to kill the goats..."

"And because maybe I've been with this outfit too long," I said. Martin smiled and stood up, stubbing out his cigarette in the ash tray on the table.

"Okay, Sebastián, thanks for the drink. Catch you later."

Tilting my head back against the wall, I blew out four smoke rings.

"Yeah, catch you later."

Martin paused, turning in the doorway.

"France next week!" he said with a broad grin. I took another drag on my cigarette.

"Yeah, France again; can't wait." He shut the door behind him, and I was alone again.

Chapter Six

Nîmes, France, Spring 2001

The first time I ever saw Carole, she was having a drink at a small bistro in Nîmes with a friend of hers. Martin and I had gone there one Friday evening after work.

As we grabbed the first table by the door, I caught sight of them both sitting on stools, sipping coffee at the bar. She was older than me, I guessed around forty, and sophisticated too. I was much taken with her stylish, low-cut top; her skirt just below the knee; her strawberry-blonde, shoulder-length hair, and green eyes.

It was her eyes, and the way they sparkled like emeralds, and the creases in the creamy skin around them that deepened when she smiled that got me.

Both she and her friend saw us walk in. Not that they could miss us. We were both in uniform, and as everyone else in the place was a civilian, we stuck out like a bulldog's bollocks, as they say. They glanced our way but made a show of ignoring us, and chatted on. We settled into our seats and ordered a couple of beers.

Martin noticed my distraction but said nothing as I stared spell-bound at the strawberry-blonde over his shoulder. He tried to engage me in a conversation about sport.

"Shame we are both on duty tomorrow, Sebastián," he began. "We could have gone to the Stade de Costieres to watch the game, eh?"

"Yes... well, there'll be other games, Martin, don't worry," I replied. But it was too late for him now, as I had already fallen under Carole's spell. We wouldn't be having a full conversation about anything now; not in the collaborative sense, anyway. I couldn't take my eyes off the exquisite creature at the bar: the way she tilted her head to one side when she laughed, the way she ran her fingers through her hair, the way she did absolutely everything.

"Martin," I said. "Look behind you; isn't that woman sat on the stool with the brunette stunning?"

"Fuck you, Sebastián. Don't you ever stop pussy-hunting; she's a bit on the old side isn't she?" I didn't answer him, but still, the Strawberry Blonde entranced me. Martin's voice quickly became distracting as I tried to make eye contact with the girls at the bar.

"You know, Sebastián, one thing I miss about Quebec and civilian life is Monday night football."

"Oh, really?"

"Yeah, really; getting in from work, sitting back in a Lazy Boy recliner with a six-pack of Molson dry, beer nuts, and chicken wings…"

"American football isn't my thing, really, Martin. I prefer soccer," I said. "It has more flow to it for me, more poetry and spontaneity."

"You know what I think, Sebastián?"

"What?"

"I think there's no point in talking to you about anything when you're on a pussy hunt; but if you're going for it I'll take the brunette, she's pretty hot."

"You're right, mate - fuck football. Keep me covered, I'm going in…" I said.

Martin smiled. "Remember, the brunette's mine…"

Soon enough, I was next to the girls at the bar without a single line or merry quip prepared.

"Hi girls, would you like to join my friend and I for a couple of drinks? We don't get out much," I said as I sidled up next to them.

Dropping her head, the brunette turned away and laughed whilst the strawberry-blonde looked me up and down coolly with a mild disdain.

"Haven't you got a war to fight somewhere?" she retorted.

"Done that, now I'm back. So I've got time to buy you two a drink and we can all get to know each other!" I laughed.

The brunette chuckled - at me, not with me - whilst the strawberry-blonde remained aloof. "I don't think we would have much in common, but thank you anyway," she said. Undeterred, I continued.

"I love girls like you; all hard on the outside and soft in the middle."

By that I meant that some women often develop a hard outer casing in order to protect that which they feel is soft and vulnerable in them. I always found women who followed this pattern of behaviour attractive. The challenge was always to break through the hard exterior.

Putting her coffee down on the bar, the strawberry-blonde crossed one leg over the other, and straightened her skirt as she turned on her barstool to look me square in the face.

"Well, soldier," she said, "I don't love people like you, and unless you have a Ph.D. like I have, then I doubt that we would have very much to talk about at all, don't you?"

Things weren't going my way at this point, but I was determined to turn the situation around, so I persevered.

"So, you know what I do for a living. What do you do?" I said.

She gave me a withering look.

"I'm a lecturer in history at the university."

"Okay," I said. "Ask me a question about anything at all, and if I get the answer right you two must come and have a drink with my friend and me. Deal?" I smiled. Her friend chirped up.

"I'm Celine, by the way, and this is Carole."

"Nice to meet you both; I'm Sebastián," I said, as I gave them both the most charming smile in my armoury.

"May I ask the question please? I like games!" said Celine. Carole seemed bored.

"Oh, do…" she said wearily. Celine turned to me with a playful look on her face.

"What's the chemical symbol for silver?" she asked.

"Ha ha, that's easy!" I laughed.

"Go on then… what is it?"

"Ag!"

Celine looked surprised.

"Are you a chemist as well as a soldier, or does the Foreign Legion give chemistry lessons these days?"

"No, I know that the chemical symbol for silver is Ag because I'm from the land of silver - Argentina," I said with satisfaction.

Carole reclaimed her coffee and carried on drinking it, without looking at me.

Taking a nonchalant sip of my Kronenburg, I tried to look as cool as I could.

"So, you'll honour our deal then and come and have a drink with us?" I said. Carole put her empty coffee cup back on the bar.

"Yes, okay, a drink," she said, as Celine beamed a naughty smile.

Looking impatiently at her watch, Carole got off her stool, and together with the mischievous Celine, she left the bar to join us at our table.

As soon as I had introduced Martin and the girls were seated, I ordered a plate of cold meats and cheeses with a bottle of red wine.

When Carole protested that they had only agreed to have a drink, I said that they definitely didn't seem like the kind of ladies who would be so rude as to just watch us as we ate.

The food arrived, and despite their initial reservations, the conversation flowed easily. Both women were seemingly fascinated by the company of two Foreign Legion sergeants, one from Argentina, the other a native of French-speaking Quebec.

Forgetting time altogether, we polished off the meats and cheese, then ordered a veal *blanquette* with wild mushrooms and a goats-cheese salad.

As one bottle was emptied the waitress brought another, and so on. Martin got pissed, reminding us time and again that he wasn't a Canadian but a Quebecois. Carole relaxed as I told her about the time I had visited the Colon Theatre in Buenos Aires; and about how it had originated in Paris, was dismantled there and then rebuilt in the Argentine Capital, brick by brick, during the early 1800s.

Celine drank like a fish, constantly reaching across the table to finger the medal ribbons on Martin's uniform, while I joked that he had bought them from a market stall in Marseilles. As we cleaned our plates with chunks of bread, Celine asked us how many languages we spoke.

"Just Spanish and French," I replied.

"Just French," said Martin.

"What? You are from North America and you don't speak English!" Carole enquired incredulously.

"I'm not a North American," Martin declared, "I am Quebecois! The English occupy our land, that's all. They go around the world taking what doesn't belong to them, but they never took our language."

"Yeah, the English took our islands, too," I said. "But I do believe I am an American. I'm a Latin American. I was born there. I don't feel Spanish, and I've never been to Spain."

As I emptied the last of the wine into the two

women's glasses, they said something to each other in English that I had no way of understanding. Martin glanced around the room blankly as the waitress approached with yet another bottle.

Celine and Martin were not alone in their excessive alcohol consumption that night. Soon after leaving the bistro as a foursome, Carole and I said goodnight to our friends before sliding into the back of a taxi.

Back at her flat, I did to her what I had wanted to do since I had first set eyes on her earlier in the evening. On the Persian rug in front of her cream living room sofa I slid my hands along her smooth thighs and up her skirt, before pulling down her knickers and fucking her hard against the floor.

Her mouth found mine and our tongues clashed as she broke out of her rusty cage. Opening her legs wide, she gripped my hips with her thighs, consuming me as I entered her with all the hunger of a man that has known loss, and loved living.

Later, as we lay together in her soft bed, I craned my neck to look at the framed picture hanging above us on the wall.

Lit by the light coming into the bedroom through the half-open door, the picture showed a man, covered in animal hair and with horns sprouting from his head. Cornered by a pack of hunting dogs, the man stood beside a lake verged with cypress and pine trees. At the edge of the lake stood a woman wearing a rose-coloured dress that left her right breast exposed. As the dogs savaged the man, the woman fired an arrow over the top of them at him.

"What does that picture mean?" I asked Carole,

"It's *The death of Actaeon,*" she whispered. "Don't ask me about it now; I'm sleepy."

As Carole fell asleep in my arms, I recalled how earlier in the evening I had lied to her and the others about visiting the Colon Theatre in Buenos Aires; how I had let them all believe that I was from that city and never once mentioned Black River Province or Patagonia.

Then I thought about Martin telling us of his disdain for all things English and pretending that he couldn't speak it, even though I knew full well that he could.

I realised then how hard it is to be honest, even with ourselves, when we are all so full of ego and insecurity. I felt sad to be lying there in a bed so far from home, trying desperately to not confront my past, because if I couldn't accept it then surely no-one else could. But that's how it started with Carole. I lied, and perhaps she did too. I stayed until the early hours.

Chapter Seven

Djibouti, East Africa, 2003

The 13th Demi Brigade is reinforced every six months with a company of soldiers from either the Second Foreign Infantry Regiment in Nîmes or one from the Second Foreign Parachute Regiment based in Corsica. With its harsh desert environment, Djibouti provides an excellent training ground for units from the whole of the French Army, and allows France to affirm its power and presence in the Gulf region of the Middle East.

For six months we had worked hard and trained hard. With only four desertions during the whole tour, we were ready for home, or whatever it was that any of us decided we wanted to call France.

The deserters had been 'recovered and retrained', and whilst they would be coming back to Europe with the rest of us they would not be enjoying a period of leave, and would be confined to the barracks upon our return.

The day after receiving my brother's letter, I got up before dawn and dressed in a tracksuit and trainers. Around my waist I wore a standard-issue bayonet secured in a scabbard attached to my belt. Over at the kitchen, my six-man barbecue team of five Legionnaires and one corporal were ready and waiting for me with coffee and cigarettes.

We passed ten minutes with the coffee, fags, and disposable chat before I took them over to the goats in the compound. As the sky turned pale grey over the compound walls, the goats nibbled happily on hay scattered around the dusty floor.

"Right, any one of you, go and grab a goat and bring it here. I want this all done in ten minutes flat," I said.

A young Turkish legionnaire named Turan was first

to catch a goat by the horns and bring it to me. Grabbing its curly horn with my left hand, I took charge of the struggling animal, securing it between my knees with its own legs facing away from me. Gripping the bayonet firmly in my right fist, I stuck it hard into the goat's lower neck.

The blade cut the goat's last cry short, covering my left thigh, right wrist, and hand with its warm blood, before I dropped the beast at my feet. Turan quickly picked up the twitching animal and carried it over to a tarpaulin spread on the earth a few feet away.

Ten minutes later, my hands, feet and tracksuit bottoms were all drenched in rich, sticky blood. When all the goats were dead I walked over to Corporal Stolt, who was standing with the lads next to the slain beasts.

"Give me a cigarette, Corporal," I said.

The Legionnaires stood around, looking down at the goats on the tarpaulin. Some of them smoked in silence, others muttered praise for my abilities with the bayonet. A couple affected indifference. I took a couple of drags on the cigarette, flicked its blood-soaked remnants into the dirt, and addressed the men.

"When you are told to kill, you just do it, okay? It's only blood."

Sucking my thumb, I spat blood in the dust, then spent the next three quarters of an hour preparing one of the goat carcasses as the Legionnaires copied my every move on the other goats with their own knives. Corporal Stolt started the three fires with his Zippo, then tended to them as I had instructed to him earlier.

Confident that the men would carry out my instructions, I returned to my room to change and shower before trying to call Carole in France. She didn't answer the phone. I went to breakfast, then to my office to finish some paper work relating to inventories, before rotating back to the regiment in

France. I was still feeling unsettled by my brother's letter, and I found it difficult to concentrate.

From time to time I got up from my chair, went to the office window, and glanced up at the African sky. I was itching to get back to France and a period of leave.

Chapter Eight

Return to France from Djibouti, 2003

The skies above Nîmes were fresh, cloudless, and blue. It was good to be returning from the heat of Djibouti after a full-on, six-month tour of duty with the Company. The sun was shining as students and locals alike mingled in its early rays, while the ancient Roman *Maison Caree* basked in the attention of tourists.

Nîmes began as a Roman colony around 28BC. The City was built along the route taken by the Emperor's Legions from Italy to Spain. In order to make the journey more easily, the Roman army built a road across what is now southern France in about 118 BC, calling it the Via Domitia.

They founded Nîmes roughly halfway along its length, on the edge of the fertile alluvial plain of the Vistrenque River. Here, in what was to become the Languedoc region of modern-day France, they built a city of communal baths, temples, gardens, and an amphitheatre that they completed in the first or second century AD, and which stands in the middle of town to this day.

Modern-day Nîmes is a vibrant city of museums, cafes, bars, and galleries. Rock concerts are staged within the walls of the amphitheatre.

During the summer months the city is gorged with tourists and locals alike, as its parks and gardens throb to the sounds of buskers, child's play, families, and guided walking tours. At night the air fills with the hum of traffic, and cigarette smoke mingles with the aromas of coffee and food. Strolling along the street, one hears bar music, loud, easy chat, and throngs of people letting their hair down.

We were all looking forward to a breather before recommitting to garrison life with the rest of the regiment. The fresh air of Europe, laced with birdsong, was a chance to drink in what we thought of as civilisation after the privations of the previous half-year. Those of us with women in our lives had even more reason to be cheerful.

The day after our return, following lunch in the mess, I headed to my room to shower and change before going into town to surprise Carole with a gift from Africa. I had dinner planned, as well as a night in a Nîmes hotel. On the way to my room, I bumped into Captain Duriuex.

"Aah, Sebastián!" he fawned as we shook hands in the corridor. "Listen, I am sorry I didn't have a chance to thank you properly for your hard work and efforts in Djibouti before we left. You understand, we were both very busy organising the Company. Your magnificent barbecue was much appreciated by all who attended, by the way."

"Thank you, Captain," I fawned back. "I try to please. I am just sorry that four of the lads felt the need to leave us midway through the tour. I felt it personally, you know; like I had failed somehow."

I didn't actually mean that, and I'm sure he knew it. Just like he knew we didn't like each other. Duriuex was a prick. It wasn't his fault; he just wasn't a soldier.

"Sebastián, try not to think too much about things in that way. Without its deserters, what would the Legion be?" he said. "Men come here to forget... and then sometimes they forget that too, eh?"

He laughed and patted my upper arm, the scent of his cologne arousing my contempt for him even further as it wafted around him in the corridor. Laughing back in the sycophantic manner of a subordinate, I played along with our tedious charade of social niceties.

"You're right, of course, Captain," I said. "And I'm

sure they have benefitted from the retraining they received from Corporal Stein, also."

"Do you have plans for the weekend, Sebastián?"

"Yes, actually. I'm going to surprise my girlfriend over in Ecusson this afternoon. She has an apartment there. I got her a little something from the tour, and I have a room booked at L' orangerie."

"Very nice!" he replied. "Well, enjoy yourself, Alvarez, and thank you again." Parting in the corridor with icy smiles, we went our separate ways.

I didn't know it then, but within two years Duriuex was to jeopardise not just my own life, but the lives of everyone in our forty-man Infantry section. Far from Nîmes and the trappings of Western civilisation, Duriuex and his upper-class arrogance would put my life and those of my colleagues and friends in serious peril. In a cold and stinking Afghan ditch, his ineptitude would lead us all into a violent and deadly trap. But all of that comes much later in my story.

Back in my room, I changed into a freshly laundered uniform before heading over to Carole's apartment in the Ecusson neighbourhood of Nîmes.

Before leaving Africa, I had bought Carole a necklace from a market stall in Djibouti City. It was made of silver coins from the lands on the other side of the Arabian Gulf. Turquoise stones hung between each of the coins, and from the loops of silver hung delicate silver chains of varying length.

Catching a taxi from the barracks into town, I sat in the back and pulled the necklace from my pocket. Feeding the silver chains and Arabic coins rhythmically through my fingers like a set of prayer beads, I ignored the drivers' puerile moans about road works and immigrants.

Through the cab's window, I saw lots of women, black, white, and coffee-coloured, strolling along the pavement, confidently wearing low-cut tops and expensive sunglasses. Carefree couples enjoyed the sunshine hand in hand. The sight of Western girls going about their business, freely exposing the flesh of their arms, legs, and cleavage, ignited that which was primitive in me.

As the driver attempted to offload his petite grievances onto me about the traffic and *"Africans"*, I thought about my impending physical reunion with Carole.

It is usual for many men to talk about how they are a tit, ass, or leg man. Under normal circumstances I would have been the same, but today wasn't normal.

Not only had I spent the last half-year in a fly-blown Third World outpost where I had endured insufferable conditions, but I had also borne responsibility for a clutch of wayward young Legionnaires and all their youthful inconsistencies to boot. Right now what I wanted—no, needed—was to bask in the warm intimacy of Carole's sex.

As my driver negotiated the rush-hour traffic, I revelled in the anticipation of what was to come. Memories of the first moments of coupling with Carole filled my mind. I remembered, with easy satisfaction, the times she had given herself to me in the dark; the feeling I'd got, like every birthday and Christmas present I had ever unwrapped as a child; every cuddle, every warm, wet kiss, and every thrill that I had ever known, all encapsulated in that first sweet instance of union with her.

Yes, it was going to be a great weekend; the food, the soft bed, the feminine smells, and the fucking.

Chapter Nine

I first heard her moans as I put my key into the lock of her apartment door.

As I let myself in, I was confronted not only by Carole's breathless voice coming from the bedroom, but the sight of a three-quarters-drunk bottle of white wine and two glasses on the low living room table.

From the bedroom in which I had enjoyed so much comfort, and moments big as years, I heard Carole enjoying someone else.

"Beautiful, beautiful…" she breathed.

I had brought a bottle of wine with me to surprise her with. Throwing it onto the sofa, I walked through the open door into the bedroom.

Carole was naked on the bed, her back arched, as some middle-aged bastard with a heavy film of sweat covering his forehead heaved himself into her. She dug her fingernails into the sallow skin of his hairy lower back as they joined. The heavy scent of their sex, mixed with her perfume, reached me on the light spring breeze wafting into the room through the open window. Carole opened her eyes as her head turned in my direction.

"Oh my God!" she shrieked, as the fat old bastard leapt off her like a cat shot with an air-gun.

"Who the hell…?" he blurted.

This was the point where advancing years on my part and an adherence to the ethos of military training and controlled aggression kicked in, much to the benefit of all concerned. I had no wish to jeopardise either my rank or my pension on behalf of this fat bastard or a woman who wasn't who I'd hoped she'd be. Jutting my thumb over my shoulder in the direction of the door, I issued an order.

"Out you go," I said.

He looked at a sheepish and humiliated Carole. "Carole? Who…"

"Never mind who," I interrupted. "It's me, that's who. Now get out."

Feet apart, with my hands on my hips, I glared down at him as he looked up into my eyes, fixed like jet stones. They were eyes that had seen things beyond his imagination, and he instinctively knew it.

Leaving Carole on the bed and stepping over her discarded underwear, he stooped to gather his crumpled clothes with his left hand whilst reaching for a pair of spectacles on the bedside table with his right.

Stepping forward, I pinned his clothes to the floor with my right foot, casually swiping his glasses off the table and into the waste bin next to it with my left hand. I looked down at my usurper.

"Get out," I said.

"My clothes and my spectacles… please…" the fat git whined.

At this, Carole gathered the white bed sheet around her nipples, still hard from the memory of his tongue. She put a leg out of the bed, placing it on the floor as her green eyes blazed and flashed with anger.

"Sebastián, you are an animal!" she spat.

"Yes of course I am; that's what you pay your taxes for, isn't it, bitch?"

Seeking sanctuary from her guilt in arrogance and superiority, Carole raised her chin and lowered her voice.

"Let him have his clothes, Sebastián." Her tone was haughty and loaded with authority.

"Listen, fatty," I said. "if you're still in this apartment in thirty seconds, I'm gonna kick your balls out the back of your ass. Now fuck off!"

The fat man left without his clothes. Dropping the sheet, Carole reached for her underwear in a silent rage.

Back in the living room, I swigged the last quarter from the bottle of wine she had enjoyed with her lover before taking him into her bed.

Carole dressed, angrily. Her panties and bra-straps snapping against her peach-coloured skin were like firecrackers declaring her fury. She stormed out of the bedroom, then left the apartment without speaking and slammed the door; the scent of Coco Chanel hanging in the air behind her.

I lit a cigarette. Opening the red wine that I had brought with me, I sat on her couch and drank from the bottle. I looked around the room at the things Carole had filled it with: books, paintings, house plants and ornaments, things that normal people surround themselves with. The things I didn't have because of the stupid shit I had done so long ago.

On a shelf amongst her books, Carole had placed a plaster bust of Minerva, wife of Mars, the god of war. Getting up from the sofa, I hung the necklace from Djibouti around its neck.

"Fuck you," I snarled into the figure's passive and disinterested face.

Soon, half the wine was gone.

Back in the bedroom, I glanced at *"The Death of Actaeon"*, hanging on the wall above Carole's bed. I remembered the time shortly after we had first met, when Carole had explained its meaning to me as we drank wine under her duvet one evening.

Whilst out hunting in the forest with his comrades, Actaeon, Prince of Thebes, had tired of the day's sport. After ordering everyone to rest and seek leisure amongst the trees, Actaeon wandered off alone.

Arriving at a cave filled with the clear waters flowing from a fountain in its side, Actaeon spied the goddess Artemis as she bathed naked in the pool. Enraged by Actaeon's invasion of her privacy, Artemis turned him into a half man, half beast, and reached for her arrows.

Actaeon fled the cave as Artemis dressed angrily and gave chase. As he ran, Actaeon was spotted by his own hunting dogs. They promptly brought him down by the side of a lake. With Artemis now firing arrows over the dogs at Actaeon from a distance, they tore him apart, and he was killed.

Turning away from the picture, I picked up Carole's lover's clothes and took them into the bathroom. I crammed them into the toilet and pissed on them. At the washbasin I leaned over and stared into the mirror, then punched my reflection with an angry growl. The mirror broke. Cracks like a spider's web spread from its centre to the outer edges.

Looking at the image of myself in uniform, I realised that that's just what it was: an image. The immaculately ironed creases in my walking-out shirt, the hand-sewn insignia of the rank I'd earned emblazoned on the shoulder boards, together with the braided lanyards and the medal ribbons that affirmed me in the eyes of others.

What did that fat bastard have that I didn't? What was so attractive about him that she would open her legs for him on a spring afternoon that should have been ours?

I registered the angry look on my face, reflected in the mirror, and the spit coming out through my clenched teeth. I knew well the feeling of alcohol intoxication that had been so much a part of my existence since I had buried myself and my guilt in the Legion of the lost and damned. It was all so clear.

He didn't need to wear a uniform or carry a gun to make him self feel like someone. He probably had an apartment of his own, with books and *things*. *Stuff*, just like she had.

He probably contributed to society in ways that weren't reduced to the level of violence in the name of ideologies or nationalistic concepts. He probably lived his life in accordance with his own agendas and priorities, and not those of an institution that offered a safe haven to the broken.

I looked again at his clothes in the toilet, and I understood for the first time that his clothes were *his*. He got to decide what he wore from one day to the next, unlike me. I couldn't blame Carole for the choices she made. Outside of being a curiosity and a distraction for her what value did I have, for her or anybody else?

The sophisticated intelligence and maturity that drew me to her in the first place was also what allowed her to see that underneath the uniform and badges of this professional soldier, there was a lost and frightened little boy. A little boy who had prospered within an organisation whose strength he had borrowed and used second-hand, an organisation whose boundaries protected him from himself and from his own lack of boundaries.

Back in the living room, I slouched on the sofa. The windows were open to the balcony overlooking the Place aux Herbs and the cathedral beyond. The spring breeze brushing past the white curtains carried the sounds of young people laughing.

Thinking about the dream I had secretly harboured of staying on in Nîmes after my Legion service and getting a place to study at the university, I played through my mind one last time the fantasy that Carole might one day have my child, and we could make a life together.

The gently billowing curtains fell still, and as the wind died, so too did a little more hope. I had been in

France for thirteen years, but still I was that same teenager on the run.

Chapter Ten

Argentine Patagonia, January 1990

Standing alone and shivering by the side of the tree-lined Ruta 237 highway in Rio Negro at the age of nineteen, I realised that everything was over: my career, my relationship, my future, and my whole damned world. I was suddenly a criminal and a desperate fugitive.

They would be coming after me very soon. If I didn't get away, I was going to prison for a long, long time. I *had* to get away.

I had jumped from my horse in the forest during a storm a couple of hours beforehand. I removed his bridle and sent him galloping through the rain-soaked trees with a slap on the arse. Then I unbuckled my spurs and tramped through the brush to the highway. It had been dark for half an hour.

The mid-summer thunderstorm was over. It had stopped raining, but I was shivering with shock and feeling the cold. I was frightened and beginning to despair. Soon, and much to my relief, a trucker pulled his lorry over and gave a couple of short toots on the horn. I climbed into the cab.

"Come far...? Going far...?" the driver asked as I pulled the door shut.

"Where are *you* going?" I said.

"Buenos Aires, or as near as."

I tried to look both friendly and innocent. I sat back in the seat as he lifted the clutch and eased the vehicle back onto the dark strip of tarmac that was to act as the bridge for me from one life to another. Looking across the cab, the driver smiled at me like a priest.

He was a short, thick-set man in his early fifties with a healthy tan and jet-black hair that was swept back from his face and down over his ears. A streak of grey ran from just above his right eye back over his scalp like a moonbeam.

Every silver strand seemed to tell the story of the years he'd lived. Each hair a medal commemorating an episode of a life punctuated with mini-victories against the odds. The skin between the forefinger and thumb of his right hand was tattooed with three dots in the shape of a triangle. I knew its meaning: *My Crazy Life*.

"You've been out in the rain, my friend. Are you hungry?" he asked as the lorry picked up speed and headed north into the night.

"Yes, I am. I'm hungry."

He nodded to a canvas satchel lying between us on the thick, sheepskin-covered seat.

"There's food in there. Take what you want and don't worry about me. I'm fine. I always bring a lot of food. See, I pick up hitchers a fair bit. It gets boring out in the desert. Besides, everyone's got a story, eh?"

Opening the satchel flap, I reached inside and grabbed a large steak, lettuce, and mayonnaise sandwich on white bread. With my other hand I fished out a large ripe tomato and started to eat with both hands. The meat was good, and the juice from the tomato was soon running through my fingers.

"My name's Juan Cruz," said the trucker. He turned on the windscreen wipers and sprayed water over the dusty glass in front of us, clearing a splattered moth from the windscreen.

"Hello, Juan Cruz," I replied through a full mouth.

"There's some chicken flan in there, hardboiled eggs, and some Chubut cheese as well if you want," he offered.

"Yes, thank you, I saw it."

"So, what are you doing out here in the desert all by yourself, without even a bag?" His eyes were fixed on the highway in front of us.

"Oh, it's a game I'm having with some friends from University in Buenos Aires. We are trying to get back to the capital by any means necessary, without using any public transport, and in the quickest time possible." The lies I was to tell and live by for the next twenty years had begun.

"And where did you set out from on this game of yours?" he said, as he kept his eyes on the road.

"Rio Gallegos," I said, wiping tomato juice and mayonnaise from my hands onto my dirty jeans.

"Aaaah..." Juan Cruz smiled. "That's some game, my friend." He ran his hand through his hair in one smooth action before turning to me with a dry smile. "But if it amuses you..." He turned his attention to the road once more. "Personally, I prefer my own transport, and at least I get paid."

I nodded and forced a grin, before pulling another tomato from the satchel.

Juan Cruz smiled on serenely, cradling the large steering wheel in his fat hands as if it were a newborn baby. The crucifix and rosary beads that hung from a nail above the windscreen in the cab rocked gently with the movement of the truck on the undulating highway.

Finishing the steak sandwich, I reached back into the satchel and grabbed a slice of flan and an egg. Once I'd devoured the flan, I cracked the egg on the knuckles of my left fist and finished it off in two bites. Then I licked the mayonnaise from the corners of my mouth.

"Thank you," I said.

"You're welcome, amigo," Juan Cruz replied affably.

The lorry pushed on through the young night, and as the wheels beneath us ate up the miles we adopted the stance of two strangers in a bus station waiting room, a kind of silent tolerance. I remember the stars that night, and the white lines in the middle of the highway coming at us like bullets from a machine gun.

I remember the smell of cigarettes, oil, and sheepskin, fortified by the warm air from the cab's heater. Yes, even now after all these years, I remember the lines and the warmth, my full belly and my empty heart.

Anyone who has travelled the desert highways of Patagonia at night will be familiar with the sight of the *chillo*. This is the South American grey fox. Chillos are most often spotted as apparitions of silver emerging from the inky blackness of the roadside. They offer the briefest glimpse of their flanks as they dart from one side of the road to the other, through the alien beams of the lonely cars and overnight coaches that strike out across the vast emptiness of the desert. Despite their fleeting nature, they are a common sight. Many times I had seen chillos appearing like guilty ghosts in the headlights of vehicles in Black River Province. Now on this night, as I sat wrapped in the warm air of that cab next to Juan Cruz, I saw one again. I didn't know it then, but it would be the last time.

This chillo was different from all the others. He wasn't crossing the highway as if he had the hounds of hell on its tail. He sat quietly at the very edge of the road, his eyes illuminated by the lights of the truck like freshly minted silver pesos. They were fixed impassively on our cab; they seemed to be fixed on me. As we cruised past him at 70 mph, the Chillo's head turned calmly and followed our route.

I stared back into his eyes, shifting uneasily in my seat as Juan Cruz turned to look at me with a knowing smile.

"See that chillo...?" he said. "He was looking at you."

I squirmed further into my seat.

"Huh? No, I don't think so. Perhaps he was sick," I replied.

"Yeah, could have been. It's a sick world out there, after all. Eh?"

I crossed my legs and tried to change the subject of our non-versation.

"How long will it take us to get to Buenos Aires, amigo?"

"Around about this time tomorrow. I'm passing straight through Neuquén, stopping at General Acha, then again in Santa Rosa, and after that my beautiful Buenos Aires, and my even more beautiful wife!" With that he wound down the window, and spat snot from the back of his nose into the night. "That's not set in stone, of course. If we need a piss and a leg stretcher, there's nothing stopping us, is there."

He wound the window up again. "I'm actually going to General Rodriguez, on the edge of the capital proper. Do you know it?"

"Yes, yes I know it," I lied again, then I fell asleep with my temple pressed against the window, without taking a last look at the only home I had ever known.

I woke with a start as Juan Cruz jabbed a finger into my left shoulder, then pointed out of the windscreen. He had stopped the truck by the side of the highway. Shifting in my seat, stretching and rubbing my eyes, I looked through the windscreen and saw the sign welcoming drivers to La Pampa Province in the head lights.

"I'm having a slash," he said. "I always have a slash here at the sign to keep me safe."

"Keep you safe?"

"Yeah, it's just a superstition of mine."

Opening the door, Juan Cruz disappeared from sight as he jumped down into what was becoming the wide expanse of the pampas. I got out my side, walked to the back of the truck, and had a piss while Juan Cruz did the same on the metal post of the road sign up in front.

"I'm coming home, baby!" he shouted towards the horizon as his urine scattered the dirt in front of him. "I always say that for my wife too!" he laughed.

Back in the cab he opened the satchel, reached inside, and brought out two eggs.

"Here, shell these whilst I make tea. It's gonna be light soon."

Reaching up into a shelf above the windscreen, he retrieved a mate gourd and silver *bombilla* straw. Then, from under his jacket, he grabbed a packet of *yerba mate* green tea. As he did this I picked up the thermos flask lying next to the satchel, unscrewed the top, and passed it to him.

Mate tea to an Argentine is like coffee to a New York office worker, but more so. The gourd it is drunk from is a small, pumpkin-like squash with its insides scooped out, then dried until rock hard. The rim is often capped with decorative silver or tin.

With the gourd packed almost to the top with tiny shredded tea leaves, Juan Cruz poured in the hot water, allowed it to settle for a minute or so, then passed it to me. I thanked him, took a couple of refreshing sips, then passed the gourd back to him.

I then shelled the eggs, passed him one, and downed mine in two bites.

"Hey! There's some bread and *dulce de membrillo* somewhere in that satchel. Let's have a proper breakfast, eh?" he said. *Dulce de membrillo* is a quince jelly that we always used to have with bread or toast at home whilst I was growing up.

My mother always gave it to my brother and me with orange juice for breakfast, and then again when we got in from school in the afternoons. As I spread some on white bread for Juan Cruz early that morning back in 1990, I couldn't help giving in to the realisation that things weren't ever going to be the same again.

Passing the gourd back and forth, we drank the tea as pampas's moths used the truck's headlights as some kind of silent floating disco in front. Once in General Acha, we stopped at a wayside diner and had black coffee and pastries before hitting the road again.

We now headed westwards on Highway 35 towards the town of Santa Rosa. Back on the open road, the sun had risen on the first day of the rest of my life.

Juan Cruz started talking.

"You know, when I was younger, I had a lot of trouble with the police. Nothing like the young people now with drugs and everything; just stupid stuff like fistfights and a bit of stealing. But I took my fair share of thrashings off the cops, you know. They were always knocking on my parent's door and upsetting everything at home."

"So what happened to turn things around?" I asked. Juan Cruz laughed.

"I got called up for the army! Ha ha! That fucking sorted me out, I can tell you. They were real bastards, but you know what? It taught me to take responsibility for myself and work together with others for a common result that benefited me and my friends. You know, the people I lived and worked with." sunlight filled the truck's cab as Juan Cruz got into his stride.

"When I got back home, I knew I could make a life for myself. It might not give me easy money and riches in this world, but I could look after my family, keep my nose clean, and put food on the table regularly. I learned to drive trucks in the army, see, and here I am."

I took off my jacket as the day warmed up, and my host carried on talking.

"When I get home from this trip there are my wife and kids, who are everything to me. They give me joy, understand?"

"Yeah," I said. "Joy."

I wanted to break the conversation off. Coughing loudly, I scratched the back of my head, then delved into the satchel for an egg that I didn't really want.

Before I had got myself into the situation I was now in, I had come across a book in the Gendarmerie Academy library about the French Foreign Legion. Like a lot of young men, I was spellbound by the concept of this multi-national legion of desperadoes fighting against the odds in far-flung outposts in an attempt to leave their pasts behind.

Recalling this book as I sat looking out of the window of Juan Cruz's truck, my mind started working overtime. I really did have to get far away and stay away if I was to avoid going to prison.

From what I remembered from reading about it, the French Foreign Legion would take any man from any country on earth. It would offer him both a refuge and a fresh start in exchange for the man's loyalty and willingness to fight for France.

All one had to do was present oneself at a Legion base with a passport, and the door would open and then close behind the old you forever.

Perhaps all was not lost. I couldn't change the past; but if I could get to France, maybe I could start again. In any case, I couldn't think of any other options open to me. As Juan Cruz drove on into the rays of the rising sun, flecks of hope shimmered across the wide pampas in the light of the new day.

Over the next few hours I heard about the six children of Juan Cruz, his wife, his mother, and the puppy that he hoped wouldn't be shitting on the floor by the time he got home. I feigned interest in the details of his life, as the concept of getting to France and hiding in its legion of foreigners solidified in my mind.

By the time he dropped me off later that night, at a petrol station in General Rodriguez on the outskirts of greater Buenos Aires, my mind was made up. I would make my way to France. However, I had to get there. I would manage. This would be the way to kick over the traces and start all over again.

As we shook hands and said our goodbyes, Juan Cruz mentioned that he had heard nothing about me. I offered to buy him a coffee in the diner attached to the main building, but he refused.

"Got to get home," he said. "Find out if that puppy has shat on the floor, and then do my husbandly duties for the wife, if you know what I mean."

Forcing a polite laugh, I turned to go inside.

"Hey!" he shouted after me. "Whatever your name is, I hope you win your game..."

I smiled and waved as he winked and climbed back into his cab, drove away, and got on with the rest of his life.

Inside the diner I bought myself a coffee, then sat down at a table to smoke a cigarette. That's when a young man walked over from a nearby table. He was a couple of years older than I, and tall. His hair was cut short and smart, and he was dressed in casual grey jogging bottoms, a thin dark blue sweater, and well-worn training shoes.

"Hey, do you have a light, my friend?" he asked.

"Sure," I said. I pulled one from my pocket before lighting the cigarette he held between the teeth of his smile.

"What do you think my chances of hitching a lift from here into downtown Buenos Aires?" I asked.

"Good," he said. "When I finish my coffee, I'm going there. You can come with me if you want. I'm Lucio..."

"I'm Juan Cruz," I lied as we shook hands. Walking

across the car park to his little cream Datsun, I noticed how much warmer the air was up here than where I had set out from. Lucio opened the driver's door and got in. He picked up a large white polystyrene box and held it out to me as I got into the passengers seat.

"Here, you'll have to hold this on your knee, my friend. It won't fit on the back seat," he smiled.

"Okay, sure," I said. I took the box and held it with both hands, realising that it would just fit between me and the dash board if I kept my stomach in a little. "What's in it?"

"Just a load of shit. I'm working part time as a courier to help fund my legal studies. I'm taking that from the hospital to a medical centre in town." He smiled.

"What kind of shit is it?" I asked.

"Shit type shit, you know; Stool samples." His smile broadened as we drove on. Keeping my face tilted to the window and away from the box with my stomach drawn as far in as I could, I tried not to think about the contents of the box.

Luckily for me, Lucio liked to talk about himself and hadn't asked too many questions by the time he dropped me off with a smile close to the Casa Rosada on the Plaza, the 25th of May, right in the middle of the city.

Since abandoning my horse near the highway somewhere outside Bariloche two days earlier, I had hitchhiked in just two rides up through Rio Negro Province and into La Pampa. Then, travelling westwards along Ruta Five, I had crossed the greater Buenos Aires province and into the heart of the capital.

Chapter Eleven

I knew I couldn't go to my brother's rooms at the university or anywhere near it. The men, who until recently had been colleagues of mine in the Gendarmerie Nationale, would have a heads-up on that one already. Luckily, I knew where my brother worked part-time as a bartender. The bar was on the Plaza Doreago in the Old San Telmo quarter, a five-minute walk from the Plaza de Mayo.

After a day of making coffees and Cokes last as long as possible in the burger joints and cafes along the Avenieda Santa Fe and Avenieda Florida, I cut through the city crowds, crossing the downtown area and arriving in the Plaza Doreago. I found my brother's place of work and went inside.

"What the fuck are you doing here?" he said as I approached him at the crowded bar.

"Raul, I'm in the shit, and I need you to help me."

He took me back to the toilets.

"I know what you've done, you crazy fool. What the fuck were you thinking? The police came to see me. They told me to let them know if you turned up." Raul pulled a card from his pocket and showed it to me. It held the contact details of a detective from the Gendarmerie Nationale. I took my brother by the shoulders.

"Okay, look. What's happened has happened. I can't take it back now. I just need to get away and stay away, that's all. But I need you to help me. It will be better for everyone if I just fucking disappear and never come back."

"You're right, it would be, but what am I supposed to do?"

"Okay, listen. I need your ID card and passport, and I need you to give me some of the money that Mum left us so I can get going. I'll give you my bank details and you can take what's left in my account later."

"Where are you going to go?" he asked.

I pulled out a cigarette and lit it.

"Probably Paraguay; Ciudad de Este is just a day away from here on the bus." I didn't like lying to my brother. Once you start telling lies they tend to build and feed each other, until you are a slave to the stories you've told in order to free yourself from whatever it was you have tried to run away from.

Snatching the packet from my hand, Raul helped himself to my last smoke.

"Be here tomorrow, and I'll see what I can do. In the meantime, take my ID card and book into the Hotel Bolivar. It's over on Avenieda Estados Unidos. It's not far. Go. Get out of here!"

A narrow white four-story building in the Parisian style of the 1800s, the Hotel Bolivar was a shabby *pension* with rapidly-fading charms. Using the last of my money, I took one of the small rooms set around the building's inner courtyard, which was lined with potted plants and open to the sky.

The room was without a toilet or washbasin and looked like it had seen a lifetime of loneliness. As soon as I had shut the door and locked it, I stripped to my underpants and sank into a deep, unhappy sleep on the tiny single bed in the corner.

I was woken early the next morning by the sounds of bedsprings in pain and people in ecstasy, as some anonymous woman eagerly responded to the sexual overtures of some equally anonymous man, or vice versa.

Getting out of my own bed, I dressed in the first heat of a summer's day, then left them to it as they raced towards a less than private orgasm.

I walked back downtown, and with the exception of

a short siesta back at the hotel, I spent that day hanging around watching people feed the pigeons in front of the presidential palace in the Plaza de Mayo. It was from there in October 1951 that Eva Peron stood on the balcony and addressed a packed throng of emotional supporters.

Standing with President Juan Peron at her side and suffering from cancer, 'Evita' implored the crowd not to cry for her. Most of them wept anyway as she spoke of leaving the tatters of her life along the road behind her.

As I sat alone on a bench under that same balcony in 1990 I reflected on the fact that my own life was now well and truly in tatters, not to mention the ragged stumps that used to be the lives of the other people I had affected.

I didn't need to go back to Raul's bar later that evening. Just after dark, he knocked on my door. Even though I was jumpy and paranoid, I instinctively knew it was him. He came into the little room looking at me with a mixture of brotherly concern and exasperation.

"Are you okay?" he said.

"I'm fine. Have you got everything?"

He pulled an envelope from his inside pocket, and shoved it into my hand.

"Here, my passport, and enough pesos to get you the fuck out of South America, if you want."

I took the package. Then I looked away, wondering whether or not he had known that I was lying about going to Paraguay.

"Raul, I am sorry about everything. I'm getting out of everyone's lives, I promise. I just don't want you to hate me or not care about me any more."

Raul put his arms around me as I started to shake and cry. He spoke quietly.

"This thing is bigger than me, and I just can't do any

more than give you this." I held on to my brother for one last time.

"You have done all you can. Just go now, and make sure you look after Dad. I will contact you when I get where I'm going. Don't come back here again, Raul. I'll be gone soon after you leave." I passed him my bank cards and account details so he could at least get his money back.

We turned away from each other at the same time. That was when it truly started to sink in for me just how heavy a price I was going to have to pay for my actions. I haven't spoken to my brother since.

Chapter Twelve

Escape to Uruguay, Montevideo, 1990

The next day, I was walking down the street in Uruguay's Capital City Montevideo. After jumping on a ferry from the port area of Buenos Aires, I had travelled across the wide expanse of the River Plate estuary before arriving in the old Spanish town of Colonia, where I caught a bus to Montevideo central bus station. There began a journey that I hoped would one day lead to a life worth living.

I walked downtown from the station, and checked into a small pension ironically named Hotel Ideal. It was around the corner from the city's main Plaza de Independencia. From there I set about finding an airline to take me to Europe. In my spare time I sat on the beach, watching the people enjoying the sand, the water and the ice-cream, along with their friends and families.

On the one hand, seeing these people made me feel sad. On the other hand, it made it easier to go through with what I was committed to. One evening on the beach, as the summer sun dipped low in the sky, I watched a woman with her son of about four years old.

They were busy packing away the bucket and spade that they had brought to the beach to play with. Having put everything into their beach bag, the woman tried to hurry the little boy along, but he had decided that he would quite like to carry on playing in the sand.

"Come on, Peppito," she said. "We have to go home and have something to eat with Pappa. He'll be home from work soon."

"I can't put my shoes and socks on, Mamma."

"Its okay, Peppie, I'll help you. Come here."

She lifted the little boy onto her knee, then began

gently cleaning the sand from between his toes with her fingers as the setting sun cast a halo around her tousled hair.

Now I remembered a time when I had relied on my own mother to do similar things for me. But that was before she got a cough that wouldn't go away; before she decided after all that she had better go to the doctor's instead of the priest. Then the doctor couldn't do any more, so the priest took over again.

One day I came home from school with the huge bunch of flowers that everyone had told me would make my mother feel better. I found that she had left me. Only her wracked, empty body remained on the bed she had shared with my father, in the home where they had tried to build a new life, far from the green hills of Asturias in a country that had promised so much but delivered so little.

Looking across the sand at the little boy with his mother, a steady flow of warm salted pain ran down my cheek and into the corner of my mouth. What was done was done. My mother couldn't help me now. Feeling sorry for myself wasn't going to change anything. I licked my lips and wiped my eyes. It was time to harden up.

I hadn't eaten a thing since the day before, so I went in search of food. Up a side street near the Plaza, I found a small pub that served meals. Inside I spoke to the barman.

"What can I get you?" he said as I leaned on the bar.

"What kind of food do you have?"

"Well, are you hungry?"

"Yes, starving."

"You're Argentine, aren't you? I can tell from your accent. We know all about your meat down there, but if you are really hungry you need a Uruguayan Chivito *plata*," he chirped.

"Okay, fine. I'll just grab that table by the window."

I took a seat at a little table by the window overlooking the cobbled street. The man from the kitchen soon brought another table out and placed it next to the one I was sitting at, as if I was having company. I was puzzled by this.

Fifteen minutes later he returned with the Chivito *plata* on a huge, flattened metal dish, and placed it on the table adjoining mine. The meal consisted of a stack of thin slices of cooked beef, ham, pork, chicken, bacon, and lamb. Each layer of meat was separated by fried eggs, French fries, Russian salad, mild peppers, lettuce, and tomatoes. I found some small solace in the food.

After washing the whole thing down with an Abocados wine, I returned to my sanctuary at the nearby pension, where I lay on the bed in my threadbare room trying to come to terms with the things I had done.

The next day I bought a couple of t-shirts, some underwear, and a pair of denim jeans. I was running out of money fast. Taking a stupid chance, later that afternoon I stole a toothbrush and shaving gear from a supermarket near the bus station before skulking back to the Hotel Ideal. Back in my room, I kicked myself for putting my plans in jeopardy by shoplifting, and resolved to keep a low profile until I left the city.

As usual my good intentions didn't last, and two days later I sank low enough to grab a sports bag from behind the feet of a school boy who was standing at a bus stop close to the beach. As shameful as it seems, I justified it by telling myself I needed it more than him.

I had known what I was going to do as soon as Juan Cruz had finished telling me about his national service days as we drove across the pampas five days previously. Within a fortnight of being in Montevideo,

I had obtained a tourist visa from the French Embassy using Raul's identity, and was ready to leave South America.

After spending two weeks forlornly mooching around in the city, purchasing the required airline tickets, then funding my French visa application fee, there was practically nothing left with which to pay my bill at the pension.

The night before catching the bus out to Carrasco International Airport, I went back to the little pub up the side street. Sitting at a single table tucked away in a corner, I sat down to a meal of Milanesa breaded steak and a fish pie. As I polished off my second bottle of Abocados, the man from the kitchens came out and approached me with a broad grin.

"Enjoy?"

Under the circumstances I found it hard to make small talk, and I found the man's amiable approach irritating.

"Yes thank you, very good. Good wine as well," I said, as I sat back in my chair to ease my belly. The man chatted on as he cleared my table and began swiping the bread crumbs off it and onto the floor.

"That's how the first wines in South America were. The Jesuits planted the vineyards here in the 16th century in order to have wine for the Holy Communion."

I didn't tell him how appropriate I felt the choice of wine had been, but it felt right to be drinking such a wine there and then. I felt that the pub was the church of my last supper in South America. It's just a shame that I left without my confession being heard.

The next day I left the pension without paying the bill, and I fled South America without paying for everything else I'd done either.

Chapter Thirteen

France, Paris, Winter 1990

My new life and the great adventure on which I was about to embark began on a bitterly cold Parisian morning in January. I didn't have a warm winter jacket when I arrived. I hadn't even considered that, upon walking out of the arrivals area of Charles de Gaulle International Airport, I would be walking into the penetrating cold of a northern European winter.

Much of the Parisian architecture reminded me of Buenos Aires. That was understandable, considering it was the intention of the first Argentine settlers from Europe to build a city at the mouth of the "silver River" that would put Paris in the shade. They didn't quite manage that; in fact, they never quite managed a lot of things. Too many hopes and dreams of the first Europeans who built Buenos Aires were carried away on the hot winds of the Pampas and lost forever.

Paris was different. For one thing, everything seemed to work properly. I got the sense that beyond the city limits was a country that functioned to its maximum capacity; that Paris was the hub, and none of the spokes were broken. I had come from a country that had only ever known uncertainty, instability, and disappointments.

Suddenly, after all the trauma and upheaval of recent events back home in the '*New World*', I was starting again in the old one.

From a tourist information booth in the Gare du Nord train station, I obtained a map and guide written in Spanish. Stopping a soldier amongst the bustling crowd of anonymous commuters, I asked him where the Foreign Legion barracks was.

Not speaking French at all, and presuming he

wouldn't understand Spanish, I did this by way of pointing at his uniform and showing him my passport.

"Legion, Legion, *por favor*," I repeated.

Taking the map from me, the soldier pointed to a place in the southeast of the city.

"Fort de Nugent, *oui*? Fort de Nugent. *Legion Etranger*, okay?"

"*Gracias*," I nodded.

Understanding my mission perfectly well, he gave me a thumbs up.

"*Bon chance!*" he said, turning away and disappearing into the crowd.

Before leaving the railway station I bought a coffee and a packet of cigarettes, then sat down to steel myself for the leap I was about to take. I was worried, but I knew that back home an investigation was now underway, and that a manhunt would have been launched. Statements were being taken and evidence compiled.

That being the case, I knew that if I could get inside the Legion I could at least start again. My past was forever tainted, and what was required now was a cleansing. I needed a reincarnation. If the Legion would take me in, then I could be born again.

I people-watched for half an hour before heading on foot to the Legion barracks and the adventure awaiting me on the other side of the huge oak door of its grey stone Parisian fortress.

I don't know where the Legionnaire on the gate at Fort de Nugent was from, but he was the first I had ever seen. The brilliant white Kepi on his head stood out against the backdrop of the dark wooden door. After giving my passport a cursory glance, he opened the heavy door behind him and beckoned me inside.

Once inside the fort I got the feeling that, to some extent at least, the door now behind me offered some level of protection from what I had done, that I really had escaped.

The Legionnaire mumbled something in French. He then beckoned me with a nod of the head, before walking me to a small office nearby. Through its open door, sitting behind a small desk, a tall black corporal regarded me coldly.

After dismissing the Legionnaire, the Corporal spoke and beckoned me inside the office, pointing to a spot on the floor in front of his desk.

"*Attend ici.*"

Suddenly, I was scared. I still can't explain why. I had to make a conscious effort to stop my knees from shaking in front of him.

"*Nom?*"

"Raul Gonzalo Alvarez."

"*Parlez-vous Français?*"

"No French, sorry," I replied nervously.

He shrugged. I tried to look as confident and capable as I could under the circumstances.

The corporal was dressed in military fatigues, with the sleeves of his shirt turned up and folded immaculately above his well-muscled forearms. He pushed his chair back and stood up. The name badge on his chest read *De Silva*. I knew the chance of this being the name he was born with was slight. I started to consider my own position in this regard. For now, though, I decided that for official purposes my brother's first name would suffice.

A tall athletic man with a bald head, De Silva was the first black man I had ever spoken to. I had guessed he came from one of the francophone countries of central or western Africa. He walked around to the side of his desk.

"*Montrez-moi votre Passeport.*"

It was obvious that there were to be no concessions

to my lack of ability in the French language. I understood *passeport*, so I took Raul's from my back pocket and handed it to him. He flicked quickly through. My resemblance to my brother was obviously good enough.

"*Argentine?*" he said without looking up.

I replied with the only French word I knew and understood: "*Oui.*"

The Corporal turned back towards his desk, tossed the passport onto it, and said, "*Montre moi tes avant bras.*"

"I don't understand."

He took me by the wrist and pushed my sleeve up.

"*J'ai dit, montre moi tes avant bras.*"

Pushing the sleeve up on my other arm, he held both my wrists, inspecting my inner forearms closely.

"Okay - *tu n'as jamais pris de drogue?*"

"No, no drugs," I replied in Spanish, hoping he would understand. Tapping me under the chin, he went on, "*Ouvrez la bouche.*"

He then opened his own mouth to signify that was what it was he wanted me to do. Then he had a good look at my teeth around the inside of my mouth. Stepping away from me once more, he placed his hands on his hips and gave me a cursory glance up and down from head to foot.

"*As tu déjà eu affaire á la police?*"

I shrugged my shoulders.

"*No police?*" he asked.

"No police."

"*Est ce que tu essaie d'échapper á la police?*"

"No, no police."

He nodded towards my jeans.

"*De l'argent... francs... pesetas... dollars... tes poches.*"

I emptied my front pockets of my remaining small

change, then pulled my wallet from my back pocket. He took the money, placed it on the edge of his desk, then took my wallet and counted the francs in it before filling out a form detailing the amount. Swivelling the form around to face me on the desk with his fingertips, he thrust a pen into my hand and pointed to a dotted line running across its bottom. I signed the form.

He then took a large brown envelope from a filing cabinet against the wall and placed my wallet and money in it, followed by my watch. The envelope was then sealed and placed in a safe behind his desk.

I remained in front of his desk. The two years I had just spent at the National Gendarmerie Academy had given me plenty of insight into the values and norms of military institutions, and for that alone I was now feeling grateful.

With the bored attitude of a nine-to-fiver, the corporal strolled back around the desk and sat on the corner.

"Enlèves tes vêtements, mais gardes ton slip."

I didn't have a clue what he was talking about. He began to mime unbuttoning his shirt and undoing the zipper on his combat fatigues as he repeated:

"Tu vas enlever tes vêtements et garder ton slip? Oui ou non? Enlèves tes putain de fringues et gardes ton slip, j'ai dit."

Getting the picture now, I began to undress in front of him, leaving my clothes in a pile on the floor. As I got to my underpants and started to pull them down, he raised his voice, impatiently wagging his finger at me.

"Non! Je t'ai dit de garder ton slip, imbécile!"

He wanted me to leave my underpants on. I stood to attention in front of him, in an attempt at maintaining my dignity in spite of the cold. He then pointed towards a set of weighing scales.

"Montes sur la balance."

As I stood shivering on the scales, he proceeded to take down the details of my height and weight. Then he gave me a clean set of underpants, a blue track suit, and a pair of old trainers to wear. When I had put these on, he went to the door, turned, and said, "*Suis moi.*"

I followed the corporal out into the cold and along a series of tar-sealed roads which led to a couple of dark imposing buildings several stories high. I was struck by their similarity to prison blocks.

Black winter sycamores bobbed and swayed behind the barracks' rooftops, as ugly soot-streaked clouds jostled each other low in the Parisian sky. The similarity of the barracks to a prison didn't bother me much, in light of the fact that I had chosen to come to this place voluntarily—unlike the actual prison that I would have been in now, had I had stayed in Argentina.

For those who think that joining the French Foreign Legion is in itself an act of courage, I would say this: how much braver would it have been of me to stay at home and face the consequences of my actions like a man? In turning up at the gates of the Foreign Legion I was a mere coward, and nothing more.

We entered the first barracks building on the right. De Silva led me up a staircase to an office at the end of a long corridor. He gestured for me to wait outside. Then he entered the office to hand my papers over to an older Italian corporal dressed in smart khaki shirt and dark green dress trousers.

I stood outside, watching the comings and goings of other recruits along the corridor as they milled in and out of doorways.

They were white, black, and Asian, all busy sweeping floors, cleaning windows and any other surfaces, and carrying rubbish bins. None of them smiled. Both corporals ignored me for five minutes while they chatted. Then they said their goodbyes. De

Silva didn't acknowledge me as he left the room.

The Italian corporal got up from his chair and wafted nonchalantly past me as I stood to one side of the open door. Without bothering to look at me, he said, "*Venez avec moi.*"

He led me along the corridor to a dorm room filled with four sets of bunks. Then he pointed to a bed and left me there.

Almost as soon as he had gone, I was joined in the room by two young recruits dressed in blue tracksuits. They both addressed me in English, which I couldn't understand. Not yet speaking French, I replied in Spanish.

"Sorry, guys, I'm from Argentina."

The taller of the two now broke into a smile, gave me his hand, and said, in Spanish, "Hey, a Gaucho! Welcome to the Foreign Legion. I'm Estaban Delgado from Madrid. This is Hans, from Holland. He speaks a bit of Spanish. He says he picked it up in Colombia."

As I shook hands with Hans, I noticed a deep scar running down the side of his left eye socket and stopping at his cheek.

"I'm Hans de Jong. It's shit here, let's go for a cigarette," he said with a smile.

The three of us proceeded to slope off to the toilets for a smoke and a skive. I had made my first friends in the Legion. I had already ditched the name Raul at that point and became the Gaucho as far as my fellow desperadoes were concerned, for then, and I must say that I felt relieved.

Esteban was twenty-two. He told us he was a cat-burglar, and he claimed to have stabbed a man during one of his burglaries in Madrid. We listened to his shabby story in the toilet, huddled around a fetid shit-hole in the floor like rats at the entrance to a sewer.

"I don't think he died, but I don't care anyway. He

shouldn't have fought me, the stupid bastard," he said as he smoked. Neither Hans nor I made any comment as Esteban finished telling us about his crime.

"I have a gun buried under a bush in the Parc du Tremblay a couple of kilometres from here," he said.

"What for?" I asked

"Well, if things don't work out for me here for whatever reason, I can do some work in Paris."

While I didn't have much room to talk after what I'd done, I certainly reflected on the company I was now keeping. There and then I decided not to judge Esteban or anyone else I now had to spend time with. We had all made bad choices before getting here. I began the process of making the necessary mental adjustments that I felt would be required to assimilate into this new environment. I was no longer an officer candidate amongst other officer candidates. This much was obvious.

Over the next week, the three of us formed a clique with other recruits from Sweden, Holland, India, Denmark, and Ireland. The main character amongst us was the young energetic Irishman, Tony Fitzgerald. We called him Irish Tony. He was the loudest amongst us. He pulled his weight with the work, never shirked, and was generous with his cigarettes.

Together we worked on that same landing, cleaning shit-holes, polishing floors, and talking or lying about the lives we had left behind. We went to the cookhouse and washed hundreds of dishes together, mopped floors together, and ate together.

We quickly began picking up on the basics of the French language to the extent that we knew the words for *work*, *clean*, *now*, *faster*, and so on, within a matter of days. But we communicated amongst ourselves in the *lingua franca* of Spanish, English, and French.

Some of the recruits had a head-start in the French

language by virtue of the fact that they came from French-speaking Countries like Cameroon, Ivory Coast, Switzerland, Belgium or the Province of Quebec in Canada.

Strangely enough, only Manda the Indian spoke French fluently. He had no problem understanding instruction from the sous officers. He was listed as a francophone, and was therefore responsible for translating to mainly English-speaking recruits, as he also spoke good English.

One night, as we undressed before lights out, Irish Tony questioned Manda on this point.

"Manda, how come you speak such fucking good French, anyway?"

"I grew up speaking French in India."

"French, in India! How the fuck does that work?" spluttered the Irishman.

"Well, I'm from Pondicherry, on the south-east coast. It was a French colony from the 1790s until 1954. In fact, the British had grabbed control of the town after a military attack in 1793. After the Treaty of Paris in 1814, they handed Pondicherry back to the French in 1816."

"Fuck the Brits!" said Irish Tony.

I smiled. My own country had been at war with Britain eight years previously, and I think it's safe to say that nearly all Argentines were smarting over the disastrous military defeat and national humiliation we had suffered at the hands of a nation we considered to be imperialistic pirates.

Jurgen the Dane was a postman from the small coastal town of Lemvig, on the Jutland peninsula of northern Denmark. Tall and fair-haired, he had an affable, easy manner and got on well with everybody. A couple of days after arriving at the Fort, Jurgen, Esteban and I found ourselves in the kitchens at the side of the main accommodation blocks.

After lunch, we had been tasked with washing cutlery in a huge metal sink. It was waist-high, shaped like a trough and filled with hot water. Jurgen started to talk. His hands plunged into the greasy water, and soap suds covered his arms to the elbow.

"This isn't what I had in mind when I joined the Foreign Legion," he said.

Esteban stopped washing for a moment and looked sideways at Jurgen.

"You seem like a decent sort. What are you doing here, anyway?" he said.

"Aah, well, I fucked up I suppose. A couple of months ago I got suspended from my job as a postman in Lemvig. They were doing an investigation into money going missing from envelopes and birthday cards. Stuff like that."

"Oooh, big time crime," Esteban sneered. Jurgen gave a casual shrug.

"Maybe not, but I can sleep at night, and anyway I never stole anything from anybody."

Just then a sergeant put his head around the door to check up on us. We all shut up and carried on scrubbing the cutlery until he had left.

"What did you do, then?" I asked.

"Well," continued Jurgen, "as part of the investigation, my apartment was visited by the police. They wanted to search it for evidence relating to the missing postal items, but instead of that they found my stash of Ecstasy tablets. I had been buying them in Copenhagen and then selling them in nightclubs and bars around Lemvig. I used to make very good money. It paid for some really good holidays for my girlfriend and I for the past three or four years."

Esteban laughed.

"Holiday's over, amigo! Ha ha!"

I nudged Esteban and told him to shut up. I wanted to know where Jurgen had been.

"Well, together we visited Australia, Thailand, Arizona, and Mauritius, loads of places in Europe as well. We went to London for weekends as well, quite a bit." Now Jurgen stopped washing the cutlery and stared through the window at the grey day grinding by outside. "He's right, though. Holiday's over now," he said.

"Did the Danish pigs arrest you, then?" said Esteban.

"Yeah. I jumped bail, got on a train, and swapped my postman's uniform for a Foreign Legion one. My life wasn't going anywhere, anyway. My girl Lena was a bit of a user, and life in Lemvig was boring me stupid. I quite enjoyed my time doing National Service with the Jutland Dragoons Regiment, so..."

Esteban pulled two fists full of dripping knives and forks from the water and held them up, laughing.

"So! Here we all are, washing up, ha ha!"

The Sergeant came back and told us to shut up and work, so we did.

Over the next weeks, our days followed the same pattern of washing, cleaning, and tidying. This was interspersed with the odd preliminary medical examination, such as chest x-rays to check for signs of T.B.

Slowly but surely, with each passing day, the ties that any of us might still have had to the lands we had called home were thinned out, replaced by the bonds forged between men living and working together through adversity in a formal institution, whether that be a prison or regimental environment. We were young, lost, unwanted, energetic, and immature. The perfect cannon fodder.

At Fort de Nugent, we learned to stand 'to attention'

and 'at ease' the French way. We went to the medical examinations together and started the process of absorbing the French language together. Then, after a fortnight, the time came to leave Paris and head to the Legion's home barracks outside Marseilles. Again, we went together.

Chapter Fourteen

Aubagne, South of France, Spring 1990

Formed in 1831, the French Foreign Legion was created under the rule of King Louis Philippe, in order to put internally disruptive elements from abroad to good use on behalf of the French nation.

After the July Revolution of 1830, foreigners were barred from serving in the French Army. To get around this new legislation, the Foreign Legion was created and was based for the first 130 years of its history in Algeria. Since then the legion has fought for France across the globe, from Mexico to Vietnam, and in both World Wars.

Over 35,000 men from its ranks have died in the service of France since the Legion's inception, and it was in the wake of this tradition that we arrived for recruit training at Aubagne.

In stark contrast to the old fort in Paris, the barracks there were light, bright, and modern. Most of the buildings at the recruit reception area were whitewashed and modern. The camp had an excellent refectory that many of us thought resembled a resort complex. Artificial plants and flowers adorned the window ledges, along with large colour photographs of European cities like Stockholm on the walls. But this was no resort.

We were to spend three weeks being assessed and carrying out menial tasks here, before going on to basic military training at Castle Naudary. Our 'militarisation' process began immediately with the issue of kit, clothing and orders, before being assigned our bed spaces. We were then taken outside and lined up in four ranks on the small parade square for a session of physical training that went on late into the night.

One day during our first week, Hans and I were detailed to paint the inside of a storeroom, along with Estaban, Jurgen, and Irish Tony. We had all day to complete the work, and as we were only checked on periodically by a Czechoslovakian Sergeant, we had plenty of time to talk.

Whilst having a smoke break in the afternoon, the five of us sat on paint pots in the middle of the room and chatted. I asked Hans about the scar on his temple. He told us of its origins, and how that which had scarred him had also led him to be sitting in that storeroom with four other lost boys from around the globe.

"It was a long time ago," Hans spoke with such melodrama that at first we all thought he was joking. But he wasn't.

After taking an endlessly long drag on his cigarette, he continued his story, spears of white smoke escaping his lungs on the tail of every word he spoke.

"When I was ten years old back in Holland, I was playing in this really big park called Vreugd Veg, around the corner from Rozenbommlaan Street, where I lived with my parents. I was with my friend Peter. A man came over and asked us if we could help him look for his dog in the bushes near by."

Taking another long drag on his cigarette, Hans went on as our little group started to squirm uneasily, fidgeting with embarrassment.

"So this bastard gets me to go into the bushes with him, then he picks up a rock and hits me around the side of the head with it, here."

Hans ran his finger along the length of the scar that ran down his face, then took another drag on his cigarette.

"My friend ran away to get help, but the man raped

me whilst I was unconscious."

Now we were all taking long drags on our cigarettes, not quite catching each others eye as Hans continued.

"The next day, while I was in the hospital, my father took Peter and went looking for the man in his car. Some time that afternoon Peter spotted the man and pointed him out to my father. He pulled the car over and approached the man, who ran away. Well; my father caught up with the pervert around the corner and killed him with a kitchen knife, right there at the side of the road."

Jurgen sat up straight on his paint pot.

"Shit! He just killed him right there in the street?"

Hans turned slowly to look at Jurgen.

"Right there and then, on Oossteinde Street," he said calmly, before Irish Tony piped up. "Sounds like an average Saturday night in Dundalk." We all listened in silence from then on as Hans told us the rest of his sorry tale.

Immediately following the killing Hans's father was arrested and, following a trial, he was sentenced to life imprisonment.

Hans's mother divorced his father in the following years and married a man who didn't want Hans around, so at the age of 16 he found himself on the streets with nowhere to go.

Making his way to Rotterdam, Hans slept on the streets until a passing stranger offered him a job collecting glasses and washing up in a bar down town. The job came with a room, and Hans gratefully accepted.

Over the next four years Hans worked hard and became the manager of the bar, eventually becoming friendly with the owner's friends, many of whom came from places like Columbia and Jamaica.

Much to his pleasure, Hans soon found himself going on trips to these countries with his employer. For some reason, though, he always ended up staying a couple of weeks longer than his boss before returning to Holland with his employer's original outbound suitcase, as well as his own.

In an attempt to further ingratiate himself with his new friends, Hans learned Spanish to a reasonable level and found he was going on more and more trips to places such as Cartagena and Bogota.

A couple of years later, the man was so pleased with Hans that he bought him a massage parlour all of his own and set him up in business for himself. Not quite believing his luck, Hans moved into the apartment over the salon with his girlfriend.

After a period of around twelve months, a couple of foreign men knocked on his door telling Hans that his old employer had sent them, as he was apparently owed a favour by Hans. They then produced a gun and a photograph of an old associate of theirs whom they wanted Hans to shoot within a week. Hans refused, and told the men to leave.

Later that night his old employer telephoned and calmly expressed his disappointment in Hans's refusal to help out his acquaintances. He went on to inform Hans that they were no longer friends, and that Hans should return the cost of the massage parlour by the end of the week if he wasn't prepared to shoot the man.

When Hans told his old mentor that he didn't have the money, he was given a simple choice. Either he was to shoot the man by the following Friday, or come up with the cost of the massage parlour. If neither of these options were taken up, then Hans himself was to be shot.

The following Tuesday Hans was watching a movie on the television with his girlfriend in their apartment.

During the commercial break, he got up from his seat and put on his coat.

"I'm going out to buy some cigarettes, baby; do you want me to get you anything?" he said as he walked to the door.

"You could bring me some chocolate, and I think we could use some more milk," she said, with a loving smile.

She never got the chocolate or milk, and never saw or heard from Hans again. Within a week he was washing dishes inside Fort de Nugent. There was now an uneasy silence amongst us in the storeroom as we took in the story and smoked like chimneys on a factory roof. After a short time, Jurgen spoke.

"Jesus Christ, Hans, that's some shit!"

"So, where is your father now?" I asked.

Hans shrugged his shoulders.

"prison, I guess."

"Fuck them all," said Esteban

"You are in the Legion now, you've disappeared. We'll all serve together with honour, eh?"

"Yes, you're right, mate. And after five years I'll have a French passport and I'm going to settle down and open a little café some where in the Camargue countryside."

"A café?" I laughed.

"Yes, a little place where I can serve nice coffee or teas and delicious food for people."

Jurgen laughed out loud.

"What kinds of people want to go to a faggot place like that, Hans?"

Erupting suddenly, Hans threw his cigarette past Jurgen, its burning tip exploding in a brocade of orange sparks and leaving a black dot against the white wall.

"The kind of people who don't go to massage parlours, or ask you to shoot someone for no good reason, that's who!" he snapped. "The kind of people who want to fall in love and ask someone to marry them over a nice table in the shade of the trees; those kinds of people!"

Getting off his paint pot, Hans picked up his brush and carried on painting the wall with his back to us.

Irish Tony spoke up.

"Hans; its okay, relax. I think people are just freaked out by your story and don't know how to react."

"Forget it," said Hans.

We spent the rest of the day talking about sex and war.

By the end of our three week induction period we had all got to know each other better, been issued with our full kit and uniforms, and were ready for Military training. When the time came we travelled by coach to Castel Naudary as a section of forty.

Chapter Fifteen

Castel Naudary, Languedoc-Roussillon

The friends I made at Aubagne - Irish Tony, Jurgen, Manda, Hans, Esteban, and Roland - were to be invaluable support and company for me and, I hope, I for them too, as we gradually became swallowed up by the Legion. During the next four months together we endured some of the toughest military training in the world, as the Legion moulded us into fighting soldiers.

We were trained by the same team of corporals and sergeants for the duration of our time at the training camp, and they themselves came from many lands. Among them was a Briton named Sergeant Wilson, and a mean little sadist from Morocco called Corporal Amar.

Wilson was a tall thickset man with a full moustache and eyes of steel. The tattoos covering his badly scarred forearms spoke of Armagh and Crossmaglen, indicating previous service in Northern Ireland with the British Army. A stickler for hygiene and cleanliness, Wilson never seemed to sleep or have the need to do so. Waking us each day at five am, he would enter the room banging a metal bin with a wooden stick whilst barking orders at us.

"This room is a HAVEN for disease!" was one of his favourite remarks at room inspections.

Amar couldn't have been more different. No taller than five foot four inches,' his skin had the appearance of aged leather, and his eyes were like raisins. Originally from El Jadid on the Moroccan coast, Amar smoked Camel cigarettes, which he broke the filters off before crushing them into the ground with the tip of his combat boot, as if they were burning like a full cigarette.

He often bragged that he was still carrying a bullet lodged in his lower back, fired at him by a guard as he broke out of Kenitra prison. He told us he had been serving a sentence there for armed robbery, having been wrongly convicted of the crime.

"Don't talk to me about pain!" he would bark viciously as he put us through our paces. "I've been shot, and it wasn't so bad!"

Amar always carried a small paper bag of crystallised ginger candy in the map pocket of his combat fatigues, and when not smoking a Camel he would chew a lump of it, munching slowly on the sugared spice like a man with all the time in the world.

Each time he pulled his bag of sweets from his pocket, he would offer one to Sergeant Wilson before helping himself. Every time Wilson would pull a face and wave the sweets away. Working together, this unlikely duo were the main enforcers of discipline where our section was concerned.

"What you are going through is nothing, you rats!" Amar would snarl whilst venting his bitter little spleen at us during physical training sessions. "I was in Kenitra central prison for a crime I didn't commit, but you wanted to come here."

Each day for a whole month began with the same routine. After washing and shaving in double quick time we had to strip our beds, leaving our sheets tightly rolled into tubes and placed in the shape of a cross on the bed, then clean the room thoroughly. Once these tasks had been completed, we were lined up in the corridor outside our rooms.

Our boot tips had to be in line with the second tiles on the floor, away from the wall, before counting ourselves off in French in front of Wilson, starting with one, from right to left. Anyone making a mistake - and there were many - quickly had a boot or fist delivered to the solar plexus or stomach. This counting procedure was not as easy as it might seem.

We were invariably lined up in a completely different order each day, so learning to count effectively in French was essential right from the beginning. Breakfast was black coffee and bread, which we were given exactly ten minutes to consume.

After eating, there were kit inspections and physical fitness training. Boots were polished thoroughly, including the soles. Every task was expected to be completed in double-time, and the hours of the day seemed endless.

For many amongst us, this introduction to the realities of military life came as something of a shock. After only three weeks in training, Manda was one of them.

"I can't keep up with all this; I'm going to crack," he said late one night, as we washed our filthy uniforms together by hand. Irish Tony gave him a friendly punch on the shoulder.

"Manda, we are all in the same boat, we just have to get through it all together, yeah?" he said.

Nevertheless, Manda looked dejected and fatigued.

"It's Sergeant Wilson, he's just brutal. I hate him; he enjoys what he is doing, in a sick way."

Now Jurgen stopped washing his own kit, and spoke up.

"You *have* to hate him, Manda; that way you can get satisfaction out of taking anything he throws at you and keep on going."

"That's right," said Tony. "I hate the bastard, but it's easy for me, I hate the British anyway."

I myself didn't hate the British, I didn't hate anyone, but I certainly had no warm feelings for Wilson or the relish with which he carried out his duties.

The next morning, however, I did come close to

91

hating both Manda and Tony, after they both hesitated too long during the morning count off in the corridor. Worn down by lack of sleep and over-exertion, neither of them got it right when expected to shout out their number amongst the rest of the section lined up in front of Amar and Wilson.

We all paid the price for their shortcomings, and it was time for us to collectively learn and execute the *March du Canard* or, "The duck Walk".

With Manda and Tony standing next to Wilson and Amar outside the accommodation block, the four of them watched as the rest of us were forced to "walk" up and down before them in a squatting position, with our hands clasped behind our newly shaven heads. This went on for a painful and exhausting thirty minutes, as Amar ranted, "You see now, how the whole section suffers if individuals amongst you don't get simple things right?"

The agony building up in the muscles of our thighs and back increased minute by minute, as Tony and Manda were forced to watch us ape the walk of a clutch of ducklings desperately in search of their mother. Now we were all paying the price for their lapse of concentration under duress. Neither was popular amongst the section for the following couple of days.

After a month at Castel Naudary we spent three weeks at another training camp situated in an old farm complex building in the Pyrenees, known as "Belle Air".

It was now March and the weather was warming up across the south of France, as we were gradually introduced to the legion speciality of the forced march. Weighed down with heavy backpacks ammunition pouches and rifles, Sergeant Wilson was ever-present, the veins in his neck and at his temples bulging with rage as he urged us on to exert more and more effort.

Marching for miles and miles, day after day in all weathers, we learned to live off the land, sleep outside, and attack the enemy - whether he was in a forest, mountainside or holed up in a building.

Communication was in French, and French only. Non-francophones were paired together with French speakers who would translate orders and instructions for them. Other than that, each non-French speaking recruit was expected to pick up the language simply by being immersed in it twenty-four hours a day. Any formal lessons in the French language were conducted by bored junior officers, and were rudimentary.

Whilst at Belle Air we learned how to handle and use our personal weapon, the FAMAS assault rifle.

After every firing of this weapon, its working parts became badly soiled with carbon deposits and had to be cleaned thoroughly; an arduous task made worse by the fact that we were made to do it standing up, whilst at the same time having to learn and memorise the names of all its working parts in French.

Each week we were put through a ten kilometre march carrying full loads of combat gear and rifles. Hans struggled and suffered badly on these marches, and I did my best to help him. If he lagged behind I would grab him by the shoulder straps and pull him along.

"Hans, just look at the boots of the guy in front, concentrate on them and keep your legs moving," I would say.

"Thanks, mate. I'm okay," he would gasp.

In return for my help and encouragement, Hans helped me with my French.

"Think of it as a code, Sebastián. Don't think you're learning a language, it's too daunting."

"How so?"

"Everything in the world has a name, just exchange

it for a French one and REMEMBER it. Just get how, where, when, what, if and then. Hang your sentences off words like that. You can't say anything if you don't know the names of things!"

Jurgen picked up French with outstanding speed, and curried great favour with the training team as a consequence.

"It's so easy for a Dane to learn a foreign language," he said one day, as we stripped and cleaned our weapons after a session on the firing ranges. "There are only five million of us on the planet and since nobody else speaks Danish, we need to be able to talk to the rest of the world."

I stopped pulling the cleaner through my rifles' barrel.

"I never really thought of that," I said.

"People speak Spanish all over the world, and English and French."

"Exactly," said Jurgen,

"One of the first things Danish children do is to learn English, so our brains are already trained in a way to absorb other forms of communication."

Esteban turned to us with a stupid grin on his face as he announced sarcastically, "How fascinating!"

At this, the normally mild-mannered but exhausted Jurgen lashed out in English.

"Fuck you, you little Spik, I've had enough of you talking shit every day; now shut that fucking sewer in the middle of your face!"

"Make me!"

Seconds later, and fists were flying between the Dane and the Spaniard; the short stocky Iberian and the tall lean Scandinavian resembling a mongoose and a snake as they kicked, punched and wrestled on the ground. Soon, Tony and I were pulling them both apart. Amar quickly appeared on the scene as if from nowhere, like an evil genie.

"What's going on here?" he asked, his slow sinister voice relishing of the opportunity to mete out a severe punishment. No-one spoke.

"I'm going to ask just one more time…" said Amar.

Jurgen spoke up. "It was just an argument over nothing, *mon caporal*."

Esteban shifted uneasily from foot to foot with his eyes to the ground.

"And what language did I hear you speaking?" enquired Amar further.

"*Anglais, mon caporal*," replied Esteban. Amar spat on the ground in disgust. "Come here both of you; stand side by side. I'll teach you better than to speak the language of barbarians."

Esteban and Jurgen presented themselves to Amar, standing to attention side by side in front of the furious corporal.

"Open your mouths, both of you," ordered Amar.

The rest of us in the section now felt sick with anticipation at whatever fate the two offenders were about to suffer. Stooping to the ground, Amar gathered up two half-handfuls of gravel and dirt. He then rammed them hard into our comrade's open mouths. In an apoplectic rage, Amar proceeded to berate the two miscreants in front of the whole section.

"You will both keep that shit in your mouths for the rest of the day! You will remove it in front of me at inspection this evening! This is the French Foreign Legion; you will speak French and French alone!"

Dribbling grimy saliva down their shirt fronts, Esteban and Jurgen stood to attention for the next forty-five minutes as the rest of us were ordered to assume the squatting position and execute the *March de Canard* on their behalf. Amar was now in full flow, stamping his feet as he harangued us.

"There is only one language here, *petit canards*; French! Just French!" he yelled.

Catching a glimpse of the two reprobates out if the corner of my eye as I waddled up and down in agony, I saw the eyes of two young men who were obviously feeling completely wretched and were without a doubt wondering what their lives had come to.

Belle Air, with all its brutality and exhaustion, was not, however, a singularly awful experience. There were nights when we sat around huge bonfires singing Legion songs and drinking sugared wine, as the feelings of comradeship and sentiment running through the Legion ethos began to settle on us.

Even during the hardest moments, I was encouraged by the individual acts of humanity displayed between us as recruits; acts of kindness and compassion that began to act as a type of glue, binding us together with a sense of commonality.

Our three week training stint at Belle Air culminated in a fifty kilometres forced march through the countryside, carrying full fighting order. Afterwards we were all covered in sores and abrasions, caused by our equipment straps rubbing constantly on the same points of our bodies through our sweaty clothing. Our feet too were blistered and sore, and it was obvious most of us were becoming leaner by the day.

On completion of the march we assembled as a group and were presented with our "*kepi blancs*", the white caps famous the world over as the headgear of the French Foreign Legion. We wore them with genuine pride, and as I placed mine on my head for the first time I made the conscious effort to try and move on and leave the past behind.

Chapter Sixteen

Returning to Castel Naudary and hardened by our experiences in the Pyrenees, we were ready to continue our training to become fully fledged fighting Legionnaires. As the proud owners of the famous white *kepi* of the French Foreign Legion, we took a renewed sense of pride in our appearance, spending hours at a time ironing our uniforms through the night.

Besides the standard green working uniforms of the Legion, a Legionnaire is issued with two other main uniforms; the "*Tenue de sortie*" ("walking out shirt") and the "*Tenue de Parade*" ("parade uniform"). Corporal Amar took great pleasure in not only showing us how to iron these uniforms, but informing us of the consequences for anyone not achieving the required standards of smartness.

"Nobody gets past me and into town for a beer with one single crease out of line; understand?" he said with a cold smile, as he laid a *tenue de sortie* across the ironing board in front of him in the classroom one morning. "There are fifteen creases to be ironed in the shirt; they will be ironed properly each and every time."

He then proceeded to iron three sharp creases efficiently above each pocket on the front of the beige shirt, two down the length of each arm, a further two across the top of the back of the shirt, and finally, three more creases running vertically down its back.

To say that we looked both smart and efficient in our uniforms is an understatement. Personally, having already completed two years at the Gendarmerie Academy back home in Argentina, I found much of the physical aspects of the training well within my capacities. What was hard was the sleep deprivation, and confusion surrounding the language difficulties, but that was true for nearly all concerned.

The fact that I had already received two years leadership training showed itself early on in my time with the Legion. Whenever a fellow recruit was hurt or injured I immediately sprang to their aid, instinctively taking control of the situation.

I rarely needed showing things twice and was easily able to pick up on and follow the logic of our training program. These traits were noticed early on by the training staff, and I was given a little extra in the way of responsibilities.

Towards the end of basic training, I was informed that if my French reached a high enough standard there was no reason why I shouldn't be eligible for an early promotion, if that's what I wanted to aim for. With this in mind, I obtained a small French grammar book and filled the few available moments of spare time with cramming French into my head.

Luckily I didn't have much time to think about the recent past. Our basic training with the Legion concluded in May 1990 with an arduous 150 kilometre route march from Perpignan back to Castel Naudry. The march was known as "The Raid."

Situated approximately fifteen kilometres from the Mediterranean coast, the town of Perpignan was the continental capital of the Kingdom of Majorca during the 13th and 14th centuries. After years of fighting between France and Spain, Perpignan was ceded to France by the Spanish in 1659 and has remained French ever since.

With a population of around 300,000 it now lies roughly thirty kilometres from the border of Spanish Catalonia. To drive the 150 kilometres from Perpignan to Castel Naudry by car should take an hour and a half. We were to walk that distance across the country, weighed down with backpacks and weapons, in three days.

As we prepared our rifles and gathered our equipment together behind the trucks that had dropped us off, Wilson gave us a short pep talk. Amar stood at his side.

"This is it," said Wilson solemnly. "This is the Raid; for the next three days you will dig deep into your reserves of physical and mental strength. Anyone not completing this march will do it again. It will behove you to overcome any weaknesses in either mind *or* body that you might experience." Amar stepped forward.

"Not that any of you have anything to worry about; I will be right at your side, every step of the way..." he slithered.

Soon enough, weighed down like pack mules in the bright spring sunshine, we headed north on foot towards Castel Naudry and our destiny as fully-fledged Legionnaires.

We found out early on that the pace of the march was unforgiving, as was the ground we covered. Taking us across tracts of grass-carpeted rolling countryside, our route passed through rural hamlets and skirted around the edge of villages.

The local inhabitants in these places would pause to stare at us blankly, as our ragtag snake of shuffling misfits wound its way through their cosseted inward-looking worlds.

Once out in the country again, skylarks sang in the air above us, as grasshoppers sprang from the ground around our feet, deftly escaping the impact of our heavy footfalls in the lush grass.

It wasn't long before we started to feel the weight of our packs and the rubbing of our boots against our already battered feet. Wilson, Amar and the other NCOs pushed us on mercilessly.

"You want to be Legionnaires? Then march or fucking die!" screamed Wilson, as he forged on alongside us in the heat of the late afternoon.

Carrying a heavier pack than the rest of us, Wilson displayed his physical prowess by running up and down our marching column, giving constant *'encouragement'*, without ever appearing to be out of breath or struggling with the demands of the task.

Looking up from the ground at one point, I was disheartened to see stretched out in front of me a curving line of recruits winding through the fields like a slow green snake. Each sweating recruit's footstep was one I had yet to take.

Towards the end of the first day, I could barely bring myself to even think about the further two days to come. Eventually, I was relieved when we neared an oval-shaped copse of chestnut, beech and oak. In it, around two hundred trees stood guard over a shallow stream, cutting across the wide pasture we marched through. This was where we were to spend our first night.

Chapter Seventeen

Entering the copse in tactical formation, we barely made a sound as we infiltrated the trees an hour before sunset. Even so, we disturbed a tawny owl with our intrusion.

Leaving his woodland sanctuary on the western side of the copse, the solitary bird spread his wings and cut low across the meadow, silently skimming the grass in the direction we would ourselves be taking the next day.

The air was cooler inside the wood, and its floor was more or less completely covered by a carpet of forget-me-nots. The light of the evening sun streaming in through the trees onto the countless tiny flower heads gave the appearance of a dusting of blue powder over the ground. This contrasted sharply with the dark green of our uniforms and our black boots.

Spreading out amongst the trees, we took up sentry positions, cleaned our weapons, and prepared food. Wilson and Amar unfolded a map in the middle of the trees and conferred quietly over it with a young lieutenant.

In the ethereal light of the scene around me, I was reminded of a church's interior, lit by the light pouring in through stained glass windows.

The trees now became columns of wood supporting a high ceiling of ever-shifting translucent leafy green tiles, each tile edged in ecclesiastic gold. Soon, our band of exhausted Legionnaires was hunched in twos over mess tins of bubbling stew like world-weary Parishioners in prayer.

I was partnered together that night with Roland, the Swede from Gothenburg, and after being stood down from sentry duty we both sat on the ground to eat and to rest our aching limbs.

Opening our rations like seagulls descending on a morsel of food thrown by some passer by, we feasted on sardines, liver pate, and chicken casserole. We ate like starved men, shovelling spoonfuls of grub into our mouths as if there was no tomorrow.

"I like it here in this wood," said Roland as we gorged ourselves.

Somewhat puzzled by his unexpected statement, I asked why, as I filled myself up on chicken casserole.

"It's springtime," he said. "It smells new in here; I like it."

The gravy from Roland's casserole spilled over his spoon, spreading across his lips to the corners of his mouth and glistening in the fading twilight as he spoke.

"You know, Sebastián," he went on, "when I get out of the Legion in five years, I'm going to get myself a puppy."

I swallowed a mouthful of chicken, stopped munching, and waited for a punch line; but there wasn't one.

"A puppy?"

"Yeah, a puppy."

It was getting dark in the wood now, and we spoke in whispers.

"Why do you want a puppy so bad that you would wait for five years?" I asked. Roland didn't look up from his meal.

"Because that puppy's going to love me, that's why,"

"Hasn't any *person* ever loved you?" I whispered back to him.

"No, nobody," he said, as he opened a tin of sardines the size of his palm.

Famished by the day's excursions, I carried on eating and talking at the same time.

"Everyone gets loved by someone sometime, my

friend," I said as we finished our food. Roland licked tomato juice off the back of his spoon.

"No they don't," he said matter-of-factly.

With food in our bellies and darkness now reining in the wood, we crawled into our sleeping bags without removing our boots. With our rifles clasped securely in our hands, Roland and I settled in for the night. Around us in the soft blue blackness, forty human islands littered the forget-me-nots, as Roland continued to talk. He began to tell me about how he had loved a Pakistani girl back in Gothenburg, and how his love for her was doomed by cultural differences between his own family and hers.

With the spring breeze bending the treetops playfully above us in that virgin hour of darkness, I heard Roland say something about how he had ended up in prison.

Then, somewhere around the point in his story where he was having sex with his attractive young probation officer, I was snatched from his soliloquy by Nyx the goddess of the night. Offering no resistance, I allowed her to kidnap me; taking me from Roland selfishly, like a jealous mistress in the dark.

Like a good woman, sleep has the capacity to temporarily liberate one from the vagaries and cruelties of life. That night in the wood as Roland talked I willingly surrendered to her irresistible pull, beneath the gently swaying branches of a chestnut tree. The young Swede would have to wait another two years to offload his woes onto me.

Just before dawn, the perimeter of the wood erupted to the blistering sound of blank rounds being fired at us, as our position came under a simulated attack by a section of Infantry from the 4th Regiment in Castel Naudary.

Wilson and Amar's training methods served us well,

the whole section falling straight into the standard operational procedures we had been taught repeatedly for the last four months. Fire control orders were delivered and received; ammunition expenditure was measured and controlled correctly. Everyone reacted just as they should have done; every one except Roland, that is.

For some reason, probably adrenalin and fatigue, Roland laughed manically through out the attack. Taking on the appearance of a madman as he fired his weapon wildly in the direction of our "attackers", I caught sight of him pulling the trigger in a state of hysterics.

Afterwards, the thought did cross my mind whether or not it really had been a case of cultural differences that had sabotaged his past relationship, and whether or not he would be fit enough to even look after a puppy in five years time anyway.

For the next two days, with our packs and weapons becoming heavier and heavier by the hour, we marched on in the late spring heat. I began to struggle considerably. Remembering Wilson's words about relying on our reserves of strength, I went inside myself mentally and trudged on determinedly through the French countryside,

Finally, three days and 150 kilometres after setting off from Perpignan on foot, together, we marched through the main gates of the barracks in Castel Naudary. With blood-soaked socks and our heads held high, we were now proud soldiers of the French Foreign Legion.

A few days after our return to the barracks the whole section assembled for a briefing about regimental postings, and the Legion's expectations of us as newly-qualified Legionnaires.

Jurgen had excelled in basic training and come out

with top marks. Consequently he could choose any regimental posting he desired, and picked the Legion's Parachute Regiment. Along with two British recruits, he would train and be based on the island of Corsica in the Mediterranean. Jurgen had been a good friend to me, and I would miss him.

Back in Aubagne, the rest of us were informed as to which regiments of the Legion we would be sent to serve in. Irish Tony, Hans, Roland, Esteban, Manda, and I would be going to the Second Foreign Infantry Regiment in Nîmes. Others went to the Legion's Cavalry Regiment in orange, some, to the Third Jungle Regiment in Tropical Guiana in South America. Some recently-qualified Legionnaires went straight to the 13th Demi brigade in Djibouti, East Africa.

"You lot are in luck," said Corporal Amar, as he addressed my little Gang after the talk. "The Second Etranger is my Regiment; I'm coming with you to Nîmes..."

"Oh shit," we thought, especially as Sergeant Wilson was coming too.

Those of us going to the Second Foreign Infantry Regiment boarded a truck from the barracks in Aubagne, having said whatever goodbyes we thought were necessary to those going to other regiments of the Legion. We were then driven northwest up the motorway for an hour and a half, until we reached the barracks on the edge of the ancient Roman city of Nîmes.

Chapter Eighteen

Nîmes, Second Foreign Infantry Regiment

In order to avoid cliques forming, new arrivals at the regiment were split up for the purposes of sleeping and accommodation. I found myself allocated to a room that was already home to two German Legionnaires named Gruber and Faust, a Peruvian named Carlos, and a twenty-three-year-old soldier from Takayama in the Japanese Alps, Hiroki Ito.

Most of our days in the Regiment began with room cleaning, inspections, and a run or a session in the gymnasium before a short parade for orders of the day. Our section commander was a young lieutenant from Fontainebleau. He was obviously a posh boy, and the day after we arrived at the Regiment he introduced himself and gave us a short pep talk after the morning parade.

"Welcome to the unit," he said. "I'm Lieutenant La Roche; anybody here not speak French, put up your hand now." Nobody put their hand up.

"Okay, good. This Regiment has high standards, and so do I. You won't let me down, or yourselves, or the Legion as a whole. Any of you who haven't completely forgotten your past lives, I suggest now is the time to do so."

La Roche then dismissed us as he pulled a packet of Gauloises cigarettes from his trouser pocket. Heading back to the block to get changed, Hans skipped alongside me and slapped me on the back

"We are in the Legion *now*, my friend!"

"Looks like it," I said. But I wasn't really listening. I was pondering what La Roche had said about forgetting our past lives. If he was meaning that we should take this opportunity to move on, fine. But forgetting was not going to be possible. Not for me anyway. In the meantime, I got to know my new roommates better. Carlos was twenty-five and from the city of Cuzco in the Peruvian Andes. He was due to leave the Legion in a couple of weeks time, after completing his five-year contract. The Germans, Gruber and Faust, were both twenty-one years old and from Dresden. They took their roles as soldiers of the Legion very seriously indeed.

"You do things right here, understand. We don't pull any extra duties for sloppy kit or dirty room and failing locker inspections here, okay?" Gruber repeatedly told me during my first few days in St Nicolas.

"We keep this place tidy and clean, okay, Alvarez," Faust continued to inform me, whilst staring at me with his Teutonic blue eyes.

Ito had an entirely different approach to welcoming new recruits. He was the first guy in the Regiment to take me under his wing and let me know about life in the unit, and what was to be expected of me.

Having joined up in 1986, he had already served four years. After watching a television documentary about the Legion whilst living at home with his parents, Ito Quit his job as a ski instructor and boarded a train for Tokyo. Phoning his parents from Narita airport, he told them that he had things to do in Europe, and to look after his younger sister.

"I need to spread my wings and find out who I am," he told his weeping mother, before telling her not to worry if she didn't hear from him for a while. Ito was calm, centred, and mature for his years. Not surprisingly, he was the section's sniper. He talked to me as we spent one evening ironing uniforms in the corridor outside our room.

"Life here can be pretty good. Keep your fitness

levels up and try and get into the sports. I was nineteen when I got here; I'm going home in about a year. On the whole, I'd say it's been a worthwhile experience."

"Thanks for the advice," I said. "I'll remember it."

"One more thing," said Ito.

"Yes?"

"Make friends by all means, but don't get too close to people. You'll be posted all over the place and move around a lot; be self reliant."

I took notice of Ito of course, but still, it felt good to make another friend, and I started to fit into Regimental life with my new colleagues and the guys I had come from Aubagne with.

If there weren't elements of culture clash between Gruber, Faust and myself when I arrived in the room at the end of May, there was certainly a definite tension between the three of us up to and including their country's defeat of Argentina in the World Cup semi-finals at the Stadio Olimpico in Rome. Both of them were ecstatic at Germany's victory.

"*Deutschland, Deutschland*!" they chanted as they came into the room late that night in July.

"Well done," I said as I got into bed, aware of the need for sleep before the following day's activities. Gruber had other plans, and pulled the bed clothes off me aggressively.

"We beat you, you greasy Diego!" he taunted as he drank from a bottle of Kronenburg. Seeing the way things were going, I took control of the situation straight away.

I might have been the new guy, but I wasn't going to eat shit off these two for anything. Springing from my bed space I smacked Gruber in the trap hard, breaking one of his front teeth, and giving myself a deep gash to the skin of my right knuckle in the process.

Gruber slumped to the floor, clutching his mouth as Ito jumped between Faust and I, preventing the other German from retaliating on his mate's behalf. Holding us both back with a hand to the chest, Ito spoke calmly.

"Enough!" he said.

From his bed space on the other side of the room, Carlos propped himself up on one elbow. Through the thick fog of his half-sleep, he spoke drowsily.

"I'm so fucking glad to be leaving here," he said, in a *seen it all before* fashion, before slumping heavily back onto his mattress.

Backing off, I stepped away from Gruber. I then fetched him a towel doused in cold water and handed it to him on the floor.

"Merci," he offered reluctantly.

We all retired to bed, and with the wounded German nursing his damaged mouth, each of us now had a clearer understanding of the pecking order amongst us.

I soon introduced Ito to Hans, Tony, Esteban and the others, and over the next couple of months we enjoyed a few free nights out on the town in Nîmes.

It was on one such evening, as we drank in a rowdy bar just outside the town centre that Irish Tony and I got talking to a Polish barmaid. She was dressed as an American cowgirl in tiny denim shorts, blue bikini top, and a huge pink cowgirl hat made of foam. Two water pistols sat in real leather holsters on her slim waist, like she meant business.

In a sexy twist to her outfit, she sported a pair of half-glasses perched mid way down her prominent nose. Her short dark hair hung cheekily around the rim of her big silly hat. Her fellow barmaid was French and having the time of her life dressed up as an Indian squaw, with a feather in her hair and a red stripe painted across her nose.

Tony introduced me to Guinness and Jameson Irish

whiskey (neither of which I enjoyed), as we tried our best to engage the interest of both the girls behind the bar.

After a bit of the usual banter, I learned the polish girl was called Anya and she was twenty nine. She gave me her phone number and she and her 'squaw' Veronique, agreed to meet up with us for drinks the next time we were free.

A few days later I tried the number she had given me and was surprised to find that she actually answered, especially considering she must have been asked for her number many times a night as a matter of course in her line of work. I asked if they would like to meet up soon with Tony and me.

"Well," she said. "You know I carry two water pistols on my belt, yes?"

"Yes, what about them?" I replied.

"One is filled with water and the other with Jack Daniels. Next time you come to the bar, I'm going to shoot you with one of them. Open your mouth when I do," she said.

"Okay... and...?"

"And if you get J.D, me and Veronique will come out sometime with you and your friend, okay? And if you get water, then you piss off," she said. Before I could answer, she hung up abruptly. Two weeks later, after taking a shot of bourbon in the mouth at the bar, the four of us went out for pizza and beer in Nîmes.

Anya shared a small flat with Veronique, who was studying a degree in hotel management at the Vatel Institute in the city. Though we got on well with both of them, as Tony and I had just recently arrived at the Regiment and had limited free time, we were acutely aware of the limitations on the lives we had chosen.

We couldn't go and stay the night with Anya and Veronique and they obviously couldn't come and stay with us. We did, however, meet up with them a few times between June and September that year, and enjoyed the times we spent together.

One evening they got us all worked up by taking us to see the new erotic French Movie, *Le Mari de la Coiffeuse*.

In it, the Italian actress Anna Galiena played the part of a sultry hairdresser who agrees, for some undivulged reason, to marry an old lech with a penchant for sexy women who cut hair for a living. Nothing unusual in that, Tony and I figured.

But then the lech, who was called Antoine, and played by the French Actor Jean Rochefort, spent the whole film sitting in the corner of the shop looking down his wife's top and up her skirt as she gave him sly glimpses of her tits and panties, whilst at the same time satisfying the male grooming needs of half the town.

I can't say that Tony or myself fully appreciated the cameraman's efforts at giving us an 'Antoine's-eye' view of his sultry wife, as we happened to be sitting in the dark right next to a pair of very sexy women whom we knew would definitely *not* be screwing us later that night.

Nevertheless, I was now looking forward to making some kind of a life based in Nîmes. With Argentina behind me, a place to live in a new country, new friends and some semblance of a new start, life began to balance out and take some sort of form and structure.

In the meantime, a few thousand miles away, the seeds were being sown for a storm which was to whip up a wind that would carry Tony and I far away from Nîmes, and our frivolous encounters with Anya and Veronique.

111

Chapter Nineteen

To the Middle East, Autumn 1990

The Ortolan bunting is a sparrow-sized bird with buff shades of green and brown feathers, interspersed with dashes of dull yellow plumage. Weighing no more than twenty-five grams or so, and no longer than fifteen or sixteen inches long, the Ortolan nests on or near the ground across Europe, and lays a clutch of up to fifteen eggs.

Every year, at the end of the summer, large flocks of these small birds leave Germany and Scandinavia for North Africa, where they spend the winter in a climate both warmer and drier than that of the European Peninsular. That is, if they manage to evade the nets of the Gascon countrymen who set out to catch them in order to fill the plates of gastronomes across France.

Since living here at the farm I've spotted the odd Ortolan from time to time while out walking with my dog, Caesar, or hunting in the countryside. This little bird reminds me of what I always think of as 'The Last Supper' I enjoyed with my comrades before we left for War in the Persian Gulf, when I was twenty-one.

Whenever I see an Ortolan in flight from tree to tree, or sitting on a branch delivering its repetitive song, I congratulate it on evading the delicate nets of the bird-catchers of Gascony. I spare a thought too for the men I once knew and lived alongside. Men who I hope have managed to evade the various nets of fate and circumstance that can catch us all.

Eight months after leaving Argentina and two months after arriving in Nîmes, Anya, Veronique, whiskey, and beer were soon pushed to the back of our minds, as the material of war fighting was drawn from stores and vehicle bays around the camp in preparation for war in the Persian Gulf.

Saddam Hussein had ordered his army to move across his nation's southern border with Kuwait in order to "liberate" what his Government referred to as 'the nineteenth province of Iraq'. Kuwait is the largest oilfield on Earth, and at some time someone drew a line around it and called it a country. It was August 1990 and the Western world, led by the United States, reacted immediately. As a regiment, we started preparations to move.

Once it had been confirmed that the Second Foreign Infantry Regiment would be deployed to the Middle East to help liberate it, the whole unit literally bristled with professional excitement as preparations to go began in earnest.

Less than a week before we boarded car ferries from the south coast of France, bound for the Saudi port of Yanbu on the red Sea, Corporal Amar held Hans, Tony, and I back after morning P.T. and orders of the day.

"Alvarez, De Jong and Fitzgerald," he said, "I have secured you some work in the kitchens over at the officer's mess today, so change into your tracksuits and I'll take you over there in ten minutes - move!" Just as we were ordered, ten minutes later we accompanied Amar over to the officer's mess.

Arriving inside the Neoclassical style building, a crisp autumn breeze rushed eagerly through the open windows and along the corridors like a child with a happy secret to tell. Corporal Amar led Hans, Tony and I to the kitchens where we reported to the Cooks, Sergeant Belcourt and Corporal Challe.

The two chubby Belgians were sitting down dressed in chef's whites, smoking cigarettes and drinking anise as we walked into the kitchen.

"Sergeant Belcourt, Corporal Challe. Here's the extra sets of spare hands you asked for; Alvarez, De

Jong and Fitzgerald," announced Amar.

"Okay, thanks; we'll send them back when we've finished work later. See you," said the glassy-eyed sergeant as he and Challe got up from their chairs with all the enthusiasm of a pair of hamsters.

"See you," said Amar, He then paused in the doorway and looked at Hans and I with contempt.

"Work hard," he said, with as much menace as he could muster, which wasn't much since we were now both full Legionnaires and no longer his recruits.

"Come with me," said Belcourt when Amar had left.

"This is going to be great," mumbled Tony sarcastically as we followed the sergeant.

Belcourt showed us into the adjoining dining room where two other recent arrivals to the regiment, a Briton and a Romanian, were already at work moving chairs and tables around and carrying plastic trays of dinner-plates and cutlery. The podgy Belgian spread his arms out wide and told us the deal.

"A group of junior officers will be entertaining some fellow 'gentlemen' of the Legion's Cavalry Regiment from orange in here later this evening." I smelt wine and anise on his breath as he spoke. Gesturing towards the two Legionnaires already busy readying the room, Belcourt continued.

"These two will tell you what needs doing, okay? Work hard and don't fuck about, or I'll stab the pair of you," he barked drunkenly. "I'll stab you all!"

Turning abruptly and unsteadily on his heels, he went back into the kitchen, leaving a trail of sour alcohol vapours in his wake.

The British Legionnaire had a skinhead and a gap in the top arch of his teeth where his incisors should have been. He came over and shook our hands, whilst introducing himself and the Romanian.

"I'm Smithy and this is Bojin," he said, "Don't

worry about that fat bastard, Belcourt. He's all talk. There's not that much to do this afternoon, just moving stuff around and helping them in the kitchen. We just have to look like we're busy. The shitter is that we're going to be here until the early hours." Hans blew out his cheeks.

"Oh, great. I hope we get to eat some of their food, then," he said.

"Yes we do," said Bojin, a tall skinny redhead with pale skin. "And you're lucky, because I'm here to make the Romanian red wine and cherry sauce to go with the wild boar these toffs are going to be eating later."

I chipped in, "Who cares how long we are here, as long as we get to eat some decent food, yes?"

Bojin continued.

"I want them to train me to be a chef. I haven't been here long, but I'm a good cook and I want to show them what I can do."

Over the next few hours, the five of us swept and buffed the floors, polished the dining table, folded napkins, and ran around in the kitchen for Belcourt and Challe; together they prepared mushrooms stuffed with snails and herbs, foie gras with pickled pears, and a side of wild boar meat. As the day stretched into evening, all seven of us stopped for a smoke, a chat, and a glass of wine.

Belcourt was well-soaked by now and began going into great detail about how he enjoyed having sex with women who were heavy smokers.

"I like to fuck a chick who smokes a lot. It's the way their vaginas contract when they cough." We all laughed. Probably out of embarrassment more than anything else. We were young and I don't suppose we had really thought about things along those lines before.

Belcourt went into full swing, holding his right fist

out in front of him, pumping the fingers of it tightly in quick succession as if it were the most intimate part of some lady who had abandoned all reason, self-respect and standards, before succumbing to his not very obvious charms. Just then, Lieutenant La Roche walked into the kitchen, entering the room from the side door directly behind Belcourt.

A full glass of wine sloshed merrily in Belcourt's free hand as he made it quite clear what he was talking about.

"COUGH, OH! COUGH, OOH! COUGH! COUGH! OH! YES! Take another drag. COUGH! OOH! COUGH! OOH!"

La Roche interrupted the Sergeant from behind. "Working hard, Sergeant Belcourt?" The rest of us laughed openly, out loud.

"Everything's under control sir," replied Belcourt as he stopped pumping his fist and put his wineglass down on the work-surface.

The young lieutenant continued, "Yes yes, I can smell the cooking, Sergeant, and I'm sure we all look forward to entertaining our guests from the cavalry tonight. I think it will be a real 'Feast of the Ortolans', present circumstances considered," he said.

Manoeuvring my own glass of wine behind my back, and emboldened by the early evening booze, I ventured to address the lieutenant myself.

"Feast of the Ortolans, sir?"

La Roche turned to me, took a Gauloises from his pocket, and lit it.

"The Feast of the Ortolans," he said, "is a play set in the late 1700s. In it, there's a dinner party for members of the French nobility. One of the guests at the table proceeds to upset everyone as they try to enjoy their evening. He describes, in great detail, the fate about to befall each of them in the revolution to come." Taking a bottle of wine from the work-surface next to him, La Roche poured himself a glass.

"Oh?" I said.

No-One else seemed to know where to look, or seemed particularly interested either, for that matter. Nevertheless, taking a sip of the wine, La Roche went on.

"Considering we are about to leave France for the Persian Gulf, where we are told Saddam Hussein is preparing the *mother of all battles* for us, I think that however portentous it might seem, an Ortolan feast is quite appropriate," he said pragmatically.

Now Challe decided to chip in. "Sir, the buntings are ready and waiting in dark boxes in the pantry. We have fed them on oats, millet and figs for the last three weeks. They are about three times their usual size."

La Roche downed his wine, then stubbed out his cigarette in an ashtray next to the sink.

"You'll drown them in armagnac first, of course..." he said.

Belcourt clapped his hands together in his eagerness to please the young lieutenant.

"Each and every one shall take its last breath submerged in a 1952 vintage, sir," he beamed. Before turning to leave, La Roche smiled.

"I'm sure everyone will enjoy the fruits of your labours, Sergeant Belcourt; we shall see you later on this evening." With that, the young officer walked out of the kitchen and left us alone.

Showing his appreciation of the short but concise insight into French history and culture provided by Lieutenant La Roche, Smithy immediately returned to our earlier line of conversation.

"Well back in England, I only used to fuck homeless women," he said.

We all looked at him at once,

"Why's that, then?" we chorused.

"Well, I could just drop them off anywhere afterwards..." Smithy laughed.

I'm sure it was the wine, but we all fell about laughing. All of us except Belcourt, that is.

"That's not funny, you little bastard, my sister's homeless. Any more of that, and I'll stab you!" he snarled. We all stopped laughing, Smithy turned pale, and then Belcourt giggled.

"Ha ha, got you! You little turd! He he, hee hee!"

Irish Tony looked across at the belittled Smithy, and sneered, "Fucking English, never can take a joke when it's on them."

Smithy didn't hear him, or pretended not to. Now Belcourt began to get into his stride.

"You know, I'm only the temporary chef here; the usual one ate some flower bulbs by mistake, thinking they were onions. He's very poorly in hospital..."

Innocently enough, Hans fell for it.

"Do they think he'll be all right?" he asked. Belcourt kept a straight face.

"Oh yes; they say he'll be out in the spring..."

Poor Hans didn't get it and couldn't understand why I was laughing.

Now, for the first time since leaving home, I was enjoying myself and starting to believe that, even in here, I could possibly have a life worth living. Smithy wandered off and returned to work in the dining room as I turned to Challe.

"Could we have a look at those birds, Corporal Challe?" I asked.

Belcourt and Challe both said that it was time to start preparing the buntings anyway, and led Hans and I into the pantry at the back of the kitchen.

The birds were held six at a time in blacked-out boxes one foot square, stacked along two shelves on the pantry walls. Reaching up to the top shelf, Sergeant Belcourt took down a box and placed it on the pantry's work-surface.

Raising the lid slightly, he pulled one of the buntings out with his left hand. Blinking in the light, the doomed bird struggled in vain against the grip of the drunken fat chef. Belcourt turned to Challe.

"Get the brandy and four or five glasses, Corporal Challe," he said, somewhat ominously.

Challe fetched four large brandy glasses and filled them with the vintage armagnac, before lining them up in a row.

Taking the first bird, Belcourt pushed it headfirst into the glass before holding his hand over the top. The bunting momentarily tried to flap its fragile wings within the confines of the glass, kicked its legs, and then died in the autumn coloured drink. Pulling another box down from the shelf, Challe grabbed a bird from inside and did the same with that one in another glass full of brandy.

"Okay, you lot," said Belcourt as he drowned another bird, "Grab boxes, grab birds and get them ready to cook."

We did to the birds exactly what the two Belgians did, and a very short time later twenty-five armagnac-soaked Ortolan buntings lay lined up on the work-surface of the pantry.

Now we all drank from the guilty brandy glasses without shame as the evening turned into night. After taking a gulp from his glass, Challe pulled a sad lifeless feather from his tongue and looked at it.

"That's what I call dead drunk!" chuckled Belcourt, "Has either of you ever plucked birds before?" he then asked Hans and I.

"Yes Sergeant, I have," I said, feeling quite relaxed and contented.

"Okay, then get plucking; and don't tear the skin."

He then turned to Hans,.

"You can get the floor cleaned up de Jong".

Returning to the main kitchen, Belcourt switched on a cassette-player near the dishwasher and turned the volume up.

"Now you bastards can have some culture, whether you like it or not,!!!!" he bellowed.

As I stood there, tipsy in the pantry, plucking the sodden buntings, the first movement of Beethoven's Fifth piano concerto oozed like syrup from the speakers of the cassette. Beside me, Corporal Challe stopped working and leaned against the open pantry door, a glass of armagnac in one hand and a drowned bunting limp in the other.

Hans stood in the kitchen leaning on a wet mop, staring intently at the floor. Belcourt stood in a trancelike state by the kitchen window, sharpening a carving-knife.

As the gentle strings of the concerto's first movement gave way seamlessly to the dominant notes of a piano and a three themed sonata, I thought about what I would be missing out on in life if I didn't return from the Gulf.

I realised then how dismissive I had been of art, books, music and culture, and how, if I got out of the coming conflict alive, then I would surely seek out these things in the future. I resolved there and then to write a letter to Raul in Argentina, letting him know I had joined the Legion.

After all, there was the chance I could become a casualty, and the thought of being killed and nobody knowing who I really was unsettled me. I knew one thing for sure, and that was that my brother had no interest in telling anyone where I was.

The Cavalry Officers arrived later and enjoyed a

hearty feast of foie gras, snails and boar, followed by the Ortolan buntings washed down with wine from the Legion's own vineyards.

The dinner table had been waited on by a couple of stewards, who now helped clear it before resetting it for ourselves. Bojin had done a wonderful job of the cherry sauce, having soaked the fruit in red wine and Juniper berries before reducing it in a large pan together with honey and sprigs of Thyme.

We were all quite happily pissed when we took our seats around the mahogany table, as Belcourt announced that it was time for them to reward us all for our hard work with an Ortolan feast.

Standing in the doorway between the dining room and kitchen, he declared loudly, "Don't listen to that little Toff La Roche about that feast of the Ortolans bullshit, or that French Revolution nonsense, or even that "mother of all battles" crap! I'm coming to the desert with you all and I'm not scared. If any Iraqis kill me, I'll stab them!"

We all laughed as he then tottered in a slightly unsettling light-footed way back into the kitchen, to retrieve the roasted birds.

"Fuck, I'm glad I don't smoke," Smithy mumbled with his mouth in his glass. Challe fired a menacing look across the table at him.

"What was that?"

"Nothing, Corporal."

Challe then lit six candles in an ornate holder in the middle of the table, and turned out the main lights. From the kitchen, Belcourt could be heard continuing his rant with his head in the oven.

"And as for their Revolution," he went on, "if it was such a success, then why are they on their fifth republic?"

He was talking to himself by now, as filling our

stomachs was the only thing on our minds. Challe handed out large white napkins, then placed a single white plate in front of each of us. No knives or forks; we weren't going to need them, just the plates and napkins.

"When sergeant Belcourt puts the bird on your plate," he said, "cover the whole of your head with the napkin. It keeps the flavours from escaping, and anyway, you should never let God watch you eating one of his Ortolans." Returning to his own seat, he carried on.

"Pick up the bird with your fingers; place it in your mouth with its head hanging out. Bite off the head and put it on the plate before you start to chew the Ortolan."

Letting out a loud, impudent belch, Bojin asked Challe, "What does it taste like, Corporal?"

Challe replied slowly, his eyes half-closed in the candlelight as if savouring a sweet memory.

"Its' like... It's like a... *m o u t h g a s m,*" he purred, conjuring up images of gastronomic delight beyond the wildest dreams of mere mortals. Smithy raised his eyebrows and rubbed his hands together.

"Can't wait!"

Belcourt returned to the dining room, holding the buntings on a large platter. Challe got up to help him serve. No-One spoke, not even Belcourt, as a reverential silence descended on the room.

After Belcourt and Challe had placed the roasted birds on our plates, each of us around the table draped a napkin over our heads. We now leant, heads bowed, over the dead buntings, like monks performing an ancient candlelit ritual.

Picking up my own bird, I pushed it piping hot, ass first, into my mouth before biting off its head. To begin with I had to hold it between my teeth, breathing in and out quickly to cool it down. Then, I started to chew.

The delicate gamey sweetness of the fig-infused flesh and bubbling fat of the roasted bunting was luxurious to say the least, and the soft mushy texture of the bones took me by surprise as they disintegrated between my teeth.

The Ortolan filled my whole mouth, and it was a few minutes before I had worked my way through its wings and body flesh. In time, I chewed my way into the slightly bitter internal organs.

Just as my taste buds registered this shift from sweet flesh to bitter innards, my teeth cut through the tiny heart and lungs of the bird, one little bite releasing a decadent deluge of hot armagnac over the breadth of my tongue.

The sounds of gastronomic pleasure wafted out from underneath the napkins of my companions around the table as I'm sure we all thought about how glad we were to be there, doing what we were doing, instead of doing just about anything else.

When we had finished eating, Belcourt, bunting grease dribbling down his chin, raised his glass at the head of the table. The wine in his glass glowed deep ruby-red in the candlelight. "Now you don't have to worry about dying in the Gulf and going to hell," he beamed drunkenly, "because you have already tasted Heaven!"

Days later, like a flock of Ortolans, we headed south for the winter.

Chapter Twenty

It took nearly 300 of our vehicles to move the Regiment and its equipment from Yanbu on the Saudi coast up to our forward positions in the desert, closer to the border of Iraq.

With helmeted soldiers, weapons and radio antennae protruding skywards along its length, our convoy projected an image of menacing efficiency, rippling in the heat haze like a distorted reflection in a fairground mirror. Ito was there, as was Esteban, Hans, Gruber, Faust, and Lieutenant La Roche.

We sat in the back of an open truck towards the rear of the convoy. Corporal Amar and Sergeant Wilson, Roland, and the rest of the section occupied vehicles in front and behind. Each of us now dressed in recently-issued sandy-coloured combat fatigues mottled mid-brown, all of us armed to the teeth.

With the lead elements of the convoy snaking out over the barren landscape into the far distance, I remember Tony in his helmet, turning to me and pulling the scarf from his mouth. Above the speeding vehicles engines and hot desert wind he shouted, "Fuck, man, if only they could see me in the Emerald bar in Dundalk now!"

At this, his Celtic blue eyes sparkled with life in the Arabian sun. Gripping my assault rifle with one hand and giving him the thumbs up with the other, I smiled back. Like Tony I was young and excited, but behind my own smile lay shadows of doubt and fear. Looking north over the top of our winding convoy to the horizon and beyond, I wondered what lay ahead. Physical pain; death? My blood in the sand, or the blood of others....?

Glory or redemption?

Much later that same day, we made the first of our desert camps and began the process of settling into our new surroundings whilst far away, old men in grey suits, safe in their offices, organised the coming violence.

The section and the Company as a whole spread out in the desert as together we set about covering our vehicles with camouflage, distributing water, organising sentry rotas and getting ourselves fed.

In a freshly dug hole in the ground, Tony and I sat under our helmets, opened a pack of rations each, and shoved tuna and potatoes, followed by crackers and cheese-spread into our mouths. Chicken liver pate was scooped from the tin with our bayonets and eaten off the tips. We didn't need to eat this way, but it made us feel like warriors.

"So, what's it like in Ireland?" I asked as we ate.

"Ireland's a great place all in all, people like a drink and a singsong - rains all the time, though," said Tony as he munched. "But I don't know all of it. I'm from Dundalk in Louth, I haven't travelled around the country that much. Louth is the smallest county in Ireland. There's a bit of money around the county but not in Dundalk, it's poor as shit. No decent work."

"Are the people poor?" I asked as I put some cheese-spread on a cracker.

"It depends what you mean by poor. I was unemployed before I came here. You do what you have to do. People get by. Then there are always the troubles, of course."

"You mean the bombings?" I said.

"Well, there's a war on against the British, you know. Well, you *should* know, coming from Argentina..."

"Yes, I do know. Are you ever going to beat them,

do you think?"

"Who knows? But we keep fighting, that's all we can do."

Finishing off our modest meal, we washed our forks and spoons, surrounded by comrades who were all doing the same thing with the minimum amount of precious water allocated to us. Tony carried on talking as the sun began to lose its grip on the immeasurable desert sky.

"I'm not here for the fuckin' French or the UN, you know," he said, as he dried his spoon on his sleeve. "Dundalk's right on the border that the British control. It's known as El Paso. I'm here on a five year training course, and then I'm going home to do my bit there," he said.

I began repacking my knife, fork and spoon set as we talked.

"I don't think it matters why we are here, now that we *are* here, does it?" I said.

"It might not matter to you; but I have a moral and historical obligation to resist the British," he replied indignantly.

I didn't answer. Something about the way he spoke and behaved smacked of thoughts and ideas that had been put into his head by someone else from an early age.

At that moment in time, as far as I was concerned, his fight in Ireland was his fight. Both the green fields of his home country and the vast expanses of Argentina were a long way from where we both were now. As were my own self-inflicted problems.

When we had finished packing away our kit, the Company took up positions around the sleeping area where the senior officer, his radio operator and bodyguard party slept, defended by a system of riflemen and machine-gunners, who in turn were

126

defended by a series of fixed sentries circling the position.

Further out still were the two man wandering patrols and chemical-warfare sentries, who carried equipment that detected the presence of poisonous gasses in the air. Wearing charcoal-lined body suits, gas-masks and hoods, they looked like Satan's agents as they wandered silently through the deep velvet night.

As the hours of darkness crept up on us during our first twenty-four hours in the desert proper, I felt comforted to be sharing a hole and an uncertain destiny with another soul walking the ragged margins of life. I enjoyed the feeling I got from being out there under the desert stars, all of us together; each man with his own story and his own reasons for being there. Whatever lay ahead of us, I knew we would be facing it as one.

That night I dozed in my sleeping bag between stints of sentry duty and for the first time since fleeing Patagonia, I didn't have that place on my mind as I went to sleep. I could only think, instead, of the physical dangers that lay ahead for all of us.

As the weeks passed, in order to take a break from repeated battle drills and the monotony of waiting, the various sections organised games of football and volleyball between themselves as a way of letting off steam and keeping fitness levels up.

One evening after a game of five-a-side, our little gang got talking over coffee. Ever the comedian, Smithy decided it was time to have a laugh at someone else's expense, as usual. He chose Esteban as his target for the night.

"Hey, Esteban!" he said. "You know that homo/singer from Spain who all the old women fancy?"

"Who's that?" said Esteban.

"You know, Julio Iglesias."

Aware of Smithy's habit of trying to humiliate

people, Esteban answered cautiously.

"Yes... what about him?"

"Well," said Smithy, "Is it true that his name translates as *July churches*?"

Again, Esteban replied with caution.

"Yes, it does; why?"

"Because that's what my mum told me once, and I didn't believe her. Fuck, you have some weird names where you come from, don't you?"

Esteban wasn't as green as he was cabbage-looking, and was quick off the mark with his response.

"Oh really?" he said. "What about Mr Ramsbottom - that's English, isn't it?"

As the translation went around the section we all had a good laugh at Smithy, before settling in for the night with our guns facing north once more.

On a couple of occasions we were visited in the desert by television crews from Paris, and once by the BBC. Interviews were carried out with officers, and we were filmed performing drills and training exercises. Whilst the cameras rolled, many of us with pasts to hide and secrets to protect covered our faces with scarves and ski goggles.

In a world of global news coverage, it wasn't worth taking the chance of being recognised and identified by organisations, or the people in them back in the places we had disappeared from.

The Regiment stayed out in the desert for what was left of the rest of the summer and into the winter. Christmas and New Year came and went, with Saddam Hussein insisting that Kuwait was staying under his control.

Sometime shortly after New Year 1991, Ito, Esteban, Tony and I were sitting on the floor under a camouflage net stretched out over a Jeep, eating rations and sharing a smoke. Through a mouthful of Chicken and vegetable casserole, Tony moaned out loud.

"Fuck, man, why don't they just let us charge over the border and kick their asses? I'm dying of boredom out here!"

Esteban, lying on his side, propped up on one elbow, casually pulled out his bayonet and lazily stabbed at the sand in front of him.

"Yes," he said. "If they don't move us north soon, I might just go up there myself and start on my own. I'm bored with all this waiting for something to happen."

"It's true," I said. "It feels like we've been here an eternity."

Ito pushed his cigarette into the ground, blowing out a long stream of smoke; his sniper's rifle and telescopic sight lay across the lap of his crossed legs.

"I couldn't care less how long we have to wait. Your problem is your Western culture," he said.

"What do you mean by that?" replied Tony,

"You have no patience or proper concept of time. Don't take it personally; it's a Western thing that's all, just your culture."

"Why? What's your concept of time, Ito?" I said.

"You say that it feels like we have been here an *eternity*. Well, back home in Japan, an old man told me about the finch that lives in the moon and what this little bird's relationship to time is. It makes perfect sense to me."

Esteban unwrapped a piece of chewing gum, pushed it into his mouth, then scoffed, "Ha! This should be good."

Flicking his Zippo open, he left his bayonet rammed in the ground and lit a smoke. Tony looked at the Japanese Sniper, and giggled.

"Yeah, lets hear about the little birdie in the moon, Ito. We've nothing else to do right now."

"Well," said Ito, "There is a small finch that lives on

the moon. Every fifty years he sets off and flies all the way to Earth to take a drink from the Shinona River, which emerges from the foot of Mount Kobushi in Japan. The journey takes him twenty years and makes him very thirsty indeed.

When he has taken a drink from the river, he flies thousands of metres up to the mountain's peak in order to wipe his beak on the summit.

Then, when he has wiped his beak on the mountain-top, he sets off on his flight back to the moon, which takes another twenty years. Fifty years later, he repeats the journey again, and so on."

After a slight pause, Esteban responded.

"And what's that got to do with Eternity, Ito?"

"Well," said Ito, "every time the finch wipes his beak on the mountain, he wears it away ever so slightly. Ultimately, given time, he will wear the mountain down to nothing, and when the mountain has been completely worn down, *that* is equivalent to just one percent, of one second of eternity."

"Shit man!" said Tony,

"I can't even think about that much time!"

"Exactly," said Ito.

I looked across at Esteban. His cigarette drooped forlornly from his half open mouth. His right hand rested half heartedly on the grip of his buried bayonet, his face, screwed up in the expression of someone trying desperately to understand something beyond his powers of comprehension. As the conversation moved on to football, I lit my own cigarette and thought my own thoughts.

We didn't have to wait for the finch's next trip to Earth from the moon to put an end to our waiting....

Chapter Twenty-One

Diplomatically and militarily, tensions were mounting; and so it came to pass that in January 1991 Esteban and I found ourselves making up a two man team of a six man observation patrol on the border area between Saudi Arabia and Iraq. Truth be told, we were probably just inside Iraq.

We had laid our positions out in a semicircle over a few hundred yards the night before. The one on the far left was held by Lieutenant La Roche and Ito. This trench faced north. Corporal Amar and another Moroccan Legionnaire waited and watched the night skyline from the middle position, which faced north by northeast, whilst Esteban and I crouched silently under the thick low cloud of a dark desert night in the third position, facing directly east.

We were there simply to observe the area and report on any movement, or lack of movement of Iraqi Forces that may or may not have been evident.

At around two o'clock in the morning, as I stared out across the grey desert floor, the horizon was barely discernible. Next to me in the dark, Esteban slunk into the bottom of the trench and decided to light a Gauloises.

Not quite believing my eyes, I immediately kicked the Zippo from his hands and hissed sharply, "What the Fuck are you doing? That light could be seen from miles away!"

"Relax, Gaucho, there's no-one out there; there's nobody out there for miles and miles." He straightened up next to me in the darkness. I didn't answer him, except to say, "Hush!", before turning back to the east and the horizon.

Moments later, and I couldn't be totally sure because the light from Esteban's Zippo had ruined my night vision somewhat, but it appeared that a dark rigid shape was moving steadily towards us under the skyline. Tracking right to left diagonally in front of us, the thing moved steadily closer.

Nudging Esteban with my elbow and pressing down hard on his left foot with my boot, I whispered into his ear, "Do you see that thing moving out there in front?"

"I think so, yes; there's a dark shape moving from right to left?" he whispered back meekly.

My heart picked up a pace as I strained my eyeballs out into the night and tightened the grip on my rifle. Now Esteban whispered again.

"It's a vehicle, isn't it Sebastián?" He sounded guilty and scared.

"You prick." I hissed. "It was you, flicking that fucking light on!"

I turned to our left and looked into the darkness. Staring into the middle distance to where I knew the rest of the patrol was dug in, I observed nothing; no sound, no movement, silence.

Looking back to our front, I noticed the dark shape making its way cautiously towards our position in the ground. It was a pick-up truck. The vehicle, with its headlights turned off, was a Toyota-type truck, much like the ones often used by ranchers back home in Patagonia.

The flat-bed behind the drivers cab was open to the elements, and carried three figures that were evidently armed with Ak47s. Neither Esteban or I moved for the minutes it took for the vehicle to drive over the flat ground, before coming to a stop just 100 yards from the lip of the trench that I was desperately hoping wasn't about to become my grave.

My mouth was bone-dry and my heart drummed manically in my ears, as the driver and passenger doors of the truck opened. Two armed men stepped from it and out into the night.

The three men on the back of the truck jumped down and stood in a huddle, whispering as the two from the driver's cab had a conference at the front. Their language, unintelligible to us, carried on the night air like the scattered chitter-chatter of small birds in a park.

Standing in that hole, frozen with fear, I genuinely felt that the two figures standing out in the open directly in front of us could hear my heart beating. A tangy metallic taste filled my mouth as my adrenaline gland went into overdrive. The taste now in my mouth was the taste of fear; pure fear.

The second man out of the Truck lifted his rifle and casually covered the first guy as he began stepping cautiously over the cold hard ground in our direction. As he drew closer, only a few feet away from us now, I could make out the outline of his large Moustache and the scarf wrapped around his neck, above the bulky parker jacket he wore with the zip undone.

Just spitting distance away from us now, he stopped walking as I felt the fear in me turn my muscles and bones rigid as steel. Pausing in front of our position, the man scanned the horizon behind us from left to right.

Quick as lightning, and without warning, Esteban stood up straight like a Jack-in-a-box, raised his weapon in one quick action, and fired three shots at the man, hitting him squarely in the upper body.

With the Spaniard's gunfire shattering the quiet of the night, the man let out a sickening sound like the startled clucking of a chicken, his body arcing backwards like a felled tree as his fellow soldiers scrambled for cover around the truck.

Along with the other members of the patrol, I aimed my rifle at the men crouched around the vehicle. I pulled the trigger frantically as they in turn fired back at us wildly and shouted in Arabic,. We killed them quickly as they crouched on the ground, their last moments filled with the terror that comes from the ultimate 'kill or *be* killed' situation.

Lieutenant La Roche got on the radio as we scrambled from our holes in the ground and in the excited aftermath of the brutal violence, our heightened voices bounced off each other in the night air.

"Get these fuckers searched!" ordered Amar. "Make sure they're fucking dead!"

Reaching the bodies of the dead Iraqis, we began removing bloodstained paperwork, maps and personal effects from them.

Kneeling over the corpse of the soldier he'd shot, Esteban tried to search inside the man's jacket. As he did so, his hands fell to the floor and he vomited violently onto the ground. *Not the actions of a man who claimed to have killed so easily before,* I thought.

I went to him, offering water from my bottle and placing a reassuring hand on his shoulder.

"Here, drink some of this, it's alright." I whispered.

"Thank you Sebastián, I'm okay. He's... he's got his eyes open, it's like he can see me."

"He can't, Estaban; he can't see you," I said gently. "It's alright, here; I'll help you."

Esteban gulped the water from my bottle as I went through the dead man's pockets and retrieved a map, wallet and notebook.

After smashing up the dashboard and steering column of the Iraqi's truck, we slashed the tyres with our bayonets and rendered the engine useless.

Shortly, a French helicopter arrived to take us back to the rest of the Company, twenty to thirty miles south from where we were. We had survived our first encounter with the enemy.

During the de-brief the light from Esteban's Zippo

wasn't mentioned, so I didn't either. I knew that inwardly Esteban acknowledged his part in what had happened, and I was also sure that he had learned a lesson he wouldn't have to learn twice. The next day the chaplain came to our trench, asking after our wellbeing.

"I hear you two had some action last night?" he said as he sat down on the edge of our hole.

Esteban reverted to his usual persona.

"That's right, Chaplain; we bumped into the enemy and shot them up bad."

Giving us both a paternal smile from the edge of our hole in the ground, the chaplain carried on with his work.

"I hear it was all a bit up close and personal; are you both all right with what happened?" he asked. Esteban shrugged.

"Suppose so."

"And how about you, Alvarez?"

"I'm still alive, Chaplain, that's good enough for me."

Looking at the pistol strapped to the chaplain's hip, and being of an enquiring mind, perhaps somewhat audaciously I probed him on his religious stance.

"How come you carry a weapon, Chaplain? Surely the Bible says *Thou shalt not kill,*" I asked.

"Yes that's right," said the chaplain. "It does; but what it means is, thou shalt not *murder*. There is a difference, you know."

Looking down at the sidearm he carried on his hip, the chaplain proceeded to pat it softly with the palm of his left hand.

"This pistol is for self-defence only," he said quietly, as an uncomfortable chill ran through the warm words he purred.

As far as I was concerned, however, killing was

killing, so changing tack slightly, I questioned the chaplain further.

"With all due respect, Chaplain, I find it interesting that a man of God would be drawn to military service in the first place, especially in a violent outfit like this," I said.

Clasping his hands piously in front of him, the chaplain continued talking at us. His fingers loosely interlocking across the lap of his clean combat trousers, and a righteous smile spread across his *holier than thou* face as he spoke.

"I find hope here in the Legion," he said.

Esteban raised his eyebrows.

"Hope?"

"Yes, hope." replied the chaplain. "Look at us; different nationalities, different races and backgrounds, united and working together towards a single aim."

Listening to him intently, I reflected inwardly on things as they were for *me*, now; and as they had been the night before, when concepts had become grim facts. Whilst I could see his point and reasoning, the pistol still bothered me somewhat, although I listened carefully as he went on.

"We in the *Legion Etranger* are a model and an example of cooperation and egalitarian unity for all men. There is no reason in my mind why the whole world couldn't be the same one day," he said piously. "It is, after all, God's plan."

"Yes, I see, Chaplain," I replied.

At this point in the conversation, sitting there in our hole in the ground, and having just fought for my life the night before, I just wanted the chaplain to go away quietly and leave us alone.

Because despite his facile talk of unity and God's plan for the world, he wasn't the one being asked to kill other people's brothers and fathers in the dark at point-blank range, and then rummage through their shot-to-pieces blood-spattered clothing for personal effects.

He wasn't the one who'd had to throw his filth-splattered gloves away and then feel dirty for ever more, because the muck and gore of the violent deaths he'd caused were smeared all over him in a way that he could never ever wash off.

After offering to pray for us and accepting our polite decline, the chaplain did finally go away and leave us alone. Esteban turned to me as the chaplain wandered casually away from our trench.

"Shit, Sebastián! That fool will have us out of a job if he gets his own way!" He said. I lit a Gauloises.

"He has a girlfriend you know, Esteban…"

"Really? I can't see it myself."

"Yeah really, apparently she's an angel!" I smirked.

We both laughed for a minute or two, until Corporal Amar appeared at our trench, wiping the smiles off our faces as the air turned cold around us. Addressing Esteban in measured tones that carried all the warmth of a Viper, Amar asked, "Were you drunk last night, Delgado?"

"No, *Mon Caporal*," replied Esteban meekly.

"Oh, really?" countered Amar. "Then you must be a baby, yes?"

Looking ashamed, Esteban squirmed uncomfortably as Amar carried on.

"You see," said Amar, "in my experience, only drunks and babies spew up for no apparent reason, like you did last night…"

Humiliated, Esteban peered into the bottom of our trench.

I said nothing. Amar raised his voice.

"Were you drunk, Delgado?!" he snapped.

Esteban looked defeated.

"No, *Mon Caporal*, there is no drink here."

"That's what I thought," replied Amar. "So you are simply a fucking baby then; well, that's fine with me, as that's what I thought about you all along," he sneered.

Neither Esteban nor myself had anything to say in the face of this despicable little establishment-backed Reptilian bully. Now satisfied with himself, Amar stood up and walked away. I turned to Esteban.

"Now I understand what the chaplain means about unity!" I said. "There's obviously a job for Amar when he leaves the Legion; as a chaplain!"

Again, we laughed out loud in our hole, whilst bravely giving the finger to Amar's back.

Above the low clouds blanketing our position, the sound of heavy bombers droned overhead.

Chapter Twenty-Two

The next morning, whilst returning from the latrines to my hole in the ground, I encountered the chaplain again. Walking in the opposite direction to me, he was on his way to perform his morning '*constitutional*' in the same toilet I had just used.

"Morning, Alvarez," he said, as our paths crossed in the sand.

"Morning, Chaplain," I replied respectfully, with a smile, before pausing. "Could I ask you a question, Chaplain...?"

The chaplain stopped walking. Standing in front of me in the sand, he held a roll of toilet paper in both hands.

"Yes, Alvarez, what is it...?"

"Chaplain," I asked, pointing over his shoulder at the early morning sunrise;

"What do you see behind you?"

Turning on his heel to face eastward, the way he had just come, the chaplain looked blankly across the empty expanse of flat desert. In the distance a glorious sun was climbing gracefully in the sky; a ball of milky-white light, rising above a horizon dashed with delicate hues of pink and violet. After a moment or two of staring east, the chaplain turned back to face me, with a puzzled look on his face.

"I don't see anything," he said. "Why, what's there, Alvarez; what do you see?"

Now it was my turn to smile piously, before answering. "Hope, Chaplain," I said. "I see hope..."

Walking away, I left him to go and have a hard think and a good crap in peace.

For several more weeks, planes from the Allied Air Forces continued to pass overhead on their way to drop bombs on the Iraqi Army, softening it up prior to our invasion. In February we heard that we had been tasked to capture the Iraqi Airport at Al-Salaman. Preparations to fight began in earnest.

The day before we set off on our mission, Lieutenant La Roche faced a challenge to his authority in the form of a Gabonese Corporal named Cresus.

Emerging from the rear of an armoured personnel carrier, La Roche found Cresus sitting against the vehicle stripping and cleaning his weapon. A large gold earring hung from his left earlobe.

"Corporal," said La Roche, "since when did regulations allow for the wearing of jewellery?" Cresus stopped what he was doing and looked up.

"I'm a warrior, sir; my tribe back home in Gabon always wears an earring when going into battle. We are going into battle tomorrow, so..."

"We are not in Africa now, Corporal, and as far as you should be concerned the Legion is your tribe. Is that clear?"

With both soldiers aware that other members of the section were watching and listening, Cresus held his ground.

"I'm not going into battle without my earring, sir. If I can't wear my earring, I'm not going."

Standing there watching the stand-off, as much as I liked La Roche, the rebel in me was rooting for Cresus.

"*Stay strong, Corporal,*" I muttered under my breath.

Pausing uncomfortably, La Roche hesitated, aware that his authority over Cresus and the rest of the section was in danger of being undermined.

On the eve of battle he couldn't afford to look weak, yet at the same time he needed Cresus to be *on board* and not resentful of authority.

"Cover it up with a plaster," he ordered, whilst turning and walking away, the tension in the air not quite dissipating.

Roland was there amongst us, and as La Roche got out of earshot, he turned to Cresus,

"Nice one, Corporal - do you have another earring for me?" he said.

Cresus didn't answer, and simply returned to methodically cleaning his weapon.

Afterwards I reflected on the fact that whilst Cresus may have represented a threat to the order of things as far as the rigid discipline of the Legion went, as a soldier and a man, perhaps Lieutenant La Roche secretly acknowledged the value of an individual with the courage of his convictions when going into battle.

In the last week of February we crossed the Iraqi border en masse, and as part of the French battle group, we in the Second Etranger captured the airport at Al-Salaman. We fought hard, but I can't say the Iraqis did, and I killed again. Within the next three days the Iraqi Army surrendered, and we had played our part in the liberation of Kuwait.

Crowds turned out to welcome us back to Nîmes, and we received medals. We marched in a parade and we got drunk.

Our return to France, with all its accompanying affirmations and accolades, engendered feelings in me of pride, for both me and my comrades; feelings not associated specifically with victory or soldiering. Rather, they sprang from the notion that in spite of the broken lives and broken dreams many of us had left behind, we had all somehow managed to salvage some vestige of self respect and dignity from the wreckage of our pasts. Whatever routes through life we had taken, whether damaged, broken or corrupted, none of us had ultimately written ourselves off entirely.

It is not uncommon to wish that life had dealt us a better hand. But there were those amongst us, like

Hans, who had taken a rotten deal and refused to give in. One way or another, we were all survivors.

Chapter Twenty-Three

Nîmes, France

One evening shortly after our return, we had a raucous get together in the packed foyer. War stories were recounted and embellished as more than enough beer was drunk.

Roland tied his t-shirt in a knot at the front as if it were a bra, and danced with Ito. Esteban got completely pissed; taking all the cigarettes from his packet and cramming them into his mouth, he tried to smoke them all at once. Faust and Gruber were there too.

Gruber, arrogant as ever, stood on a table well after midnight, wearing a pair of shorts in the colours of the German national flag. Dancing away to 'The Winds of Change' by the Scorpions, he held a bottle of Kronenburg in each hand as a cigarette drooped drunkenly from the corner of his mouth.

"*Deutschland, Deutschland!*" he sang again and again, much to the annoyance of all present. By the time the celebrations were over, he lay unconscious in a heap in the middle of the floor.

Before the last Legionnaire had left the foyer, someone (it wasn't me) had pulled down Gruber's shorts, before inserting a condom full of yoghurt into his backside with a toothbrush, then removed the toothbrush, leaving half the johnny hanging out of his ass. We all noticed a much humbler Gruber for some time after that. He deserted three weeks later.

Returning from a tattoo parlour one night following our return, I bumped into Sergeant Belcourt as he emerged unsteadily from a bar on the corner of a side-street in Nîmes.

"Alvarez!" he slurred.

"Sergeant Belcourt," I said respectfully.

"I don't give a fuck where you think you're going," he spluttered, "you're coming in here with me for a drink!"

Who was I to say no to a senior rank? Inside the crowded little bar I let Belcourt buy me a lager, whilst he drank brandy and railed against France and all things French.

After giving me his rambling version of the history of the Gauls and the Romans, he went on to explain why, in his opinion, the Vichy Government should have stayed in place after World War Two, and how the French resistance was a myth.

Four or five drinks later he told me, after a fashion, how he ended up in the Foreign Legion.

"You know I worked in the kitchen at the Lilac Tree in Paris Alvarez?"

Fatigued by what had obviously been a day of drinking, he was starting to sway. Holding on to the bar tightly with one sweaty hand, he went on.

"Those bastards at the Lilac wouldn't know talent if it walked up to them and slapped them one," he griped.

"So what happened? I asked, not really giving a fuck about the answer.

"It doesn't matter now. Who cares?" Belcourt placed a sweaty palm on my chest; "We are back from the war, I'm drunk, and you are so good-looking." This, as far as I was concerned, was my cue to make my excuses and leave.

"Where are you going?" demanded Belcourt. "You don't just walk away from a sous officer!" He glared as I started for the door. Turning to look over my shoulder, I abandoned protocol.

"Get a life," I said, before placing my *kepi* on my head and stepping outside into the street. An enraged Belcourt followed, staggering on and off the pavement

144

like the bewildered jackdaw with a broken wing I had once seen in the same street.

"Get a life? Get a life?" he shrieked after me as I walked away. "What do you know about *LIFE*?" he ranted pathetically, his voice filled with bitterness and desperation. "When I was your age my ass was for sale on the streets of Paris, you little bastard!" he shouted.

Turning to look at him as I crossed the street in search of a taxi, I saw only a sad bundle of human disappointment wrapped in the uniform of a soldier. Realising he wouldn't remember the next day anyway, I shouted back, "We could have all done other things! We could have all lead other lives! But we didn't, so here we are!"

I walked away, melting into the traffic and night time strollers to the sound of a desolate and angry little man. I didn't get a taxi. Instead I found another bar and drank Remy Martin alone, brooding darkly about my own sad past.

I didn't know what was at the heart of Belcourt's problems, not that I could have cared less, but looking down at my new tattoo and its still bleeding words - *Je ne regrette rien* - I did wonder if Belcourt's failings as a man outweighed my own shortcomings as a person.

Suddenly feeling wretched myself, I went in search of a prostitute, spending a shabby hour with an ageing Romanian hooker and making myself feel even more wretched in the process.

With tattooed tits and a plump backside, the woman's vice-ridden face showed the years of pain and disappointment. I didn't enjoy the sex, much preferring the glass of Cassis we shared afterwards.

Her room was the archetypal whore's boudoir, with a thick red carpet and reproduction impressionist paintings on the wall.

Lace shawls and silk scarves hung everywhere and

over everything; the sickly smell of sandalwood, heavy in the air.

On the ceiling above her bed, instead of the mirror one might expect, there was a quote from Oscar Wilde. It was framed in ornate gold and written in Romanian. She translated it for me.

> *"We are all in the gutter*
> *But some of us are looking up at the stars...."*

I was now twenty-one years old.

Chapter Twenty-Four

La Rochelle, Charent-Maratime, Western France, 1991

Only once during our long months in the desert had Tony and I heard from Anya and Veronique. A Christmas card had arrived addressed to both of us in December 1990. Inside, Veronique had written,

"Tony, Sebastián! We saw the Second Regiment Etranger on television! You all look very dangerous with your guns!
See you when you get back to Nîmes! Bon Noel! X X"

On the opposing page, she and Anya had both planted firm kisses with lips daubed in rich red Lipstick. In our temporary desert home, entirely void of anything remotely female, we relished taking it in turns to smell the once-greasy cosmetic which had been pressed onto the card with lips that had touched our own, months ago and far away.

Soon after returning from the Middle East and my encounters with Belcourt and the prostitute, Tony and I met up with both girls for dinner, drinks, and sex back at their apartment in town.

We both had a week's leave coming to us, and Veronique invited us to go with her and Anya to stay for a few days at her parent's holiday apartment in La Rochelle on the Atlantic coast of south western France. Having finished her studies, she was heading home to Paris via the west coast.

Veronique owned a lime-green Volkswagen Beetle, which the four of us piled into at midnight one Thursday in July, before heading for the coast. Anya and I squeezed ourselves into the back seat, whilst

Tony and Veronique sat up front. I still knew little of either Anya's or Veronique's lives, and took the opportunity to find out more.

"How did you end up in France, anyway?" I asked Anya as we neared Montpellier on the motorway.

"You don't want to know," she replied.

"Well, I do, because I asked you," I said.

"Just tell them, Anya," said Veronique from the driver's seat.

"Okay," said Anya. "Three years ago, I was working as a wine stewardess on the QE2. We were on a worldwide cruise. We were going to see the whole world; but not me."

"Why, what happened? I asked.

"When we got to Marseilles, I got off the ship and went into town. I got too drunk and woke up the next afternoon with some guy in his bed in an apartment; I didn't know where I was," she said.

Turning around in his seat up front, Tony looked over his shoulder, as I noticed Veronique glancing at us in the rear view mirror.

"Shit, did you miss the boat?" said Tony.

"Yes, that Bastard put something wrong in my drink to knock me out; the ship left without me"

"So what did you do then?" I asked.

"I got a job in a bar straight away and found a room, but I hate Marseilles. It stinks. The people have no class, so I jumped to Nîmes."

Anya was from Krakow in Poland and had begun studying medicine there. During her second year of study, her father died of a heart attack. Soon afterwards, an infant child had turned blue and died in her arms at the hospital she was training in.

She immediately stopped studying, quit medicine, and started to party hard. When she tired of the same old scene in Krakow, she expanded her horizons (after

148

a fashion) by getting herself a job on a cruise-liner in the West Indies, before landing a job on the British Liner *The QE2*.

Every six months of the previous three years that she had spent in France, Anya had set her mind on returning to Poland six months hence. Back at home in Krakow she would start life again, settling down and looking after her mother. At the end of every six months, however, Anya always seemed to find another excuse to remain in France for "*just six months more...*"

In writing his poem, 'The Road Less Travelled,' Robert frost encouraged the curious and the frustrated to strike out and seek that which is new, richer and more fulfilling in life.

I suspect that many of those choosing that alternative path in search of the sweeter, more abundant fruits that undeniably grow there, often find themselves lost, bewildered, and brutally cut by its overhanging thorn bushes. It is, after all, the 'road less travelled' for a reason.

Despite her feisty facade and seemingly robust nature, I got the feeling that Anya was just as vulnerable and lost as a lot of people. After hearing her story I reflected for a while on how fragile people's lives can be, and how things can turn on a sixpence so easily and without warning.

One thing I knew for sure though, as the four of us motored along the dark highways of south western France that summer night in 1991, was that perhaps, with the exception of Veronique, the rest of us in that car were definitely already on our way down the road less travelled.

Soon after Anya had stopped talking I fell asleep next to her in the dark, and slept soundly most of the rest of the way to La Rochelle.

With Nîmes, Montpellier, Toulouse and Bordeaux all behind us, we arrived first thing in the morning at the ancient seaport of La Rochelle. The town is built around a picturesque harbour, the entrance of which is guarded by two stone towers at its mouth.

It was from here that the French ventured to the New World. Far beyond the stone towers of La Rochelle they established colonies in what is now Texas, New Orleans and modern-day Quebec, which they named *Nouvelle France*.

The French established a presence all the way from Canada, down through the swamplands of Louisiana, and on to the Antilles in the Caribbean Sea.

When the British arrived in Canada they defeated the French, and pushed them from Quebec down through the Appalachian Mountains, and virtually into the sea.

Today, only the small Cajun communities of Louisiana and the six million or so French Canadians remain as a legacy to French ambitions in North America.

Veronique's parent's second floor apartment was close to the harbour itself, the large living-room window giving a wide view across the blue water to the two stone towers at its entrance. Her mother and father were restaurant owners who lived in Paris, and they kept the apartment as a holiday retreat.

That first evening, as we strolled with the girls to a harbour-front eatery dressed in our short sleeved summer walking-out uniforms and white *kepis*, we drew stares from locals and tourists alike. Taking a table on the pavement, Tony ordered a bottle of white wine on ice and some bread, and began to chat.

"I'm not keen on seafood, to be honest with you," he shrugged. "But as we are by the sea, I guess I'm not going to have much choice, am I?"

"You haven't tried La Rochelle lobster yet, Tony, so don't be in such a hurry to say you don't like something," said Veronique as I filled her glass.

The sun slipped easily down the sky as we drank wine and chatted amongst ourselves, eventually disappearing below the horizon and lighting the glassy waters of the Harbour as if from below with an otherworldly orange light. Veronique ordered lobster tails in tarragon butter, and mussels steamed with garlic and parsley.

"Anything else?" said the waiter,

"Yes,- and the octopus, thank you." She smiled.

"I like this place," said Anya. "I think I'll stay. Plenty of bars and restaurants for work."

"You mean it, don't you?" said Veronique. And she did.

I didn't take too much notice of what Anya was saying at the time, as just then I noticed a young couple walking past us in the crowd of evening strollers. Wearing sunglasses and jumpers hung casually over their shoulders, the arms tied loosely in front, they walked hand in hand, chatting and laughing as if they hadn't a care in the world; the whole of their lives ahead of them. Jesus! My blood froze.

It was Tania and her brother Ignacio!

No; I was mistaken, of course. It wasn't possible. It couldn't have been them. Yes, they looked remotely similar, but that wasn't the point. My heavy guilty conscience had come with me to France, and I was seeing ghosts.

The waiter arrived, grounding me back in reality as he placed a bowl of smoky octopus stew in red wine sauce on the table. Watching Tony happily dipping a chunk of crusty white bread into the steaming bowl of seafood sprinkled with freshly cut Parsley, I envied his *joie de vivre* as he pushed the sauce-soaked bread past his easy smile.

"This is great, Veronique! So much better than the tinned sardines and sand we were eating down in the desert," he said with his mouth full.

"So you like seafood now, Tony?" laughed Veronique.

Suddenly, I didn't feel part of the scene any more. I couldn't relax. Along with feelings of guilt, I felt envy. Although surrounded by people, I felt lonely. Tony had a home to go back to in Ireland, a community, and a cause which gave him a meaning and direction.

I had none of that, and therefore felt quite empty inside. Tony had simply fled unemployment as far as I knew. He was on what could be described as a great adventure. I was a fugitive, and a criminal.

After polishing off the main course, Veronique ordered *nougat semifreddo* in orange honey syrup for us all as dessert. I ordered a bottle of Remy Martin.

The next five days were mostly spent on the Beach at Mineimes on the outskirts of town. We drank wine from cardboard cartons, relaxed, and chased the girls into the curling foam of the Atlantic Ocean.

Standing in the sea with the water up to our chests one afternoon, Anya and I cooled off in the midday sun.

"Some thing is different about you, Sebastián," said Anya.

"What's that then?"

"Your eyes; they've changed, you look older."

"Well, I am older!" I joked. Anya looked serious.

"Did you kill someone or some people in the desert?" she asked quietly.

I didn't want to talk about the night of the patrol into Iraq and our first encounter with the enemy, or the bloodshed at Al-Salaman Airport. As far as I was concerned, I had found myself in a situation where I had done what I had to do to stay alive, and that was that.

"Let's not talk about it," I said. "We're on holiday, let's just enjoy."

"Okay," said Anya.

Then, putting her newly suntanned arms around my neck, she kissed me on the mouth then said, "I'm glad you and Tony came back safe, anyway."

"Me too," I said.

If only I could have found the words, I would have told Anya about the horrors I'd seen with the eyes she now looked into, but I couldn't.

I would have told her about the horror; and the beauty as well. Yes the beauty. Because besides the bloodshed and the destruction, there *had* been beauty.

Helicopters in loose formation sweeping low over the sand like the Valkyries of Valhalla, flashing silver from their windows. High-velocity tracer bullets streaking lasers like rods of crimson light through the black night under starlit skies.

And the sunsets; orgasmic sunsets, moaning in ecstasy whilst coming in colours across impossibly wide horizons,

Back then, whilst I couldn't find the words, my eyes had seen all that too. There *had* been beauty. But, of course, the beauty was in the horror, and the horror was in the beauty.

Back on the sand, as Anya slept, Tony and Veronique improved Franco/Irish relations in a tangle of warm skin, hot lips and Ambre Solaire, whilst I read *The Adventures of Tom Sawyer*.

Perhaps not so surprisingly considering my own life, I found myself a little choked when reading the part where Tom emerges from hiding at his own funeral, only to be showered with love by his Aunt Polly.

Our evenings in La Rochelle were spent eating out

and playing excessive drinking games back at the flat.

The night before we left town, the four of us went out to dinner. I don't recall what we ate that night, as it was all washed down with ridiculous amounts of wine, champagne, Remy Martin and vodka. I do remember, though, telling the girls about desert sunsets and describing how it felt to have sex with the sun.

The hangovers the next day blotted out any sentimental pangs that saying goodbye might have otherwise caused.

For reasons of her own, Anya had meant what she said about staying on in La Rochelle and Veronique let her stay in the apartment until she found digs of her own. The four of us parted company on the harbour-front.

Standing by the calm water under a strengthening summer sun, Tony French-kissed Veronique while a flock of seagulls delivered avian wolf whistles hanging in the air above us. I hugged Anya, then kissed her on the cheek.

"Goodbye, Anya; thanks for a nice time."

Anya smiled happily in the sun, a fresh breeze in her short dark hair.

"Never say goodbye, Sebastián, always say, *"See you...!"*

"Okay then... see you..." I said.

With that, Anya tweaked my earlobe and kissed me on the lips,

"See you, handsome..."

Leaving behind another chapter and another moment in time, the four of us said our farewells, as all too soon our leave had come to an end. I watched for a moment as Anya walked away arm in arm with Veronique by the harbour. Looking back, it didn't hurt then.   But it does now.

Tony and I caught three trains back to Nîmes and

the barracks via Bordeaux and Montpellier. I never said goodbye to anyone ever again.

On returning to the barracks that evening we were greeted by the sight of a taped police cordon and a Gendarme blocking the entrance to our Accommodation. Corporal Amar caught up with us after the police had waved us away, and he told us the news.

At some time during the previous night, Esteban had fallen asleep in his bed whilst smoking a cigarette. His mattress had caught fire and he had died. I was shocked. Corporal Amar was uncharacteristically sympathetic and civil about the whole thing. But only to me; in front of the rest of the section and Esteban's immediate comrades he was typically callous and scathing about the young Spaniard's demise.

"They found him curled up like a burnt match; he'd fallen through his mattress onto the floor," he said, before sneering, "Oh well, they do say smoking's bad for you..."

Two days later, after the Gendarmes and fire investigators had left, I had a look inside Esteban's personal locker and found it empty except for a book of poems by the Spanish writer Federico Garcia Lorca. Irish Tony was there in the room with me.

"I didn't know he could fucking read!" he laughed cruelly.

"Well, he obviously could," I said as I flicked through the pages of poems in the dog eared book.

If Tony didn't understand that people aren't always what they seem, I figured that that was his problem

.We all lead three simultaneous lives, I believe. The first is our public life, exposed and on show to the world. Then, there is our private life, reserved for close family and friends only.

Lastly, we have a third life, a secret one. Like

Esteban's locker, this is where we keep our most precious sentiments and private ideals. I think this is our real selves.

Life in the unit returned to normal almost as quickly as Esteban's remains were removed and the room was washed down and repainted.

Initially I couldn't understand Amar's unusually cordial behaviour towards me after we returned from leave in La Rochelle; but then a week later I received the news that my application to go back to Castel Naudry and Corporal School had been approved.

Chapter Twenty-Five

Kourou, French Guiana, 1992-1994

Lying on the north Atlantic coast of South America, a lush rainforest covers most of the 32,000 square miles of French Guyana. This relatively small country borders Brazil to the southeast and Dutch Suriname to the west.

The pristine lowland forests of this little-known land just north of the Equator are home to such venomous snakes as the South American Bushmaster and the forest Pit Viper, as well as anteaters, dwarf porcupines, Yellow Phantom fish, and a strange wildcat named the Jaguarundi.

Beneath the verdant jungle canopy the forest floor of Guyana is home to a multitude of species, many of which are poisonous and lethal. Nearly all of them rely in the demise of another life for their own survival. With an array of teeth, spines, stings and venoms, the wildlife provides an uncomfortable welcome to anyone entering the jungle by foot, riverboat or helicopter insertion.

The French began colonising Guiana about 250 years ago, first sending 12,000 colonists on a fleet of ships in 1763. Within a few years, most of them had died. Encountering hostile local tribes and Malaria-infested mangrove swamps, the early colonists had an arduous task.

This place was my first posting on being promoted to Corporal, and it was to be a two-year tour of duty in which I got to know the jungle and its wildlife well. Strangely, even though I had returned to the Continent of my birth, I felt even further from Argentina in this steaming hot tropical environment than I had in France.

Since the 1970s Guiana has been home to the European space Agency and its rocket, *Arianne*. It is the role of the Third Regiment French Foreign Legion to guard both the space rocket and its launch site, as well as patrolling the densely forested borders with Suriname and Brazil.

I never got to say goodbye to Hans, Tony and the rest of the gang in Nîmes and didn't have much time to think about them either, as I soon got used to my new colleagues and the job of soldiering in what we all came to know as *'The Green Hell'*.

Two exceptions to this were the Briton, Sergeant Wilson, and my old marching partner from the Raid march in France, Roland from Sweden; both of whom came out to the Legion Base with me and the rest of the reinforcements to Kourou on the Guyana Coast.

Wilson was a lot more human in my company, now that I was a corporal, and I would say that on some level we even became friends. Both our countries had been at war in the South Atlantic just ten years before, but we never spoke of it directly. Only once did Wilson tell me that he had actually fought against the Argentine forces in 1982.

We worked closely together on many occasions and spent up to thirty days at a time patrolling through the jungle during operations to stop illegal gold-mining and drug-smuggling across the border.

For days and even weeks on end we would patrol deep into the forest to make contact with the traditional villages of the interior, and to make our presence felt along the border with Brazil. The slightest gradients seemed like mountains as we pushed on, weighed down with weapons, radios, and chainsaws, in ninety-percent humidity. Rivers were crossed by wading through the water at chest height or placing our clothes in plastic bags and swimming across. The ever-present ticks and blood-sucking leeches had to be removed from our exhausted bodies on a regular basis.

Patrolling this environment on foot was enough to sap a man of his strength, make him doubt his capacities and often make him question the choices he'd made. I know I did. This place could truly be Hell, but one thing it did do was help one forget.

I had been in the country for just over a month when I come across Wilson, as he drank alone one evening in a ramshackle bar named *La Maison Bleue*, on the shabby edge of Kourou Township. We shared a beer and some small talk. The place was full of fishermen, prostitutes, and ne'er-do-wells.

Also there were a couple of African corporals, a Rwandan, and the Gabonese Corporal, whom I had last seen defying Lieutenant La Roche in the desert during the Gulf War the previous year.

Perhaps they both felt at home there as the majority of the other patrons in the bar were Maroons, ethnically black Africans who are the descendants of escaped slaves. I excused myself from Wilson momentarily and went to say hello to Cresus.

"You won't remember me from Saudi. I was a Legionnaire then," I said, as I introduced myself. "You were wearing the earring before we set off for the attack on the airport."

"No I don't remember you," said Cresus, "but yes, I am the one with the earring. I'm Cresus, and this is Teddy from Rwanda," he said.

The three of us shook hands across the table.

"I'm having a drink with Sergeant Wilson over there, but we'll come over in a while and have a drink with you two, yes?" I offered.

"Yes if you like, we'll play some cards," said Cresus.

We had only intended to linger for an hour or so

before heading back to the barracks, but the forces of nature conspired to keep us in that bar all night. It wasn't a hurricane or lightning, or even an earthquake that put a stop to our return to base, but an invading swarm of moths, thousands upon thousands of them.

These were no ordinary moths, however. They were the poisonous reddish-brown Hylesia moths whose flapping wings give off clouds of tiny poisoned arrows, or "*'butterfly ash'*."

This fine dust causes a painful skin condition known as *lepidopterist* to those who come into contact with it. In a matter of minutes the muggy night air was thick with these airborne hazards, and to be outside was positively dangerous.

"Looks like we aren't going anywhere any time soon," said Wilson, as the bar owner hurriedly shut the front doors, dropped the shutters onto the veranda, and switched off the outside lights. The toxic moths were rapidly laying siege to the whole area.

"*Putain Pappillons!*" the bar owner shouted. "*Quelqu un m'aider avec ces fenetres!*"

Several fishermen now put down their drinks and gave him a hand closing the windows.

Across the small tropical city the local inhabitants closed their own windows, and the town's lights were turned off. Wherever people were when the moths descended was where they stayed that night. Rather that than take the risk of running the gauntlet of 'butterfly ash' and suffering the painful and debilitating consequences for the next week or so.

"We should get a table and sit down," said Wilson, as clouds of countless moths butted, fluttered and bumped against the windows of the bar.

"Why have they turned the ceiling fans off?" I asked.

"They might spread stray 'butterfly ash' around the

place, they won't take the risk, so…"

"When will they go away?"

"The local fire brigade will park their trucks around the lakes in town and shine the headlights on the water," said Wilson.

"Oh?"

"Yeah, the moths land on the water and drown; they'll be gone in the morning," he said.

Taking four bottles of Kronenburg and a bottle of rum to a rickety table in the corner, we sat down. Wilson took a long swig of cold beer and began to talk.

"I need to be in the army, you know. I have to know what's what day to day, you see," he said.

I offered him a Gauloises but he waved the cigarette away, and carried on.

"After the Falklands war, my wife couldn't take me going away again; I had already done two tours of Northern Ireland. Anyway, I left the army, got us a small house in Glasgow, and worked as a nightclub doorman for a while."

"Did you have children?"

"Yes, two."

"What happened?"

"I couldn't make ends meet; I was stressed out and under pressure. One night I fucked someone up outside the club and spent time in prison. When I came out, the wife had been screwing the neighbour, so I fucked him up too and went back to prison."

Casually pouring rum into his beer, Wilson reached across the table and took one of my cigarettes.

"When I got out of prison again, the police told me to stay away from my old house. The wife had moved this bloke in with her."

"What did you do then?"

"I moved to another part of Glasgow and went for a job on a building site. It was summertime and I was wearing a t-shirt. As you've probably noticed, I've got some pretty horrendous scars up and down my arms..."

I had in fact noticed these scars on many occasions before, but I had considered their origins to be Wilson's business and never enquired about them. Now though, as he had brought them up, I asked how he got them.

"I served with the Scots Guards Regiment on Mount Tumbledown. We fought against the Argentine Marines in 1982. During the battle I bumped into a bloke amongst the rocks and we fought in the dark, bayonet to bayonet."

"What happened?"

"He wouldn't go down; I never knew it was so hard to stop a man. Eventually a mate of mine heard me shouting and screaming. He found me with this bloke in the rocks, and we did him in together. By then he'd done *this* to me." Wilson held out his bare forearms across the table.

"So," I said, "when you went for that job, they saw your scars and assumed you were trouble of some kind?"

"Well, the foreman took one look at me and asked me what had happened so, I just told him the way it was; that I had killed someone in a fight."

"Didn't you tell him it was during the war?" I asked.

"No, I didn't."

"Why not?"

"I don't know. I can't explain, but I couldn't have explained then either. I just knew that civilian life wasn't going to work out for me."

"And so you joined the Legion."

"Well, I didn't get the job, so yes, I joined the Legion."

"How much longer do you have to serve?" I asked.

Wilson paused, looking around the room, slowly taking everything in before his eyes fixed on mine. He now had a strangely detached look on his face.

"I'm supposed to be leaving in three years," he said, "and then I'm going to retire to a small town far away. It's called *Oblivion*."

We spent the rest of the night drinking rum and playing cards with Teddy and Cresus. That was the only time Wilson ever spoke to me of the war between our countries and he never let it, or its outcome and causes, affect the way we worked together.

Cresus won all the money on the table that night, drank more than the rest of us put together, and talked of how he had first seen the Foreign Legion whilst standing in the crowds watching the anniversary parade of the French Revolution near the Place de la Concorde.

At the time he was a student studying economics and went along to watch the famous march-past of French military forces in front of President Francois Mitterrand.

That year happened to be the two hundredth time French Troops had marched from the L'Arc de Triomphe to the Place de la Concorde to commemorate what the French know as the *Fete de la Federation*. On July 14th 1789, soldiers stormed the Bastille, releasing prisoners on to the streets and signalling the beginning of the end for the ruling Bourbon Monarchy.

The sight of the famous Foreign Legion marching past inspired Cresus to abandon his studies and join up. "My Father is a government minister back home in Gabon," he said. "My life was privileged, too cushy. I wanted to test myself, be my own man."

"Why did you stay on after your first five years?" asked Wilson,

"I need this hard life - that's the only way I can explain it," said Cresus.

We drank and played cards until the sun came up

and the moths were gone. In the morning, safe from the perils of 'butterfly ash', the four of us returned to the barracks by taxi.

Back on duty, life was constantly punctuated by seemingly endless forays into the jungle and border patrols. The sheer physical effort of keeping going concentrated the mind on the concrete matters of physical survival and left little room for introspection. At the end of any gruelling mission into the Amazon, heaven was a cold shower followed by freshly baked croissants, fresh orange juice, and a change of clothes.

After serving there and enduring its many challenges, I know from experience that the jungle of Guiana is both a good place to hide and a bad place to get lost.

Somewhere out there in the primeval landscape, uncontacted peoples still live as nature intended them to, Hunter-gatherers inhabiting a pristine yet dangerous world, beautiful and deadly at the same time.

One such group are known as the Wayampi. They have never been filmed or photographed and nothing is known of their language and habits.

Others are not known as anything at all, simply because they are not known.

Chapter Twenty-Six

Almost eight 8,000 kilometres separate the tropical jungles of French Guiana from the temperate rolling countryside of France. But it was here, under the steamy canopy of Amazonia, that Roland finally got the opportunity to finish telling me the story he had begun under the chestnut trees of Languedoc two years previously.

He and I were part of a section of Legionnaires and engineers given the task of constructing a riverside jetty to facilitate the mooring of native-style Pirogue canoes. Pirogues were the narrow river-craft used by the Legion to penetrate deep into the Amazon in the same way that indigenous peoples had always done.

The difference between the Legion's pirogues and the native's, however, was that we in the Legion utilised powerful outboard motors at the rear of the craft and were capable of delivering a devastating volume of firepower from each Legionnaire via our weapons aimed at the riverbanks from either side of the craft.

Pulling alongside the banks of the muddy river next to the jungle, we disembarked from our Pirogues and began the frustrating process of manhandling chainsaws, spades and equipment up the slippery bank and into the trees.

As we began to infiltrate the thick foliage, branches vines and warm slimy mud conspired against us, impeding the progress of our struggling column. Up near the head of the column, a black Legionnaire from England named Jackson began singing in English under the weight of a cumbersome chainsaw, perched precariously on his shoulder.

"Hi ho, hi ho, it's off to work we go, with a shovel and a pick and a great big stick, Hi ho, Hi ho Hi ho Hi ho!"

Whilst most of us chuckled at this impromptu outburst, the Sergeant Major, an Austrian named Kiesl, was suffering badly from a tumour in his humour and didn't see the funny side. He made this quite clear by shouting up the column to the Englishman.

"Jackson!" he bawled. "If you don't want that Chainsaw shoved up your black ass, I suggest that you shut the fuck up!"

Jackson duly shut up and the sound of his far from perfect singing voice was temporarily replaced with the more usual jungle sounds of tropical bird song. That is, until our section Captain took up the tune in French moments later.

Within minutes, the song was being sung by the whole section in a myriad of languages, all set to the harmonious backdrop of birds and insects. What a sight we must have made, if only anyone had been there to see us.

Forty young men, sweating, slipping, scrambling and singing up a vine-strewn jungle slope like a troupe of lost green clowns from a strange land; a land where everyone speaks their own language and everyone has their own secrets. Kiesl spent the rest of the day in a huff.

By the end of the first day of our mission several trees had been felled using chainsaws, their trunks cut and thinned before being cut into the appropriate lengths for the jetty supports.

As night time approached I sought out Roland amongst the section dispersed amongst the trees, and asked him to join me for the night under my poncho stretched out between the trees and invited him to my shelter for a chat.

"It's a long way from that wood in France, isn't it?" I said, whilst making black coffee in the half light next to my poncho.

"It's a long way away, and a lot hotter too!" he smiled.

Unlike the fresh springtime saplings of France which we had known before, the rotting foliage of the jungle floor emitted a sweet pungent scent that mingled with the aroma of our coffee in the muggy tropical air. Tony smiled as he emptied a packet of white sugar into his drink.

"Well done on making Corporal, by the way."

"Thanks Roland; if I'm going to be here I might as well get the easiest life possible, you know?"

"I understand, but this won't be my life, I'm getting out in three years," he replied.

"Yes, you have to do what you have to do; do you remember telling me about the Pakistani girl you loved back in that wood on the first night of the raid?" I asked.

Roland winced, slapping a mosquito to death against his sweaty neck, signalling the first kill of the night in our ongoing war against these ever-present parasites.

"Oh her; yeah, she really fucked me up," he said, squinting through the gloom as he inspected the mosquito's splattered corpse in the palm of his hand.

"Really?" I said.

"No; not really. I fucked myself up, I suppose, like I always did," he said, before taking a sip of coffee.

As ever more mosquitoes sought us out to drink our blood in the dark, Roland related his Gothenburg tragedy to me as the equatorial moon cast a flickering light through the high jungle canopy above us.

"Her family didn't want her seeing me because she was a Muslim, and mine weren't happy either for the same reason," he began.

"So what happened?" I asked.

"They forbade us from seeing each other. I went

around to their place one time and her Father didn't want me in the house, so I lost my temper."

"And you did what?"

"I smacked him in the mouth and smashed up the front room of the house," Roland said, with a wicked chuckle. "Problem was that at the time I was waiting to go to trial for stealing computers from my boss where I worked in Gothenburg."

He continued his story in the swarthy darkness. With his bright blonde hair almost glowing in the ambient light, and surrounded by the steam from his hot coffee, Roland had taken on the appearance of some kind of Will O' the Wisp. The world he was talking about seemed to be on another planet; a world of front doors, computers, flushing toilets and shops.

As he spoke, I couldn't help but think about my own home in far away Bariloche; the town hall and local council buildings built in the Alpine style of Europe; the restaurants and souvenir shops lining the main street through town.

Consciously pushing the images of home and feelings of homesickness from my mind, I listened to his story.

"Go on," I said.

"Well, the cops arrested me and I did a twelve-month stretch in prison. You know, you do shit and you get punished, right?"

"Right," I said as my own conscience sneaked up on me in the dark and gave me a slight tug.

Roland then went on to tell me about how he had started an affair with his female probation officer before fleeing his dysfunctional life in Sweden with some vague hope of a job at his uncle's clothing factory in Hungary.

"When I turned up at the factory in Budapest they told me he was away somewhere, so I went to his house and he wasn't there either…"

"What did you do?" I asked

"I just thought, fuck it, jumped on a train to Paris and here I am… everyone's heard of the Legion, right?" he said.

"Right," I said.

Having finished the story he'd begun in France, Roland and I again lay down to sleep amongst the leaves together.

Chapter Twenty-Seven

Guyana was a tough posting - very tough - but in spite of the hardships and privations of soldiering in the jungle, I don't think anyone ever forgets the feeling that goes along with seeing the Arianne space rocket take off and head into outer space for the first time. The sight of this modern marvel of technology rising above the Amazon, reaching for the stars, can definitely be described as a conversation-stopper, to say the least.

I remember on one occasion, during a jungle patrol in August 1992, being privy to a conversation between a Polish Legionnaire called Nowak and a black Briton from Manchester named Jackson.

Living and working with men from over a hundred and thirty different countries from around the world could lead to some interesting insights into the view points of people from differing backgrounds.

The Patrol's mission was to provide part of the protective outer cordon through the jungle around the launch site of the rocket in order to hinder the approach of any possible launch saboteurs.

We had stopped to rest and eat under the jungle canopy on an east-facing wooded slope. The section spread out amongst the trees and we opened our rations.

Above us, amongst the branches of the Ceropia and Kopak trees, a multitude of birds created a deafening cacophony of sound.

Sun parakeets, cayenne jays, crimson topaz hummingbirds and squirrel cuckoos competed with trumpeter birds in trying to drown out the sound of the ever-present cicadas.

"This food's shit, I'm sick of it," declared Jackson as he picked at a tin of sardines.

"What do you want out here, *haute cuisine*?" said

Nowak.

"I could murder a Rogan Josh Curry right now. I wish I was in Manchester."

"Manchester, for a Curry?" said an Italian Legionnaire named Evangelista.

"Yeah, Manchester. We have the best curries in the world," said Jackson. Nowak scoffed.

"That's the thing with England; it's full of Niggers and Asian types. My sister worked there for two years and she told me all about it."

Jackson stopped eating and looked up from his sardines. "Yeah? Well you and your sister would be speaking German now if it hadn't been for England, you beetroot-eating piece of shit."

"Oh really?" said Nowak, who now had a smug smirk on his face.

"Yeah, really," replied Jackson, "and I told your Sister that when I paid her for a fuck in a brothel when she was working in England, because it's full of that sort from Poland as well."

Like a cobra on the attack, Nowak sprang from his squatting position against a Ceropia tree and launched himself at the English man. Wrestling and scrapping amongst the rotting leaves of the jungle floor, the two young Legionnaires did their best to try and kill each other in a frenzy of pent-up hate and aggression.

Before anyone could react or intervene Jackson had pushed Nowak a good four feet away with a boot to the lower stomach, then kicked his teeth out as he lay prostrate on the ground.

"Don't fuck with people from Manchester, you bastard!" He shouted into the Pole's contorted face.

The fresh warm blood dripping from Nowak's wounded mouth speckled the rotting leaves scarlet. At that moment, the birds and insects which had until now been a riot of sound coming at us from 360 degrees suddenly fell deathly silent. An eerie calm descended on the scene amongst us, as a low rumble coming through the trees from a distance made the hairs on the back of my neck stand up.

Standing over the incapacitated Pole, Evangelista pointed through a gap in the trees on the slope where we stood.

"Look! It's Arianne!"

Several miles away, the pure white outline of the space rocket was clearly visible against the blue equatorial sky, a trail of smoke leading from it and back into the jungle as it hurtled on its way out of the Earth's atmosphere.

Toucans and parakeets exploded violently into the air around us as a troop of howler monkeys shook the branches of the trees above us, like hysterical inmates in an asylum.

The whole section watched in humble silence as the rocket disappeared from view and into another world. Turning to look at the Legionnaire standing beside me, a young American named Chase Zeigler, I noticed that he had a tear in his eye.

"It's religious, man… just religious," he said.

Standing there in the tropical heat, sweating amongst the trees and creatures of the earth, our faces turned skyward watching Arianne's race to the Heavens; I knew exactly what he meant.

Chapter Twenty-Eight

Zeigler was from Olympia, outside Seattle in the Pacific North West of the USA. I had known him for some time. He talked often about his home in America, which was understandable as he was close to completing his five-year tour of duty with the Legion. He was looking forward to being reunited with the family and friends he had left behind half a decade before.

Although he didn't know it, Chase Zeigler would never return to his home and family in Washington State, or even leave the jungles of Guyana.

Back in Kourou after the launch of Arianne, which had interrupted the fight between Jackson and Nowak, I got talking to Zeigler in La Maison Bleue over a couple of bottles of Kronenburg Larger.

"So, Zeigler," I said as we stood at the bar. "You're going home soon. Has the Legion been good to you, do you think? Are you being sent back to the land of the living in a better state than when you arrived?"

After taking a long draught from his bottle of cold beer, Zeigler smiled.

"Well, Corporal Alvarez," he said, "it's been a long trip, it really has. I joined this outfit in 1987, you know."

I ordered two more beers and offered him a cigarette. "Thanks," he said, pulling the smoke from the pack.

Between slugs of lager and tugging on the French cigarettes, Chase Zeigler told me a tale of an uncoordinated life; of a young man born into a North America far removed from the Southern one I had grown up in during the same period of time.

His was the story of a youngster emerging into a

culture of material plenty and individual indulgence. His America; the America of the north was a land of milk and honey.

He spoke of a land of freedom and social ascendancy, as opposed to *my* South America, which I had known as a land of strict social and economic hierarchies imported from Europe, and which lagged pathetically behind the new Northern world that Europeans had also 'discovered'.

"My dad's from Seattle, my mom's from Warwickshire in England," he told me.

"They met back in the early seventies. My dad was on an extended trip around Europe for the summer. Anyway, they got married and shit, so my mom ended up living in America and I was born, then my little brother and sister."

Chase looked around the Maison Bleue and chuckled, his blue eyes twinkling as he cast them over the human menagerie that made up the patronage of the bar.

As the fishermen, prostitutes, thieves and losers poured copious amounts of beer and rum down their necks, Chase Zeigler spilled his guts out to me; *me*, the lost boy from Latin America with plenty to hide,

After marrying his father in 1970, Chase's mother Sandra, an artist, moved from the English Midlands to Washington State and settled down to what both she and Chase's father wrongly predicted would be some semblance of the family ideal, the American dream.

As the 1970s came and went, Chase and his siblings became lost in the fight between their parents for independence and freedom.

The family moved inland, from Seattle to the provincial town of Olympia, where Chase's Father began a business making candles, selling them in shopping malls around the area. Sandra found life in

Olympia to be equally as oppressive as in the provincial English town of Rugby.

Feeling the pressure of financial and familial responsibility, John Zeigler shelved his candle-making business and used his academic qualifications to gain employment and teach class at South Puget Sound Community College.

One summer when Chase was six years old, his mother took a trip alone to the Burning Man Festival in Arizona. There she met a yoga teacher who showed her how to release her locked-away sexual energies by "accessing her chakra points". She never went home, and Chase's Dad brought his kids up alone.

"What do your brother and sister do?" I asked.

"My little brother's in college and my sister works at Disney World in Florida."

"Really? That's different!"

"Yeah; check this out. You know all those people that walk around there dressed as cartoon characters?"

"Yes?"

"Well, my sister told me that they all have hideous facial deformities and they do it as a kind of therapy."

"Really?"

"Yeah, really. And you know the chick that dresses up as Snow White?"

"Yes?"

"Well, she's always a dyke!"

I shook my head and laughed.

"Well you learn something new every day, whether it's useful or not, I suppose."

Following graduation from high school, Chase deferred a place at college and took time out to work for the US National Parks' service, clearing hiking trails across Puget Sound on the Pacific Ocean, before helping to build a church and a school for disadvantaged kids in Baja Mexico.

"After I got done with that I was about ready to go to college, but before term started in the fall, I took a trip to England to visit my mom's parents. I never really got to know them, and I felt it was something I should do." As he spoke, a scuffle broke out between two fishermen playing cards in the corner of the bar, and we were distracted for a moment.

"Did you go back to America?"

"Nope."

Zeigler dropped his cigarette butt amongst the others on the floor and ground it slowly into the floorboards with the toe of his combat boot.

"I was headed back to the airport to catch a flight home, and I met a fellow in a pub near Euston train station in London. We got talking and he told me he was leaving his old life behind and heading for France to join the Legion, and..."

"And here you are..." I said, raising my glass in the thick smoky air.

"*Que sera, sera...*" smiled Zeigler, before emptying the rest of his beer down his throat.

"Back in the states soon enough, though," he said with a smile. We can't have known it then, but Zeigler would never see America or his family again.

Some time after our conversation in Le Maison Bleue and a week before he was to return to France for his discharge from the Legion, Zeigler joined the rest of our Section on a routine patrol deep in the western jungle towards the Brazilian border.

Just before darkness fell on the night before we were to be picked up by helicopter, we spread out amongst the trees, organised sentries, fed ourselves and bedded down for the night. When morning came, Chase had disappeared.

As soon as his disappearance was noted, the whole

section immediately spread out in formation and set about the business of finding him. His fully-loaded weapon had been left underneath his poncho spread out between the trees; his rucksack and kit were also where he had left them.

None of the sentries had heard a sound during the hours of darkness, and we all knew he was looking forward to going home to America.

After sending a situation report by radio, we were joined later that day by another group of helicopter-borne Legionnaires, including Sergeant Wilson, who enlarged the search party.

Stepping over rotting logs and pushing past hanging vines, we scoured the foliage.

Nowak was the first to mention the Wayampi, as a bright red hummingbird hovered high above us in the mid canopy

"Those fucking Wayampi savages have taken him," he began to mutter as we quartered the ground looking for our colleague. "Shut up with that bullshit, Nowak!" I growled, as the humidity and mosquitoes sapped my reserves of strength and patience. Evangelista spoke next.

"They could have got him, though, Corporal. You know, they could have. I think they are watching us all right now. They know this place; it's their home, and we are in it."

Now the jungle seemed to be watching us with a thousand pairs of eyes. People were getting jumpy, and the place took on a malevolent vibe as active minds raced with the possibility that one of our own had been spirited away by a tribe of jungle-dwelling cannibals.

Wilson soon picked up on the talk of Wayampi. Gathering us together under the thick muggy jungle canopy, he addressed us in the cloying heat.

"Listen! There are no reports of Wayampi Tribes in

this area, okay. Even if there were any, they are a Stone Age people with bows and arrows. We have assault rifles. Put these thoughts out of your heads; concentrate on finding this soldier, and we shall all leave together".

The only thing to come from our subsequent two-day search of the jungle was a five-inch-long dark brown animal bone found on the forest floor. Wrapped around its length was a string of brightly-coloured iridescent feathers and some copper-coloured beads, all held together with dried animal sinews. We never found Chase Zeigler.

The journey he'd begun in a London pub five years previously was over. Sometimes, as I sit here by the window where I write, I do wonder whatever happened to him.

Chapter Twenty-Nine

Back in Kourou the day after our return to base, the section paraded first thing in the morning as usual. We were told that an investigation into Ziegler's disappearance was to be launched and we would all be spoken to about it. Before being dismissed we were handed over to Sergeant Wilson.

Standing in the front rank of the section were Nowak and Jackson. Whilst going through the details of the orders for the day, the eagle-eyed sergeant spotted a bulge in the top breast pocket of Nowak's shirt.

"Nowak," he said. "What's that bulging through your top left hand pocket?"

"It's a handkerchief, sir."

"A handkerchief?" Wilson looked and sounded incredulous. "Where does it say in the uniform regulations that a Legionnaire should carry a handkerchief in his breast pocket?"

"I don't know, sir."

"You don't know? Well, neither do I!"

Stepping forward, Wilson closed in on Nowak. Expecting him to deliver a blow to the Pole's stomach or ribs, I winced in anticipation. Instead, Wilson retained his composure.

"Nowak," he said quite calmly. "Take the handkerchief out of your pocket and hold it above your head with your right hand."

Nowak did as he was told, as we all wondered what was coming next.

"Now, Nowak, you're going to skip once around the edge of the parade ground with your snot rag above your head. Every fifth step you are going to exclaim *What a gay day!* Now go!"

Turning to the right, Nowak set off around the parade square on his humiliating run of shame. Watching from the ranks, every one stood stock-still in disciplined silence. As Nowak got halfway around the parade ground, Jackson, unable contain his pleasure and amusement at seeing his old sparring partner's humiliation, let out a loud smirk. On hearing this, Wilson shouted over to Nowak.

"Stop!" he bellowed.

Turning on his heel, Wilson now walked over to Jackson, putting his face just inches from the young Englishman's.

"Do you find this amusing, Jackson?"

"No, sir." All of a sudden Jackson had a very straight face.

"bullshit! Don't lie to me!" barked Wilson, "You will get over there and join Nowak, hold his hand, and skip with him TWICE around the parade square. GO!"

Now we all laughed at the sight of Jackson and Nowak, skipping hand in hand in the heat like two teenagers declaring their love for each other under a blue tropical sky.

Later that night, as I lay on my bed in the early hours, I was pulled from my sleep by the muffled crump of a firearm being discharged.

Imagining myself to be dreaming, I rolled over and went back to sleep.

When morning came, I changed into my PT kit before sunrise and went to meet Wilson to take the section on a three kilometre run. On the way past the refectory I came across Nowak, Evangelista, and the others, standing in a huddle.

"Corporal Alvarez," said Evangelista with a satisfied glint in his eye as he looked at me. "Have you heard about what happened last night?"

"Go on…" I answered. Evangelista tried hard, but

failed to disguise his delight.

"Sergeant Wilson shot himself in the head with his pistol in his room."

The sudden dull crack that had woken me the night before had been the sound of Wilson's early retirement.

Something about Wilson's demise didn't surprise me, and irrespective of the news, I proceeded to take the section on the run as arranged; taking them again immediately afterwards, in honour of Sergeant Wilson.

Chapter Thirty

In the absence of seasons that would otherwise mark the passing of time in the temperate parts of the world, two years in Guyana seemed more like ten.

The World Cup of 1994 provided much needed relief and a distraction for the Regiment, even if only because of the fights that broke out between us because of it. I took my own fair share of ribbings from the Romanians amongst us as their team knocked out Argentina on the television screen in the foyer.

Cresus and I became good friends and we began 'dating' a couple of beautiful local prostitutes named Cua and Ntuj. They were sisters and daughters of Vietnamese refugees belonging to the Hmong Tribes people.

The Hmong had collaborated with the Western powers engaged in the fighting in Southeast Asia during the wars of the 1960s and 70s. After the fall of the South Vietnam in 1975, a number of the Hmong had been relocated to Guyana by the French Government.

We met both girls in La Maison Bleu one evening, before employing them for a late-night screw in a dingy room lit by a single light bulb above the barber's shop next door to the bar.

Ntuj was nineteen years old, her name meant sky, and she and Cresus partnered up together. Her sister Cua was twenty-one, and her name translated as Wind.

"Lucky you!" Cresus would joke. "You always seem to get the wind!"

Both of these young girls, whilst somehow visibly tainted by the work they did and the lives they led, were playful and delicate in the manner of some other worldly findings.

With long black hair and almond eyes Cua and Ntuj were light-footed, quick to laugh, and easy on the eye.

Neither Cresus nor I could have cared less that we were paying them. We were both Legionnaires and knew the score. For the next half year that constituted the last six months of that tour of the jungle, Cresus and I kept Wind and sky on a financial retainer, in order to provide sex and company for us both during our spare time.

In between long-range jungle patrols and training exercises, the girls provided us with relaxation and *'comfort'* in return for meals, cash and drinks.

Before leaving Guyana, Cresus and I took a jeep and drove both girls down to the Capital Cayenne to visit with their parents.

They lived in a two-roomed apartment over their own fruit and vegetable store. Before arriving at their family home, Ntuj and Cua reminded us that their parents thought they worked as hairdressers in Kourou, warning us of the consequences to them if their true line of work was revealed.

Greeting us at the door of their tiny home, the girl's father, Quang, looked Cresus up and down before smiling, high-fiving him, and saying in perfect English,

"Whasss up, man, everything cool?"

With Cresus looking bemused, Quang reverted to French.

"When I worked with the Americans back home, I had a friend who looked just like you; his name was Bill; B, I, L, L." As he spoke the letters of Bill's name, Quang tapped each finger of his left hand with the index finger of his right hand like a child learning to count.

"He was from Detroit; you remind me of him!" he told Cresus.

"Oh, okay, well I'm Cresus, sorry I'm not Bill; I'm

from Gabon, not Detroit." Cresus smiled.

Quang's eyes sparkled with happy memories as he chuckled, "Bill was my friend, he taught me English. I wrote to him after the war but he didn't write back, perhaps he died, I don't know."

After introducing me and meeting the girl's mother, Nhung, we all went inside and sat cross-legged on mats spread across the floor. Within minutes we were eating lunch with the family under an old photograph of President LB Johnson hanging on the wall.

Nhung served up plates of shrimp spring rolls, followed by delicious quails and bamboo shoots, all washed down with a cold cucumber and mint drink over crushed ice. Quang told us about his time in the Hmong secret army, set up by the CIA during America's conflict with North Vietnam.

"I know about war," he said. "When I was your age I was crossing the border into Laos. We were attacking the Viet Cong's supply routes along the Ho Chi Mihn trail; I lost a lot of friends."

Nhung smiled.

"War stories, war stories. It was a terrible time, Quang, talk about something else!"

"We don't mind," said Cresus. "It's interesting."

Quang continued. "The Viet Cong suspected what I was doing, so they came to the village looking for me."

"Did they catch you?" I asked.

"No, I got away to Laos and began escorting American pilots out of the jungle to safety after they'd been shot down."

"Our father is a hero!" Cua said proudly.

"Sounds like it," I said.

"How did you end up in Guyana?" asked Cresus.

Nhung took up the story.

"When the Communists took over we had nowhere to hide; we Hmong people were singled out for

184

retribution because we had helped the Americans."

Quang and his wife went on to tell us of their escape westwards and how they had bravely crossed the Mekong River into Thailand at night. Using a small raft which they had built themselves, they crossed the river in 1975.

After two years in a Thai refugee camp they were resettled in Cayenne by the French authorities, going on to start their business and raise a family in South America.

When we had finished eating, Quang invited Cresus and I to the beach at Remire-Mont Joly the next day to fly kites with him and his daughters. Naturally we accepted his offer out of politeness, but as Cresus and I settled down to sleep in the kitchen later that night, neither of us was keen.

"Shit, Sebastián. What did we just agree to?" Cresus whispered as we lay together on sleeping mats rolled out on the floor. "Flying kites on a beach with an old man when we should be out and about drinking and debauching his daughters!"

"It's only one day, Cresus, plenty of time to party after that." I said.

In the morning, after a breakfast of noodle soup, we set out with both girls and their father for Mont Joly beach. Each of us carried a kite. Cua and Njut's resembled goldfish, whilst their father and I carried kites shaped like Phoenix birds. Cresus was given a long-tailed dragon to fly.

Once on the sand, Cua held Quang's kite for him as he ran down the beach, the warm wind of the Atlantic catching his phoenix, lifting it into the air bobbing and weaving as if suddenly alive.

Only then did we hear the melodic sounds of the delicate bamboo flutes that Quang had skilfully attached to the kite's struts. One by one, we raised our kites aloft, as the sea breeze filled with the sweet and gentle sounds of the handcrafted instruments.

For the next three days Cresus and I enjoyed the company and hospitality of some of the kindest, most honourable people I have ever known. Despite their poverty and refugee status, this simple Vietnamese family carried themselves with an aristocratic dignity that I will never forget.

Forced to chose sides in a conflict not of his own making, Quang had made a decision that had ultimately gone against him; but then again, perhaps in the scheme of things, maybe not.

In a triumph of human tenacity he had overcome adversity against all the odds to build a new life, living in peace whilst maintaining both his culture and his humanity.

Our time with his family in Cayenne taught me much. Not least, that most people in the world want the same things; to live in peace, raise their families, and have enough food to eat.

Whether one is a soldier, prostitute, rich or poor, first and foremost we are all someone's son or daughter.

Soon after our visit to Cayenne, my two-year-long tour of Guyana was over at last. Leaving our friends behind, we returned to France.

Back in Nîmes, Cresus and I met up again before going on to keep the peace in Bosnia.

Being familiar with the nightlife of Marseilles, Cresus suggested that we go down there for a weekend's drinking and carousing.

On our first evening in town we found a bar where we ate oysters, washed down with Canadian Whiskey. After getting lost in the back streets later that same night, we got into an ugly street fight with a group of Lebanese merchant seamen.

As there were more of them than us, we were soon in trouble. Whilst protecting me against an attack from behind, Cresus took a blade to the palm of his hand and was badly wounded.

Consigned to desk duties in Nîmes, he didn't make it to Bosnia with the rest of us, but I owed him my life. I had turned twenty-four.

Chapter Thirty-One

Bosnia, 1994

Sergeant Rana, the huge Maori warrior from New Zealand's Northland Cape, looked down at the pool of coagulating black blood on the living room floor of the little gingerbread house at the edge of the village. Lifting his combat boot out of the mess, he turned the sole of it upwards.

"Fuck, this stuff's gone all sticky, like jelly," he said.

Lewis, the British Legionnaire standing with us, spoke up.

"It's because it's so cold here, that's why," he said, matter-of-factly. "If it was hot enough, you'd see the plasma separating from it and going all yellow."

Lieutenant La Roche was there with us in the front room. He had been promoted to the rank of Captain whilst I was deployed in Guyana. Looking down with Sergeant Rana, the four of us shifted our feet in the viscera, feeling our skin tighten and creep under our jackets as the realisation of what we were standing in took hold.

The thick winter parkas and gloves we wore did little to keep out the miserable cold. Neither did the light blue berets of the United Nations Peacekeeping force which we wore on our heads.

At our feet lay an old couple; dead amongst the debris of the ransacked house. Close by, a young blonde woman lay lifeless in the doorway leading from the front room to the kitchen at the back of the house. All three had been brutalised, murdered, then savagely butchered. Sickeningly, it appeared that the blonde woman's underclothes and stockings had been disturbed.

La Roche turned to me, the deep dark pits under his tired eyes contrasting sharply with the light blue of his beret.

"Corporal Alvarez; get upstairs and see if anyone else is up there. Look out for booby traps and don't touch anything," he said.

Taking the British Legionnaire Lewis, up the small twisting staircase, we looked into each of the rooms of what had once been a family home for signs of either life or death.

There was nothing; the chill wind blowing through the broken windows of the house and the watery light of a winter's sun seeping inside only added to the awful feeling of horror hanging in the air.

Unnerved, I wanted to get back and join the others downstairs. Turning to Lewis on the landing and trying very hard to sound capable and unflustered, I spoke flatly as I led the way back to the stairs.

"Come on," I said. "There's nothing here, let's go."

"Wait a minute," said the Briton.

Stepping into the small bedroom at the head of the stairs, Lewis grabbed a bottle of cherry brandy from a little table just inside the door.

"They won't need this anymore, will they?" he said.

Pausing on the first step at the head of the stairs, I looked Lewis square in the face.

"Put it back," I said.

"But..."

"I said, put it back."

Lewis resentfully tossed the liquor back inside the room and onto the bed, before following me downstairs. Down in the front room we found the others still standing there in the blood. They had been joined by two military policemen and the chaplain, whom I had first met in Saudi Arabia.

La Roche turned to me as we reached the bottom of

the stairs.

"Anything?"

I shook my head.

Both MPs were smoking and looking down at the bodies, whilst the chaplain stood in the front doorway, tapping a small Bible lightly on the back of his hand as he mumbled over and over again.

"And into whatsoever house ye enter, first say, peace be to this house; and into whatsoever house ye enter, first say peace be to this house..."

I noticed the pistol still strapped firmly to his hip as it had been three years previously in the desert.

Clearing his throat uneasily, La Roche asked the policemen, "What do you think?"

"Well, these are obviously the parents and the daughter," said one of them.

"Wonder where the man of the house is?" said Rana,

"Taken away and *cleansed* somewhere else," replied the other MP,

As hardened as I had become to life's grim realities, the sight of this young woman lying dead, prostrate and violated on the floor in a room full of soldiers, sickened the part inside of me that had cherished a mother, loved a girlfriend, and felt the friendship and warmth of school teachers and other women in my life.

A kind of emotional detachment steadied me, allowing me to remain in the house, functioning efficiently enough to interact with my colleagues in a professionally viable manner.

Stepping over the young woman's corpse, Rana walked out into the miserly sunlight of the house's back garden. Welcoming the opportunity to escape from the hideousness of the scene inside the house, I followed him there.

I took just two steps outside before a thunderbolt of

shock burst inside me, as the scene in the garden unfolded. The woman's three small children had been killed, desecrated and left outside on the cold ground, a macabre shroud of pristine frost covering each of them.

The emotional detachment which I had relied upon until now deserted me like a turncoat faced with impossible odds. Turning swiftly away, I clamped my hand tight over my mouth, breathing in and out hard through my nostrils and squeezing my watering eyelids tightly shut. La Roche and Lewis joined us outside.

"In the name of God..." said La Roche,

Turning back to the house, he shouted to the chaplain inside.

"Nick!" he called out. "There are children out here!" His words, weakened by shock and emotion, sounded brittle and cracked in the cold air.

The chaplain appeared in the doorway and we all looked to him as Lewis spoke out.

"We need to find the animals that did this and string 'em up!" he said angrily.

Walking slowly towards Lewis, the chaplain pulled the soldier's hand from the grip of his rifle and then pressed the small Bible in its place, before speaking softly.

"We are peacekeepers," he said. "Here to help. The Bible tells us that the peacemakers shall be called the children of God."

Pushing the Bible back at the chaplain, the Briton transformed his shock and feelings of powerlessness into anger at the chaplain.

"Well, I'm no child, and there is no God; but the fucking Devil's been here, though."

Sergeant Rana shouted at Lewis from his position beside the dead children laid out on the grass.

"Watch your mouth, Legionnaire!"

Turning his back on our group and putting a hand on

one hip, Lewis paced about the garden, unable to find an outlet for his feelings.

Recovering my own composure, I pulled a pack of Gauloises from my pocket and looked up at the cold white sky. A lone magpie flew over the garden, protesting loudly in a rolling rattling chatter at the atrocity laid out on the ground beneath him.

As I smoked, I found myself missing the steamy jungle canopy of Guyana, its heat and its orchestra of colourful birdsong. The chaplain spoke again, this time addressing us all calmly.

"Be angry, and sin not," he preached. "Let the sun go down on your wrath, and neither give place to the Devil."

Lewis scoffed, spitting on the grass and kicking the toe of his boot into the ground. Giving him a cigarette, I told him to calm down and take it easy.

I had changed. I was no longer running scared. In my fourth year in the Legion I now felt a certain detachment from my past; from who I had been. The things I had done and the lives I had ruined didn't really bother me now so much, for some reason.

My view of the world from this lonely house in a Balkan village was pragmatic, to say the least. Shit happens. Whys and wherefores don't matter, only survival. Taking Lewis to one side, I spoke to him out of earshot of the others.

"Don't you ever touch anything in a house we go into here again," I said as I looked him in the eye. "If that bottle had been attached to a wire, it could have been goodnight Vienna for all of us; understand?"

Lewis hung his head.

"Sorry, Corporal; I'm tired."

"So am I, but we can't afford to be," I replied.

This was Bosnia, and that was the scene in one small house in one small village, in one part of a small country whose name had disappeared from the world map in 1918, only to reappear again towards the end of the twentieth century in a blaze of artillery and gunfire.

Chapter Thirty-Two

We spent the whole of that night guarding the house from looters after the bodies had been removed. Outside in the darkness other Legionnaires manned checkpoints at either side of the village access roads.

Sometime during the small hours, I went upstairs to use the toilet and found the chaplain and Sergeant Rana sitting on the bed in the master bedroom. They were drinking the cherry brandy I had earlier ordered the British Legionnaire to respect. A single candle cast malevolent shadows around the room.

"A nightcap, Alvarez?" said the chaplain as he offered me a glass.

Conveniently setting my own morals to one side, I took the tumbler and drank, fuzzy tentacles of warmth spreading from the back of my throat to my nose and ears in the sweet flush of alcohol.

The bedroom walls held pictures of the children who had lain lifeless in the back garden earlier. I stood and perused them for a moment, before draining the glass.

"Something's gone wrong here," I said. "I thought Europeans were civilised. You know, like they lived by some kind of higher morality."

Before answering, the chaplain refilled his own glass.

"A society," he said, "any society, only ever exists as a concept in the minds of the people who inhabit it. Here, the concept has been abandoned. These people have turned their backs on God and all that is good. Here, it is alright to slaughter one's neighbours in their homes because you believe they don't belong. The law has been replaced by gun law." Passing the bottle to Rana, the chaplain went on.

"Civilisation has given way to barbarism and hatred on a scale not seen in Europe since World War Two."

"No shit," I mumbled, as I cast my eyes over the pictures on the wall.

The chaplain looked to Rana and me. "As we find ourselves in the middle of this, we must use God as both our strength and our shield," he said.

Rana put his boots up on the bed. "I like it here", He shrugged.

"I feel safe; I've got a gun. It's just Sheep and Wolves here. I'm a Wolf. Everything's simple. It's just life and death, no bullshit complications."

"I know what you mean." I said.

"Do you two know what Excelsior is?" said the chaplain,

"No. What is it?" Replied Rana,"

"It is the light of human dignity which refuses to be dimmed. Remember that both of you; especially here."

Emotionally drained by the day's events, I excused myself and left the chaplain and Rana to polish off the last of the dead family's brandy.

Whilst in Bosnia, I focused on my job and my responsibilities as an NCO. In spite of everything, I suppose I enjoyed the feeling of living for a purpose. We were participating in events of global importance. My past was well and truly pushed to the back of my mind, if not entirely forgotten.

Looking back, I'm really only able to remember Bosnia in black and white; a cold sad place where everything seemed broken. In the absence of reason and order, a community had banished everything the rest of the developed world held to be civilised, turning on itself with disastrous results.

After the discovery of the bodies in the gingerbread house many of us adopted a harder, more aggressive attitude in our dealings with the male population in

Bosnia. A 'bad' attitude during vehicle and house searches was often softened with a smack in the mouth as we imposed our authority on potentially violent individuals, whether they had proven to be so or not.

It had now been over four years since my own stupid actions had set me adrift from a life worth living. I now occupied the eddies that held the flotsam and jetsam of life.

Away from the pull of the main stream, I lived amongst the dysfunctional, the broken, and the lost, and I was getting comfortable.

Soon, my contract with the Foreign Legion would be up and I would be free to go. But go where; Argentina and prison? No, my mind was made up; I was staying on. Not that I felt there were many other options open to me.

When our tour of Bosnia came to an end, we returned to Nîmes and garrison life to find out that after years of overindulgence in alcohol and eating officer's scraps, Sergeant Belcourt had succumbed to a fatal heart attack one morning whilst cooking breakfast in the Mess.

A couple of days after our return to barracks I received a postcard from in the United States; Nevada, to be exact. On the front of the card was a picture of Caesar's Palace casino in Las Vegas. It had been sent across the Atlantic to Nîmes some months previously and been passed on to me in Guyana. Obviously the card and I had passed each other in opposite directions as I returned to Europe from Kourou. It had then been sent back across the Atlantic to France whilst I was in Bosnia, waiting for me in Nîmes when I returned.

It was from Anya.

"Hi!
I am in America, everything is fun, I have job in

196

casino! I went into desert. Now I know what you meant. I had sex with the sun, and remember you…! Give a kiss to Tony. See you… Anya X

It was the last I ever heard of her.

Smithy deserted the Legion soon after our return from Bosnia. Corporal Amar left the service, hung up his *kepi* and became a Nîmes taxi driver. My good friend Cresus had been forced to quit the Legion after the hand he'd use to protect me failed to recover from the wound inflicted by the knife-wielding sailor in Marseilles. He had saved my life but I didn't get the chance to say goodbye, and sadly, I never found out what became of him.

When the time came, I signed another five-year contract with the Legion. Having completed a full five years, I was entitled to and received a French passport, allowing me to reside in France or anywhere else in the European Union permanently.

In spite of the shame I still felt at what I had done, inwardly I cocked a snoot at the Argentine authorities. The rebel inside me was still alive.

Since running away, nearly half a decade had passed, and I was now nearly twenty-five.

Chapter Thirty-Three

Nîmes, France, 1995

Shortly after New Year 1995 I was able to catch up with Irish Tony, Roland, Manda, Hans and the rest of the original gang in the refectory at St Nicolas. They were all due to leave the Legion shortly.

On completion of five years service, all those returning to civilian life pass back through Aubagne to be demobbed. Taking some leave, I went down with them all, and together we caught up with Jurgen the Danish postman-cum-Paratrooper, back from the parachute Regiment in Corsica.

We had all changed in various ways. Irish Tony had become a calmer, more solid individual. Manda and Hans seemed a little sadder than when we had all set out on our own personal journeys five years previously.

Each of us had our own tales to tell and did so late into the night. Amongst us, I was the only one staying on, and whilst I harboured warm feelings for them all I also envied them and their opportunities to restart their lives afresh.

Catching up with Roland at the bar, I posed the obvious question.

"So, Roland, are you looking forward to getting that puppy you always talked about?" I asked.

Roland looked positively bashful all of a sudden.

"You remembered the puppy, did you?" he said whilst peering into his beer, avoiding eye contact as he swished it around his glass.

"What's the matter?" I enquired. "Are you going to get the puppy or not?"

Roland downed his beer in one.

"I'm going back to Sweden tomorrow, mate, I've missed my family there. I was crazy five years ago; I just want to start again," he said.

Pushing feelings of jealousy aside once again, I persevered.

"And the puppy...?"

Roland looked up at me, his voice taking on a whimsical tone amongst the hubbub of happiness surrounding us.

"Everybody needs a dream," he said quietly.

Just then Hans and Jurgen appeared beside us. Hans, full of drink, swayed unsteadily like a half-broken branch in the wind in front of us.

Roland took one look at him and laughed out loud.

"Hans, have you seen yourself?" he said.

Trying desperately hard to focus his intoxicated eyes, Hans threw a funny back at Roland.

"Yes, I have," he said, sounding for all the world as if his back teeth were stuck together with industrial strength chewing gum. He went on, his confidence propelled by drink.

"I'm 5'10 with brown hair and a scar running down the side of my face, although it has been said by some that I'm very handsome!"

Glancing at each other sideways, Roland and I laughed out loud, whilst Hans looked very pleased with himself indeed, no doubt feeling that he had effectively deflected a criticism.

Roland made a half-hearted counter attack.

"You've got eyes like piss holes in the snow, mate!" he said.

"Okay then," replied Hans. "Well that must make me a snowman, mustn't it...?" he slurred.

Winking at Roland as if to let him know to lay off, I put my arm around Hans; more to hold him up than anything else.

"So, Hans, what will you do?" I asked.

"We'll see, Sebastián. We'll see," was all he would

say.

Realising that there was to be no sense to be had from Hans, Jurgen then piped up.

"I've met an amazing girl in Corsica, She's half Italian. We've decided to live there and open a water-sports business; you know, jet-skiing and a banana boat, stuff like that."

Putting a drunken hand on Jurgen's shoulder, I said sloppily, "I wish you all the best, my friend."

Irish Tony bit the top off a bottle of Kronenburg, spitting it out onto the floor before saying "I'm off back to God's own country to do what I have to do to get those British Bastards out of the Island of Ireland, so wish me luck!"

Still swaying, Hans turned to him solemnly, with a forlorn look on his face.

"Haven't you had enough of fighting?" he said.

Shooting Hans a sharp sideways look, Tony gave him a bullet of a reply.

"No," he shot back coldly.

Feeling the atmosphere cool, I spoke up,

"Okay, relax you two," I said, in my best Corporal's voice. "We're here to have a good time, yes?"

Tony changed gear.

"Hey, do you remember that mad little Spanish fucker Esteban? Setting himself on fire like that in his own bed?"

"Of course," I said. "I still have the book of poems he had in his locker."

"His book of poems; why?"

"Don't know," I said. "I just do."

"What about you, Sebastián?" said Jurgen.

"Back to Castel Naudry. I'm getting promoted to Sergeant."

Whilst we drank late into the night, I remember the fact that none of us actually said goodbye.

The next day I wished each of them well, before watching them line up proudly to receive their certificates of service. From the edge of the parade ground, I looked on silently as they gave their final salutes in the crisp morning light of a peppermint dawn; then they left the Legion for good.

Sitting alone over breakfast after my friends had gone I felt decidedly hollow, and I spent the rest of the day aimlessly walking around the camp without talking to anyone.

Chapter Thirty-Four

Second Tour of Duty, 1995-2000

It is the 14th of July 1995 and we are marching along the Champ de Lysee in Paris, during the Bastille Day parade. It is my first time participating in what many consider to be the defining spectacle of the French Republic. Animated crowds line the sunlit streets as we march in formation at a slow eighty steps per minute.

Whilst marching in step with my colleagues, I see two suited men amongst the people gathered on the pavement just ahead of me in my peripheral vision. They are looking right at me.

Walking in my direction, they step from the throng of flag-waving spectators. Around their necks and hanging on chains, they wear the badges of the Argentine Federal Police.

"That's him," says the younger of the two as he points at me over the shoulder of the first man. I notice the younger man's blonde hair. It picks up the sun as he steps towards me.

Distracted, I break my stride; the toes of the man marching behind me clip my heels and I stumble from the formation towards the crowd. The older policeman reaches for a pair of handcuffs from the back of his belt with one hand, whilst making a grab for my wrist with the other. As he does, I register his silver hair, cut in a short crop.

Voices from the crowd stand out above the cheering.

"What's happening?" they say.

"Look, they're arresting him!"

Bewildered, I pull away from the two men. As I do,

my mother appears from the crowd, rushing towards where I am struggling with the police. She is wearing a white dress covered in bold red roses. Across her front and between her breasts, she wears the Presidential sash in the colours of the Argentine flag.

"Leave him alone, he's my son!" she cries as she steps in between me and the policemen.

"Mamma, help me!" I say as I look into her desperate eyes.

She grabs at my uniform as the police try and make her let go of me.

"Sebastián, Sebastián!" she cries, over and over again.

I wake up. Its dawn on the 15th of July 1995 and I'm lying on the grass in the gardens of Luxembourg in Paris. Next to me on the ground, and tugging at my shirt, is the young blonde Danish backpacker with whom I'd partied the night before, after the parade.

"Sebastián, Sebastián, wake up," she says.

"Where are we?"

Neither of us can remember how we got there, but I take her to a cafe nearby and we share a coffee and croissant whilst trying to work out whether or not we'd had sex earlier. Half an hour or so later I leave her to her croissant and coffee, and make my way back to Fort de Nugent.

Standing in the shower back at the barracks where it had all begun, and feeling decidedly out of sorts, I considered my situation. I remembered that once, whilst having a conversation with Martin Bruchard in Nîmes, I had made a remark about the world being a small place.

"Yes, it is," he said. "Unless you're looking for someone..."

At the time, and for obvious reasons, it had made me feel better about everything. My dream had shaken all that up. I had been in the Legion for over five years now and since getting promoted, life had got easier in many respects.

I had more leave, more cash, and a comfortable room of my own. It may not have been part of my life plan whilst growing up, but then again neither was committing federal offences and facing a hefty prison sentence.

Getting out of the shower and dressing, the dream still bothered me. Surely no-one back in Argentina was still actively looking for me? Not after all this time.

With the old gang gone and my life in the legion firmly established, Nîmes became my home, and the events of 1990 and Argentina slipped further and further into my past as the decade wore on.

In 1997 I completed a six month Tour of Guyana where I worked as a jungle warfare instructor. Whilst there, I managed to find and rekindle my relationship with Cua, who still worked at La Maison Bleu. Being an instructor, I now had a little more free time and visited Cayenne with her several times to stay with her family there.

Like a fool, at twenty-six years old I 'fell in love' with Cua, asking her to marry me and offering to take her back to live with me in France. While she thought about my proposition, her mother Nhung became seriously ill and died. Understandably, Cua didn't want to leave her father Quang alone in Cayenne, and instead of coming to France with me, she moved there to be with him.

About a week after Nhung died, Cua and I went with Quang to the beach at Mount Joly, where we helped him launch his phoenix kite into the air at sunset. With my arm around Cua's shoulder, we watched from a distance as Quang wept silent tears for his wife, whilst the flutes of his kite sang a soft lilting eulogy over the glowing sand.

Eventually, as always, the time came for me to say farewell to Cua and Quang for the last time. It was a sad parting and I missed them both for a long time afterwards.

In many respects, life is like a train journey. You travel along the line as other people get on and off the train. You never get to know most of the other passengers, even some of those who sit next to you. Others touch your life, making your journey that little bit more interesting and special. Sometimes they get off after one or two stops, sometimes they stay for a while longer. Never the less, sooner or later we must all leave the train.

After returning from my second tour of Guiana, I deployed on more exercises in Djibouti, Chad, and around France. The world moved on. Mobile phones and the internet shrank the planet, although as Legionnaires, at that time we were denied access to them.

There were more girls of course, along the way, but nothing permanent or serious. A man joining the Foreign Legion quickly accepts that in return for a safe haven and a fresh start, he must forfeit the right to romantic attachments and domesticity. At first, whilst still young, it was the usual prostitutes or students studying in Nîmes.

As I got older there were cynical bar girls and waitresses past their prime, hardened by life and on their way down. Colleagues came and went like the seasons, as I steadily worked my way up the Legion's rank structure to become Chief Sergeant.

In 1998, the World Cup came to France. I watched Argentina draw 2-2 to England on the television, before my hopes of victory were dashed as I saw Holland beat us 2-1 at the St Etienne stadium in Marseilles. Being amongst so many Argentines at the stadium and in the bars afterwards was strange, to say the least.

Although I missed my family and Bariloche itself often, it was the first time I had felt true homesickness for my country in nearly ten years.

In a strange twist, Smithy the Briton reappeared on the scene unexpectedly. He had foolishly travelled to France to support the English Football team and been arrested for fighting in the street.

After having his fingerprints taken he was identified as a Legion deserter, and sent to Guyana via Nîmes to complete his last year of service in the jungle. I believe he spent his time there cleaning toilets and washing dishes.

There were many painful partings too, and not just Cua and her family. In the summer of 1999, after establishing a close working relationship with him, I attended the wedding of Captain La Roche in Fontainebleau.

He left the army shortly afterwards. Professional, patient and steadfast throughout, he had been there almost from the start, the desert, Bosnia and through it all, providing support and encouragement along the way.

Now, a decade after running away from home and making a new life in the Legion, practically all the originals were gone.

In 2000 the Twin Towers were hit by suicide bombers flying hijacked planes. Western foreign policy tipped on its axis, but when the United States decided to invade Iraq in 2003, the French Government refused to participate, much to the frustration of most Legionnaires. Little did we know that, in time, things (and us) were going to spill over into Afghanistan.

There were many occasions, mostly whilst alone in

my room in the dead of night, when I would think over what I had done back home. Only the coming of the dawn and my daily duties relieved me.

Naturally enough, I often thought of Tania and our child; my father and brother Raul, too. But quite honestly, the pain of what I had lost forever was too much to bear. But it wasn't just that. How selfish of me to feel sorry for myself after what I'd done to their lives? The tragedy and the mess I'd left behind.

Then there were the nightmares. Not just relating to my actions back home, but the slain children in the garden in Bosnia as well. Sometimes I dreamt that the men whom we had shot dead in the desert had sprung back to life as we searched them, angrily clawing at our faces with broken fingernails.

Many times I woke in the darkness thinking my sweat was blood. Slowly, year followed year, and I matured into a man of thirty.

As I got older, I learned to accept life as it is and not as I would like it to be; people too. We are all a mixture of good and bad qualities.

We are all responsible for the things we do and the way we treat each other. Ultimately, of course, it is ourselves with whom we have to live.

When my second five-year tour with the Legion concluded, and with nowhere else to go, I signed up for another five years.

Part Two

Chapter One

Shortly after signing my second contract I bumped into Corporal Amar in Nîmes. It was the first time I had seen him since he had left the Legion five years previously. His new career as a taxi driver had evidently ended badly.

Stepping off the pavement at dawn one morning after a night's drinking in town, I caught site of him emptying dustbins in to the back of a refuse truck on the corner of the street.

Catching my eye as he placed a bin on the ground, he made the mistake of holding my gaze for a second too long as our eyes met across the road.

Remembering his treatment of Esteban in the desert, and his response to my friends death in the fire, I took my chance to repay him in some small way for all the petit acts of inhumanity I had witnessed him perpetrate years before.

Impotently returning my callous stare, like a rabbit caught in the headlights of an on coming car in the middle of the road, Amar looked pathetic.

Whilst looking him directly in the eye, I pulled a packet of Gauloises from my trouser pocket. After taking the last one and lighting it, I tossed the empty pack nonchalantly onto the ground at his feet before brushing past him and walking away.

Looking back, I shouldn't have lowered myself. But that's the thing about the Amars of this world; perniciously corrosive and mean-spirited; they tend to bring out the worst in others. But who was I to judge him, having never walked in his shoes?

After all, during our first violent encounter with Iraqi forces as fledgling Legionnaires, had Amar not reacted with all the professionalism of a trained soldier and NCO? Had he not prepared us well; to cut no quarter to the enemy, under whatever circumstances we encountered him?

If Amar had have been soft in his dealings with us, we in turn may have been soft in our dealings with those whose job, like ours, was to kill ruthlessly and without question.

Recalling these events from where I am now, in relation to Corporal Amar, I think and hope that perhaps at some point, somewhere amongst the tossed away garbage of his fellow man, and bereft of social, military and economic status, Amar may finally have found some humility and empathy for others. Who knows? At the time, however, I didn't feel bad in the slightest.

It was during a one-year deployment to the recruit training team at Castel Naudry that I met and became friends with Martin Bruchard. Together we enjoyed nights out in Nîmes and Carcassonne; Christmas parties with sugared wine and the building of Christmas Nativity cribs at the barracks.

Whilst alcohol and violence still played their part in my life, I became a very different person from the wayward nineteen year old who had acted so foolishly, causing so much damage years before. The passing of time, however, means little to the powers behind the forces of law and order, and I remained a fugitive.

I was thirty one when I met Carole at the bistro on an evening out in Nîmes with Martin in 2002. By now I had reached the rank of acting Adjutant and was considered an *old sweat* in the Legion. For the next year, when I wasn't working or away on exercise, I enjoyed Carole's company until my final deployment on a six-month tour of Djibouti.

Carole showed me Nîmes through a fresh pair of eyes, teaching me its history and keeping me away from the bars. Together we enjoyed strolls around the Jardins de la Fontains, feeding the song birds around its impressive fountains and waterways.

We went to the movies together, and in the sanctuary of her apartment, Carole taught me how to cook a traditional Nîmes cassoulet.

Emboldened by copious amounts of Vin de Pays, I quickly became adept at combining a blend of haricot beans, confit of duck, sausages, carrots, parsley and laurel. Cooked slowly in a pot with a knuckle of pork, my cassoulets often became the main ingredient in an agreeable evening. Carole shared with me her love of the arts, taking me to the Carre D'Art Gallery and introducing me to writers such as Albert Camus, Sagan, and Robbe-Grillet.

Whilst alone in my room at the barracks, I travelled the high seas with Captain Ahab and his crew in search of Moby Dick, revisited familiar places in Argentina on the Patagonia Express with Theroux, and fought giants in La Mancha with Don Quixote.

I owed Carole much, and Just before my last deployment to Djibouti I took her camping amongst the saline lagoons of the Mediterranean coast south of Nîmes.

Chapter Two

Camargue Delta, Bouches-du-Rhône, Southern France

Fed by the waters of the Rhône River, the Camargue Delta covers almost 1000 square kilometres of low marshy plain on the coast forty kilometres south of Nîmes.

Cutting a relentless swathe for 800 kilometres south from its source on a remote glacier high above the town of Valais in Switzerland, the mighty Rhône eventually breaks up into various tributaries and seeps through the tepid marshes of the Delta and into the Mediterranean Sea.

This vast wetland is home to feral white horses, timid water snakes and herds of semi-wild black bulls. The latter-day European Cowboys, who watch over these fearsome beasts whilst proudly mounted on white Stallions, are known as *Les Guardiens*.

Above the Delta's peaceful waterways and sultry woodlands, garish bee-eaters, blue roller birds and shrikes flutter among flocks of rose finches and brash pink flamingos.

Like clouds of confetti tossed on the breeze at a gypsy wedding, they pepper the hazy horizon as they take to the wing.

It was here, in the autumn of 2002, that Carole and I set up camp next to the glassy waters of a quiet lagoon. This was Carole's first camping trip. She seemed happy and exited as I pitched our tent amongst the clumps of sea lavender growing beneath the oleander and tamarisk trees.

"You know Sebastián, this is the first time I've been camping; I'm having a really lovely time; thank you," she said, as she gathered pine needles and dried kindling from the sandy ground.

Without a trace of make up, she looked even more beautiful than usual in the clean autumn air.

"No Carole, *thank you*" I smiled back. "This makes a nice change from sleeping out with a bunch of sweaty Legionnaires!"

Before long I had made a fire and lit the dried wood with my Zippo. Sitting outside the tent in the late afternoon, I opened a bottle of Cotes du Rhône as we relaxed beneath a Tamarisk tree.

As I melted a squashy slab of brie spiked with garlic and rosemary over the fire's delicate yellow flames, we ate grapes while Carole talked of wine and the antiquity.

"Did you know, Sebastián, that the Phocaeans brought Shiraz grapes from Iran to their colony in Marseilles around 600 B.C.? Two and a half thousand years ago... All the way from Persia."

"Really?" I said. "Well, these will definitely give me a stomach ache then if they're that old!"

"You'll be fine." Carole laughed. "These are eating grapes," she said as I dipped my bread into the cheese.

Carole took a mouthful of wine, and then, with her thoughts now on the Middle East, she turned to me as we ate. "What was it like, Sebastián, in Iraq?"

I looked out over the fire and across the lagoon. The gently rippling open water reflected a bright Azure sky; the rushes and reeds on the far side shone brilliant green in the late autumn sun.

"Sometimes hot, sometimes cold, lots of empty space; some good friends..." I said. Uncomfortable memories of fear and death began to creep up on me.

As the birds in the surrounding marshes began their drawn-out evensong, and before Carole had the chance to probe deeper, I spoke again.

"That cheese was good," I said, as I poured another cup full of wine.

Carole picked up on my discomfort.

"What else have we got to eat?" she said cheerfully.

"Plenty!" I replied, momentarily forcing myself to match her cheerfulness. Reaching into my backpack, I fished out crackers, olives, and two venison and cranberry sausages laced with Genepi liquor.

As darkness fell around us, we ate our fill, as a flock of tufted duck appeared out of nowhere to land in the middle of the lagoon. We watched the birds settle on the water, and as countless bush crickets announced themselves in the surrounding scrub, I threw a handful of pine needles on the fire, then turned to Carole.

"You haven't really shared your life story with me; nothing from before Nîmes, anyway," I said.

"I haven't shared much, have I? You don't really know me at all, Sebastián."

"Okay, tell me then." And so Carole began to talk.

Originally from Quimper on the English Channel coast of Brittany, her father was a doctor and her mother a schoolteacher. Carole excelled at school and later attended the University of Strasbourg where she fell for her lecturer, marrying him at the age of twenty one.

After gaining her degree, Carole went on to study for a PhD in history. Whilst eating dinner one night with her husband in their apartment, there was a knock at the door. Carole got up from the table to answer it. A student of her husbands had arrived with the news that she was pregnant by him.

"She had the baby; a little girl," said Carole, her voice sounding somehow far away as the reflection of the fire danced in her green eyes.

"They still live together," she said, her voice hardening.

"That must have hurt," I said.

Turning to look at me, Carole straightened her back.

"I think that everyone in your life, no matter who it is, lets you down at some point or other, don't you?"

Suddenly feeling the chill of the evening air, I looked down into the fire, thought about my own life, and felt shabby

"Sometimes people do things they can't take back, that's life, but I guess you're right; everyone lets you down at some point," I said.

Carole looked at me closely.

"There's something I need to tell you, Sebastián." She looked serious,

"What is it?" I asked.

"You've got cheese all over your chin." She laughed.

With all the wine drunk, we retreated from the dying fire and into the tent, pulling down the zip from the inside. The tent was a modest-sized two-man affair with only enough room to kneel up in.

Once inside we took off our shoes, and Carole removed her fleece top. As I undid the zipper on my trousers, Carole responded to the sound of it by pushing her hand inside the open fly to massage and squeeze my cock.

"I want you," she said in the darkness, before pulling down my pants and covering me with her mouth.

Running the fingers of both my hands through her soft hair as she fellated me, I pictured her using the very mouth now around my hard cock to confidently address her students in class. I imagined the articulate words that came out of it as she gave seminars on subjects beyond my knowledge.

While she gradually increased her grip on me with the intensity of her sucking, I thought about the way I had watched her in the past, when she had pushed delicate salad leaves from the tip of an expensive shiny fork over her perfect white teeth and onto her pink wet tongue.

Remembering the way she sipped sophisticated white wines through her classically formed lips aroused me enormously, especially when I thought of the Latin, Greek and English that tumbled effortlessly from them.

This wasn't love for me. This was the thrill of crossing boundaries. Age, nationality, social hierarchies culture and class. And Carole; what was in it for her? It can't have been love, she didn't know me. How could she, when no-one really knew me. I had spent years kicking over the traces before I ever met her.

They do say that the mind is the most powerful sex organ in the body, and Carole had a finely tuned one; one that, whilst often at odds with her carnal needs, evidently lost the battle at times.

What she did know about me was that I was a foreigner, hired by her country's government to do its dirty work in the hard and ugly corners of its old and fading empire.

She must also have known that the excited hard cock now in her mouth was regularly taken out to casually piss in the street by a drunken soldier who spat, swore and fought.

She knew full well that it had been wanked off to pornographic films and stuck in places she would rather not think about. And still she sucked; she sucked *me*, a criminal, this woman who'd never broken the law or pissed outside in her life.

She sucked as if it were some kind of necessity and that both our survivals depended on it. I began to feel her spit running down my balls and in the palms of my hands as it spread from her mouth and across her smooth cheeks. Carole gorged on me like a half-starved and hungry woman; this woman who'd never known hunger in her life.

In the pitch dark of our tent, I shuffled the images of her and her mouth in my mind until I had them in just the right sequence; each image followed by another in just the right order and lasting for exactly as long as I wanted it to. When I couldn't take any more, I finally settled on one particular image.

Purposefully slowing the image down, I braced myself for what was literally about to come. It was the image of Carole slowly raising an expensive fork to her partially open mouth.

Impaled on the fork's gently curved tips, a delicate cluster of Lolla Rosso lettuce leaves dripped honey and mustard; their frills pushing and folding over between her soft lips, as creamy traces of erotic dressing smeared her lipstick.

With that, the blood moved quickly to the centre of my body and a tingling chill gripped my skin, only to be replaced immediately by the red hot rush of my powerful orgasm. I exhaled hard, my breath warm and heavy as I held on tightly to the back of Carole's head,

"You fucking whore..." I panted breathlessly, my words either pushed or pulled involuntarily from my sex-drenched subconscious. Carole kept me in her mouth after I'd come, until I eased her head back gently with my fingers.

Reaching around to hold my buttocks with both hands, Carole pressed her cheek hard against my phallus before saying quietly, "I'm sorry. I'm a dirty bitch - nothing but a dirty, dirty bitch - but it's your entire fault, Sebastián."

Her words, loaded with guilty pleasure and faux self-loathing, expanded my ego, and in return I stroked her hair, telling her that she was a beautiful woman.

Carole tensed her fingers around my ass so that I felt her nails dig into my flesh, giving me the slightest momentary sexual aftershock. She then turned to kiss my spent prick, before finally letting go. We said nothing to each other after that as we continued to undress, before climbing into our sleeping bags and embracing.

Looking back on all of that now, I suppose that in some way I felt that I was achieving some form of social ascendency in every aspect of my relationship with Carole. As for her and what she got out of sleeping with me, she'd have to tell you that herself. But I do know this.

Through her mouth, Carole had acquired the taste for fine wines and gourmet foods. She also used her mouth to communicate both her depth and range of knowledge, projecting her intellect to the world via the use of classical languages and cultural awareness.

These were the things that had come to define her. So by taking a young soldiers cock in her mouth perhaps she felt liberated, even if only for a while; free from the thin social veneer that so many people varnish themselves with daily.

Like many young men, I felt that my manhood was centred in my penis. Consequently, mine had become a seasoned veteran of many ego-driven sexploits and adventures. Countless times it had blazed a heroic trail into the pleasure-lands that lie beyond those enticing silk and lace barriers worn by the fairer sex.

Not liking myself much as a person a lot of the time, I have no doubt that by putting my cock in Carole's mouth I felt that I was bringing her down to my own level to some degree, therefore making it more comfortable for me to be in a relationship with her.

As I never asked Carole what she got out of it I couldn't really say, but when I think about it now, all I can come up with is freedom; transient and unsustainable freedom, but freedom never the less.

When it came time for me to deploy to Djibouti in

December that year, I felt reluctant to go. I would have liked to have seen Carole over Christmas and the New Year, but it wasn't to be.

At least I could look forward to being with her again when we returned to France in the spring.

Chapter Three

Nîmes, Spring 2003

With regard to people letting you down, Carole certainly proved herself right upon my return from Africa. Looking back, I didn't handle things well and provided her with every reason to leave me behind forever in the process.

After throwing her lover out and falling asleep on her couch. I woke alone in the apartment the following morning with a hangover. Realising that there was nothing to be achieved by hanging around or waiting for Carole's return, I left her front door key on the coffee table and left.

There's a peculiar thing about keys, I feel. They can often symbolise the path we take through life; their collection somehow measuring our achievements and successes.

The first key someone has as a child is the key to their money-box. Next, they might have the key to the lock on their bicycle and the shed it's kept in. Many then progress to the locker key at their school, then the front door key to their family home.

When we start driving we have car keys; at work we are given the keys to lock up the building after everyone else has gone home, or as juniors we might be the first to arrive.

As we continue in the adult world, we are given the keys to the department, the safe, then our own office and our own house. In the end, it is a simple bunch of keys that mark and measure ones life's journey; but not me. Not then.

The act of leaving Carole's key on her coffee table rendered me keyless at the age of thirty-three. No keys, and no life.

Pulling the door shut behind me as I left, I dragged myself back to the barracks. Finding Martin in his room, I spilled my guts about everything.

"Mate," he said. "When I was younger, it took me six months to get over some chick that broke my heart. The next one took six weeks to get over, the one after that, six days. It takes me six hours to get over a woman now."

Sitting on the end of Martin's bed, I rubbed my tired eyes.

"I'm leaving the Legion the year after next Martin; I thought she and I could..."

"Mate, that's the life we have chosen for ourselves." He shrugged. "What do they say? *"Dreaming of love in a life of pain?"* He poured us some coffee.

"She said she loved me, Martin."

"Jesus Christ, Sebastián, people will say *anything* when they are fucking!"

"You're a cynical bastard, Martin."

"Look," he went on. "A long time ago I was married; she was all I ever wanted. Not the best-looking girl in the world but clever, and kind."

"What happened?" I asked.

"It was a relationship, Sebastián, they end. The thing was, I thought I'd found everything in her."

"How so?

"You know, someone to share life's ups and downs, the rise and falls of living."

"Did she end it, Martin?"

"Yes, but I'm lucky!"

"Lucky?"

"Yeah, lucky; she ripped my heart out. I can't love anyone now, not even myself. No-one could ever hurt me again; I simply don't give a fuck anymore."

"I'm not sure I want that to be me, Martin."

"Do you think you'll go back to Argentina?"

Shrugging my shoulders, I took a gulp of black coffee.

"Look, Sebastián. I know it's hard, but try to forget her and move on."

"Martin, I've been seeing her for over a year. She made me feel like I had some kind of life; something more than just the Legion. I thought we might have a future. Now she's shat all over me."

"Sebastián. Love *is* like the Legion. There are no victims, just volunteers. Come back tonight and we'll share a couple of glasses of *I don't care any more juice*; yes?"

"Yes, why not," I said.

Thinking about what Martin had said later, I found it hard to disagree with him. The following Monday, I contacted my grandmother's lawyers in Spain. Using the telephone, I masqueraded as my brother Raul and pretended that I was calling from Argentina. Again, I felt shabby.

Later that year our orders came through for deployment to Afghanistan and I found myself on active service once again. By the time we got to Kabul, the emotional ties that I had naively attached myself to Carole with were fraying at last.

Chapter Four

Afghanistan, Sorubi Province, Winter 2004

Approaching the small village from the north, we travelled on foot as a section along a wide dirt track. We had replaced our combat helmets with our green berets in order to appear less threatening to the inhabitants. In some respects, the surrounding landscape reminded me of places I had known back home in Patagonia. Woods and copses of deciduous trees dotted a landscape of undulating arid ground, stretching away to distant snow-covered mountains.

Recently promoted to Major by some one as stupid as he was, Duriuex lead the section from the front. Walking in staggered formation, each man kept his eyes peeled for anything which could be considered to be amiss.

Three hundred yards or so from the village of about 250 people, we began paying close attention to the surrounding area. To the right of the track we walked along was a wide strip of short yellow grass leading to a wooded area of alder, ash and young walnut oak, their branches bare under a colourless winter sky.

Taking particular notice of a large flock of caramel-tailed starlings circling above the wood as if to land, before suddenly flying away as we walked parallel to it, was Turan, the young Turkish Legionnaire who had helped me kill the Goats in Djibouti.

Giving a silent hand signal to the rest of the patrol to take cover, Turan sunk into the undergrowth by the track. With the rest of the section now crouching in the irrigation ditches either side of the path, he called forward to Duriuex.

"There's something wrong in those trees, sir. Those birds don't want to land in there."

"No," Replied Duriuex. "It's us that's spooked them, let's keep going."

Continuing our approach to the village's scattering of small houses, I felt uneasy, thinking that we should have checked out the wood before carrying on, but it wasn't my call.

On arrival in the village itself we found a passive community who seemed outwardly accepting of our presence. Duriuex's' interpreter, Ali, asked an old man in a doorway to lead us to the Tribal elder's house, which was a low one-storey building made of wattle and daub, covered with clay.

Once inside, the Major, his radio operator, an Australian named Taylor, and myself as Adjutant made our acquaintances, whilst several members of the section took up strategic positions around the edge of the village. Others handed out sweets to the children.

The old man sat cross-legged between two others on mats spread across the ground around a central fire. As Ali introduced us, the village elder stroked his beard and smiled - somewhat nervously, I felt. After the initial pleasantries and introductions were over, they offered to share a large bowl of food with us.

This was a scenario we knew well. Upon arriving in Afghan villages it was normal to be offered food and drink with the village elders. We had become accustomed to eating local fare such as chicken and chickpea stews or meatballs and noodles tossed in yoghurt. Often the food provided by villagers was a welcome relief from field-kitchen food provided by our own Legion cooks.

Once seated, we placed our weapons closely beside us on the ground. Bowls of steamed rice with raisins, carrots and pieces of lamb were produced, served with large round pieces of warm lavash bread. Ali translated for us.

"This food is *qabli puloa*. It's good, yes?" he said as he helped himself.

I turned to Duriuex.

"Looks like we turned up at the right time of day."

Ali was right, the food was good. Duriuex asked the elder whether everyone in the village had enough to eat.

"Plenty of food here for everyone; no-one hungry here," came his affable reply.

"Do you have anyone in need of medical attention? We have a doctor with us," Duriuex went on.

"You could leave bandages and antiseptic with us if you like," replied the elder.

"That won't be a problem; I'll make sure you get some before we leave," said Duriuex, before glancing in my direction,

"I'll go and speak to the doctor as soon as we have finished eating," I replied through a mouth full of steaming *qabli puloa*. Duriuex went on.

"What about the Taliban, do you have any contact with them?"

The elder's answer was to stroke his long beard, close his eyes and shake his head slowly from side to side. I didn't trust him; my gut told me not to. Just then Taylor's radio burst into life with a message.

"Is everything okay?" asked Duriuex,

"Lieutenant Girard says that there are no young men anywhere in the village, sir; just old ones, and the women and children."

Through Ali, Duriuex addressed the village elder.

"Where are all the men folk? There seems to be only the older men here."

"They are at the mosque. They have gone to pray, that's all," replied the elder. Concerned by this, I turned to Duriuex.

"Sir, I think we should think about when we're

leaving and in what fashion," I said. Duriuex turned to me calmly.

"I understand, Alvarez. I'm sure everything's fine, though. It's important that these people get the medical supplies they need, and that we leave on good terms. Okay?"

Asking Ali to excuse me, I picked up my weapon and left the small house to go in search of the doctor. Once outside I also passed the word around that we needed to be extra vigilant and that the village and its surroundings were not to be trusted. After speaking to the doctor, I then made my way back to the elder's house and waited outside for Duriuex and Taylor to emerge.

Whilst there, Martin approached me, surrounded by several smiling children whose mouths were stuffed with chocolate and biscuits. He offered me a cigarette.

"Here, have one of these…" he said as he pulled his Zippo from his pocket. He then lit the cigarette for me.

"Thanks." I took one drag - then, coughing and spluttering, I threw the burning fag on the ground.

"What the fuck?" I said as I spat on the floor and wiped my mouth.

Martin laughed out loud, along with the village children who had been following him around in the hope of more candy. Looking me in the face as he laughed, Martin gave me a hefty slap on my upper arm and then smiled.

"It's a local one; come on, get into it, we're *here*. At least you've had your lunch!"

"Martin, listen; now's not the time." Taking in my tone, Martin straightened out immediately.

"What's up?" he said.

"There are no men of fighting age in the whole village, if you haven't noticed. Something's not right. I'm sure their preparing to zap us; and Duriuex's a

228

prick."

"Tell me about it; what about Lieutenant Girard?"

"Forget him. He's just out of the Academy, and he thinks Duriuex is God."

Like Lieutenant La Roche before him, Girard was a native of Fontainebleau, but as far as I was concerned, when I compared them both in my mind, Girard was lacking in every respect.

"Okay then; what's the plan?" asked Martin.

"How the fuck do I know? We're not the one's doing the planning, I think *they* are. The old boy says they're all at the mosque; he's lying, I can tell. We're never going to be safe over here until Duriuex steps on a goddamned mine, I'm telling you."

Martin looked unsettled by my talk.

"Steady on, Sebastián - you're not getting jumpy, are you?"

"Martin, if the balloon goes up I'm going to need your help keeping our guys steady and on the ball. It's a young section; hardly any of them are even twenty-one."

"Yes but come on, they've been in scraps before."

"I know, and it's gone to rat-shit as far as I'm concerned."

"What does Duriuex think?"

"Fuck Duriuex; the point is, things are too quiet around here for my liking, mate, and *I'm asking you*; *forget* Duriuex if the lid comes off this time, okay? Whatever happens, it's got to be *our fight*. And if you want to know the truth, yes I am jumpy, very fucking jumpy."

Martin gave me a Gauloises from his top pocket then lit it.

"Everything's going to be fine, Sebastián. I'm in the mood for a din-dong today, anyway."

"Martin, get your corporals, Dowling and Mancini;

tell them to tune in for a scrap and tell them to get behind the lads *hard* if something goes off, okay. Remind them not to feed or stroke the dogs; they've never seen a vet. Rabies, yes?"

"I'm on it, Sebastián, see you in a bit."

"Thanks, Martin."

Martin left and I stayed where I was; waiting, smoking, and thinking. Looking up, I observed an international airliner heading south east toward the Indian sub-continent, or maybe Australia. Streaking a brilliant white vapour trail across the sky, it shone like a daytime star as it reflected the winter sun.

Standing outside the Tribal elder's house, smoking a cigarette with a gun in my hands, I imagined the roles being played out by the people within the star above me.

"Chicken or beef, sir; red or white wine?"

"How long till we land?"

"Would you like a newspaper; coffee or tea?"

I felt a million miles away from the people overhead in their hermetically sealed world of comfort and privilege. The smell of my burning tobacco failed to smother the scents around me.

The aromas of human beings living as they have always lived. Woodsmoke and cooking, rotting food, dogs, chicken-shit, body odour and piss. I sucked on my French cigarette like a child sucking its mother's nipple for security.

An hour or so later, and with the bandages and antiseptic distributed amongst the village, we made our way out of the settlement and back the way we had come.

Chapter Five

They opened fire on us with automatic weapons from the wood we had passed on the way in. Turan had been right.

Taking cover from the ferocious weight of fire being levelled against us, we immediately took cover and fired back aggressively from the irrigation ditches either side of the track. Everyone, the whole section, shooting and shouting at the same time.

"Calm down! Identify targets!"

"I can see them!"

"Don't let them get around the side of us!"

"Calm down!"

Looking up the ditch I was in and trying to make eye contact with Duriuex, all I could see were Legionnaires in ones and twos ducking and firing over the top of the ditch. Turning to Turan, I spoke as calmly as I could manage with bullets zipping and cracking just inches above us.

"Right, Turan; I'm going back down this ditch towards the village. You come with me."

"Yes, okay, *mon Adjutant*."

"When I've gone as far as I think I need to, I'm crossing the track, then I'm going to give it to these bastards with grenades from their right. You cover me then join me straight away."

"Ready when you are, sir."

Crouching low, I set off down the ditch as fast as I could, guessing when I'd covered around 150 yards or so. Turning to find Turan right on my heels as I came to a stop, I gathered my breath and pulled two grenades from my webbing pouches.

Cowering in that stinking ditch amongst the chaos and din all around us, I felt a spark of anger towards

Duriuex ignite inside me. Preferring to be in control rather than listen to anyone else, he had left us unnecessarily open to attack.

Hunched over with the freezing ditch water seeping into my boots and through my socks, that spark of anger lit the lava deep inside me which had lain dormant for a very long time.

Of course, the sum of that anger wasn't just Duriuex; it was Carole too, the Whore; the filthy Fucking Whore. Right now she would be sipping wine in France with her cock sucking mouth; sitting back comfortably, effectively masquerading as a respectable and learned woman, oozing fake class and sophistication.

That Bitch had taken my last dream and shat on it; let some bloke stick his dick into it. Then there was my father; never listening, just criticising and putting me down. Why couldn't he ever have asked me how I felt instead? No wonder I went off the Fucking rails.

And my mother; dying and leaving me like that. Dying in the middle of the afternoon and leaving me when I was at school; *Why*? I never saw her smile at the Flowers I had bought for her. She never even let me say goodbye.

And of course there was France. Perhaps Sergeant Belcourt had been right about France. They *had* been happy to wave flags for us and cheer; but they wouldn't want us living next door to them. They wouldn't want us marrying their Daughters, *would they*; *NO*! Well why didn't they do their own fucking dirty work then?

And the Legion, with all its vacuous talk of brotherhood and comradeship, when all we seemed to do was argue and fight amongst ourselves.

And of course there was me. I was angry at *me*.

If I hadn't done the things I'd done, I could have had a house outside Mendoza with Tania and our child.

We could have had a garden looking out over the vineyards to the mountains. There would have been a back yard with a Barbecue and trips to the Mall; children's toys and bed time stories; a dog, a family car and a *life*.

Was it not my own fault that my world was ugly and full of violence, alcohol, whores and hangovers? Wasn't it all my own fault that nobody loved me, when all I'd ever done was suit myself and think about *me*?

Well, the Legion had given me something. It had given me a gun and bullets and bombs, and now I was going to use them with relish. With the lava inside me red-hot and lit by the spark of anger at Duriuex, I was going to have my Vesuvian moment.

"Turan, take this grenade, pull the pin; hold it while I get the pin out on this one then pass it back to me."

"Okay, I've got it."

"You're on automatic, yes?"

"Yes."

"Give me that first bomb back."

"Here."

"Okay, as soon as I move, stitch rounds along that tree line from left to right - fire low, okay - low low low - *tree line only* - don't stop until I've chucked one of these, okay? Then follow."

"I'm ready."

"See you in the trees..."

With gunfire streaking both ways across the track to our right, I bolted forwards from my position and out across the track. Turan immediately delivered a vicious volley of ammunition past me and into the trees to my front and right.

With the wind at my heels I charged through the yellow grass on the other side of the track, until a bullet cutting within a hair's breadth of my cheek instinctively made me dive for cover.

A second or so later and my first grenade exploded in the wood, followed immediately by my second. As that one detonated, a blood-curdling scream, cut through by the sound of splitting bark and breaking branches, rose horribly above the sounds of gunfire all around.

Looking through the grass to my right, I saw my young Legionnaires crossing the open ground at speed towards the trees. Firing their weapons on automatic as they ran, they looked like performers in a carnival. Streams of spent cartridge cases poured from the sides of their clattering rifles in ribbons of gold.

Swinging my weapon around on its sling to my front, I emptied a full magazine of rounds into the wood. Pausing to reload, I looked around for Turan. Writhing in pain, he lay on the ground, having been shot at a position not far behind me. Ignoring his plight, I jumped to my feet and kept the momentum of the attack going. Charging into the trees, I fired short bullet bursts in front of me as I ran.

Once inside the wood I leapt over the blood-stained body of a Taliban fighter. Then, dropping onto one knee, I raked the trees ahead with gunfire, whilst to my right comrades did the same. Figures of armed men on the run ducked through the trees ahead of me as they ran for their lives. Minutes later five of the enemy lay dead.

Five dead people.

There were three for Duriuex and my parents, one for France, and one for Carole, the whore. There was one missing; the one for *me*. The one to pay the price for my anger and my part in my own pain. I didn't know it yet, but I was going to have to pay for all that myself.

Realising the bad guys had melted away, and aware of the risk of booby traps in the wood, we called off our pursuit and reorganised ourselves.

Turan was our only casualty. He had taken a bullet through the shoulder. Rushing back from the wood to the open ground, I found the doctor tending to him in the grass. I held Turan's hand in mine.

"We got the bastards, hold on Legionnaire," I said as he gripped my hand tightly in his. Turan expressed his anguish through gritted teeth, in Turkish; the doctor turned to me, his voice steady and calm.

"I've found an exit wound in the area of his shoulder blade. See if you can find anything else."

Letting go of Turan's hand, I removed my left glove. Pushing my hand behind his back, between the ground and his body, I felt around under his clothing. As I did so, Turan became calm. Working my way from the top of his buttocks, I groped around under his clothes.

Soon enough, I felt the first two fingers of my hand slip into a warm wet hole in the lumbar region of his back. Both fingers sank into the wound up to my knuckles. The newly-formed hole in Turan felt like a rough vagina. Turan was crying now. No noise; Just tears. Tears and breathing. Pulling my fingers out, I looked to the doctor as a French Helicopter swooped in to land close by.

"Exit wound in the lumbar region."

"Okay," said the doctor. "The bullet must have hit a bone and split in two on its way through."

Now Turan's skin took on a waxy texture. He became calmer still as the doctor jabbed the needle of a saline drip into his forearm. Passing the bag it was attached to to me, the doctor maintained a professional attitude.

"Hold this up."

Holding the bag above my head with my right hand, I held on to Turan's hand with my left as I knelt beside him.

Around us, weapons were removed from the bodies of the Taliban fighters, and reinforcements arrived by helicopter to secure and hold the village.

Just then, Martin appeared at our side with a couple of stretcher bearers for Turan. Ignoring me, he looked at the doctor.

"Good to go?"

"We need to be quick, he's bleeding internally," said the doctor.

Turan began sobbing as Martin turned to the medics.

"Okay... *C'est bon....? Tu l'a; aller aller, court!*"

Picking up Turan, the medics laid him on their stretcher, and then began to run towards the helicopter parked between the ditch and the wood. I ran with them, holding on to the drip giving life into Turan's failing body as we covered the ground.

"*Tu l'a, on y va!*" shouted the medics as we ran. We arrived at the aircraft in seconds. Once there and at the open door in its side, the choppers loadmaster took the drip from my hand, and Turan was loaded on board.

The chopper lifted off and I noticed that the air along the track was filled with the smell of cordite from spent bullet-cases from the battle, much like the smell you get at the end of a firework display. As I turned away from the ascending aircraft, Martin grabbed me by the shoulder.

"Here," he said as he unscrewed the top on his water canteen, "You've got blood all over your fucking hands."

He emptied the contents of his canteen over my blood-soaked hands and I rinsed them in the cold air.

"Thanks, Martin; is everyone else okay?"

"Duriuex has a nosebleed for some reason, and the new British guy has a splinter of something in the back of his hand, but he's looking after the wound himself."

"Okay, good. Take six guys now; move fast and form a cut-off group on the north side of that fucking village. Any one trying to leave put the hard word on them, okay?"

Soon, several of the old men in the village were rounded up and taken away for questioning.

As we took control of the community, the mountains beyond the village pulsed lavender in the late afternoon sun, as if somehow saddened by the spectacle of violence before them.

It had been the latest in a series of vicious confrontations with the Taliban since we had arrived in the country four months previously. Later that night I spoke to Major Duriuex back at the base.

"Looks like our hearts and minds campaign isn't going too well, is it, sir?"

"Sebastián, we are here to do a job. I'm very proud of what we are achieving, but you must remember that we are only a small part of the picture out here."

"Yes, sir; I'm just glad that nobody got killed today."

"Sebastián, I'm putting you in for an award for what you did out there. Your actions were in the finest traditions of the Legion and you are a credit to your regiment."

What could I say? As far as I was concerned, as a mature soldier it was my job to use my experience to set an example and take care of the younger members of the section, and that's what I felt I had done. The fact of the matter was that Duriuex realised he was a total prick and an ineffectual soldier. His complete lack of intuition and abilities as an officer had fed those of us under his command into a potentially catastrophic situation. By recommending me for an award, Duriuex was simply distracting attention away from the fact that he was a total fucking prick.

"Sir, I think Legionnaire Turan deserves to be recognised. I wouldn't have made it to the trees if it hadn't been for him sticking with me."

"Sure; write a report and I'll see what I can do. Leave it with me."

Turan survived his wound and was repatriated to France, receiving nothing for his bravery.

Chapter Six

Afghanistan was a hard place to soldier. The terrain was rough and arduous to cover. Not only did we have to contend with the constant threat of anti-personnel mines laid for us by the Taliban, but also the *legacy mines* left over from the conflict between the Russians and the Mujahedeen in the 1970s.

Being on home ground, the enemy knew the terrain intimately, and in that respect we were always at a disadvantage.

One of the hardest things to over come whilst out on patrol was the pervasive fear of stepping on something that would either remove one's legs, end one's life, or even worse, blow one's bollocks off. Everyone one had their own ways of dealing with this.

"Fuck it," said Martin one night as we talked in a bunker inside our forward operating post. "I don't really care. You're either alive, or you're not. That's how I see life."

He poured us both some warming coffee from his Thermos flask as the temperature inside the bunker plummeted rapidly.

"What about your future?" I asked.

"I don't think about it. I'm a Legionnaire, and that's it," he said.

"What about Quebec; you know, home?"

"You know as well as I do, Sebastián, that everyone joins the Legion because they are either running from something or to something."

"And you?" I asked.

"I did some things back home; I can't go back," he said flatly.

Lighting a smoke, I passed one to Martin.

"That's why the Taliban get such a hard time when they fuck with us, isn't it?" I said. "Most of us have nothing to lose."

Martin didn't answer. He simply got into his sleeping bag with his weapon and gave me a look that left me with the unnerving feeling that he was looking right inside me.

"What's wrong?" I asked.

"You, Sebastián; you think too much."

"Do I?"

"Yes, you do; I look at life like this," he said. "I'm not interested in being happy or unhappy; neither thing really exists as far as I'm concerned."

Standing up, I threw the cold dregs of my coffee out over the narrow slit opening of the bunker. Outside, a sickle moon hung low in the sky like a sultan's dagger poised to strike. Its light reflected off the drops of coffee, giving them the appearance of mercury trickling over the sandbags. Picking up my weapon, I crawled into my own sleeping bag on the floor next to Martin as he went on.

"It's like this," he said. "Real simple; I just do what works for me and I get satisfaction out of that, and that's all."

"Like what?" I asked.

"Well," he said, "As shallow as it seems; when I open a bottle of liquor and drink it, pull the trigger on my weapon, or stick my dick in a woman, I always get the result I want. It's the same every time, I can rely on it, and I'm satisfied; those are the moments I live for. I'm a soldier, for God's sake... who really gives a shit about anything else?"

Not for the first time since I'd known Martin, I couldn't fault his simple logic, and felt positively envious of his world view as we settled down to face the prospect of another day of surviving Afghanistan.

Moments later, though, as I lay next to him in the darkness of our fortress bunker, I couldn't help but feel that, not far beneath his outwardly emollient attitude, there was a man slowly and quietly choking on bitterness.

After encountering many angry men over the years, Belcourt and Amar amongst them, I had come to the conclusion that only one thing makes a person angry when all's said and done, and that is injustice.

Feelings of injustice lie at the heart of every angry emotion I believe, and yet unlike Amar and Belcourt, Martin never seemed angry to me. There was something else. Something I couldn't quite put my finger on.

In time, as Martin's breathing became heavier and slower, it became apparent to me that he was fast asleep. For some strange reason that I can't explain, as Martin slept, I got the image in my mind of a middle-aged woman. She stood alone in the softly-lit living room of a warm and comfortable suburban home.

Quietly and carefully, the woman polished the framed high school graduation photograph of a son, a once bright and shining son who was difficult to love; except perhaps in absentia.

After replacing the photo on the mantle piece above the fire, the woman walked to the living room door to go up to bed. As she got there, she looked back at the picture.

"Goodnight, son," she said.

And with that, she switched off the light and the image was gone.

Having known Martin for six years at this point, I felt strongly that whatever he had done back home in Quebec, it hadn't been illegal. It is the way of the world, I think, that some of the worst atrocities human beings commit against each other are perfectly legal.

Turning to my sleeping friend on the cold floor beside me, I whispered quietly to him in the darkness from my sleeping bag,

"Goodnight, mate."

Oblivious to my gesture, Martin began to snore.

The thing with warm words is that they only hold their warmth if they are received, and as Martin didn't hear mine, they floated peacefully up through the cold dark air, dissolving into nothing as they hit the roof of the bunker.

Much has been written down the ages about the bonds of love and friendship forged between men in times of war. So much, in fact, that I feel I have little more to add through my own pen; except perhaps those few which I have just this moment written.

Over the next two months we cleared villages of Taliban fighters, only to clear them again weeks later as the war of attrition continued. We fought hard as a unit, and so did the Taliban.

In spite of Martin's pragmatic view of our situation as Legionnaires, my own thoughts were turning slowly to the time I would be retiring from the Legion and about what might lie ahead for me.

More and more I was considering settling down, at least for a while, in my grandmother's farm in Spain. The Legion had given me a place to hide and escape from my past, but not from myself. What options did I have? I could stay in France and try and carve out some kind of life for myself; but apart from the ability to shoot straight and iron perfectly, what was I qualified to do?

As the tour progressed, many of us continued to wonder what good we were doing in Afghanistan.

"We should just leave this lot to their own devices," said Taylor one day, as we refuelled our vehicle at the roadside. "I don't want to loose my legs in this shithole for nothing; gotta get back to Australia and surf."

Removing his helmet, he leaned back against the

side of the truck, scratching his head.

"I don't understand this thing about how we're fighting for freedom over here," he said. "I mean, they don't have to pay taxes, they can drive around at any speed without a licence, no speed cameras, and they can own an assault rifle without a licence. They have a lot more freedom here than the average Australian, as far as I can tell."

Our medic, a young Norwegian named Clasen, shook his head.

"This place is terrible, I hate it. The people don't even want us here, it's not worth it."

Whilst inwardly I agreed, personal feelings couldn't come in to it for me.

"Stop complaining," I said. "You signed up for this; keep your minds on the job in hand and do what you're trained to do. Everything else will look after itself," I told them.

Glancing over my shoulder up the stony slope by the side of the road, Taylor nodded and spoke.

"Oh look…," he said casually, "here comes a little friend."

Turning around to look for myself, I noticed a small child; a girl of around six or seven, walking towards us from a single-roomed shack around a hundred yards back from the road. In her arms she carried a doll made of brown and blue cloth stuffed with rags. Two orange buttons made the doll's eyes. Its hair was made from finely cut strips of hessian sacking of the kind that comes from military sandbags.

Moments later the girl stepped from the rocky slope and down onto the road. Swinging my weapon on its sling around my body, I let it rest in the small of my back before dropping down onto my haunches, beckoning her towards me, and encouraging her with a smile.

Dropping her chin onto her chest as she approached, she smiled in the way that little girls smile at fathers the world over when they want something. Reaching into my pocket to pull out some candy I stretched out my arm as she drew closer.

"Here, would you like some candy?" I said in Spanish.

I spoke in Spanish, firstly because she wouldn't have understood French anyway, and secondly because I wanted a break.

French was the language of my work; it was a working tool for me. I didn't *think* in it, or *feel* in it; and so whilst my colleagues refuelled vehicles and checked oil and water levels, I took some mental time out. Also, by speaking in Spanish, I was excluding Taylor and Clasen from my interaction with the girl.

Squatting in the dust, I met the girl face to face behind the truck. Cautiously and silently she took the candy from my hand, at arm's length.

Now I noticed her eyes; luminescent ocean-grey eyes, framed by a delicious mix of tangled honey and fawn locks, resting on caramel cheeks flushed deep rose-pink in the winter air.

Looking into her eyes from a distance of barely a foot, they took my breath away. Brilliant flecks of amber and gold shot like sparks from a furnace across her iris's from jet-black pupils. Smiling a sunbeam straight at me, the girl popped the candy into her mouth and let its sweetness mingle with her saliva. Spellbound by this child of war, I took in every detail of her face.

Whilst her long brown eyelashes could have been those of a young fallow deer, she also resembled a beautiful tiger cub; innocent and wild all at once.

She was, quite simply, the most stunning human being I had ever seen.

Pointing at myself as she rolled the candy around

her mouth, and then poking myself in the chest, I spoke softly.

"Hello, I'm Sebastián," Nodding my head and smiling, I went on. "Sebastián... yes?" Then I pointed to her. "What's your name, little one?"

"Hadia," she said, before proudly holding up her doll to show me. "Elaha..."

"*Que Bonita!*" I said,

Unlike most adults, Hadia's eyes held no secrets or enmity. Instead, within them, shadows of clouds swept across the snowy peaks of the Hindu Kush. Fields of poppies bobbed in the sunshine and campfires burned brightly.

Inside those two brightly-coloured orbs, a thousand ancient dreams flickered and danced across her gaze to the songs of her people.

This child mesmerised me, making me feel warm inside and taking me to a long-forgotten place deep inside myself; a happier, more hopeful place than the one I had known just moments ago.

Abruptly and painfully the spell was broken, as behind me French-speaking voices barked orders along our convoy, cruelly letting the cold back inside my heart.

"Okay! Everybody ready!"

"Let's go! Keep your eyes peeled! Load up!"

Unwrapping a chocolate bar, I handed it to Hadia before ruffling her honey hair.

"Thank you for showing me your dolly!" I smiled as she smiled back.

Standing up and grabbing my weapon from behind my back, I rejoined Taylor and Clasen in the rear of the truck. Turning back to the road as the vehicle's engine started, I waved to Hadia. Clutching her doll with one hand, she waved the half eaten chocolate bar at me with the other.

"*De kuday pa aman!*" she shouted above the noise of the truck's engines.

I smiled and waved once more before strapping my helmet back in place as our convoy moved slowly away. Now Clasen decided to give his opinion of my encounter with Hadia.

"I don't know why we are giving fucking candy to this lot's kids, when it's probably their fathers and brothers who are planting fucking bombs and taking fucking pot-shots at us," he griped to Taylor.

Sitting opposite him, I gave his right boot a nudge with my own to get his attention.

"Clasen," I said flatly.

"*Oui, mon Adjutant?*" he replied, sensing from my tone that he was about to get it.

"Afghanistan might be a democracy now, but the Legion isn't; if I hear you open your mouth again today, even just once, you cunt..." I said, "about anything... anything at all... I *will* knock your fucking teeth out; do you understand?"

Looking down at his feet, Clasen nodded humbly like a peasant in disgrace. The truck gathered speed and we bumped and pitched over the stony ground. With my point made clearly and to my satisfaction, I turned to look back the way we had come.

Alone in the road, Hadia stood munching my chocolate with one hand whilst holding Elaha with the other. The discarded silver wrapper of the chocolate bar sparkled and danced at her feet, twirling in the grey dust like a visiting fairy from another world.

Watching that little Afghan girl getting smaller and smaller as we drove away, jolting over the stony ground in that troubled chaotic land, I knew just two things about my own troubled and chaotic life. Firstly, I knew I was getting tired; and secondly, I knew I wanted peace. Peace for *me*.

I had given the Legion fourteen years of my life, and somewhere along the line I had shed my dreams like a snake shedding its own skin.

Watching Hadia turn to walk back up the barren slope to her family and home, I realised that I no longer had dreams. What had happened to me; what had I become?

They say that everyone has to pay the piper in the end, but I had lost so much and deep inside I was hurting.

Years after seeing hope between the rays of the rising sun in Iraq at twenty years old, I was reduced to dragging a thirty-four-year-old carcass out of a sleeping bag every day. I wasn't living; I was *existing*. Existing in a barren landscape and carrying a barren soul around inside of me.

My tired battered feet, incarcerated in combat boots for what seemed like forever, yearned to walk in soft warm grass, yearned to be kissed by the cool lips of the sea on a peaceful beach.

Sadly, if I wanted my dreams and my life back, I now accepted that I was going to have to fight for them. I was a participant in a violent conflict, and if I was to get out of it alive I had to be fully prepared to be extremely violent myself.

The soft warm grass of faraway meadows and cool wet kisses of the sea would have to wait for a future I hardly dared hope for.

Chapter Seven

We were in Afghanistan to both impose and uphold a system of democracy which was entirely alien to a people whose culture, steeped in ancient tribal traditions and feudalism, could best be described as *change-resistant*. In fact to the eyes of the vast majority of us Legionnaires, Afghan society seemed both draconian and austere, to say the least.

Any tactics employed to combat local fighters were swiftly adjusted to by them and had to be changed or altered accordingly. The best thing a soldier could do was to accept, on a personal level, that the most he could hope to achieve was leaving Afghanistan in one piece.

Tensions arising from the difficulties we faced found expression in fights between Legionnaires, even when out in the field. My own job in this regard was taxing.

The trip we made to take over duties at one of our forward operating bases in the mountainous Sorubi district was to be my last. My own tour was to end there.

Whilst organising vehicles, men and equipment in the compound before we left for the journey into the mountains, Martin came over to me for a chat as I prepared my weapon.

Wearing a wide smile and a pair of sunglasses with lenses of iridescent purple and gold, he looked like a wasp on the hunt. Martin knew as well as I did that there was a rumour amongst the local people that the particular style of sunglasses he wore enabled a soldier to see through women's clothing. With this in mind, I wore a pair of Ray-Ban aviators which Carole had bought me for my Birthday.

"Everything okay, Sebastián?" he said.

"Everything's fine; business as usual, isn't it?"

"Suppose so," he said. "Where we are going is dangerous as fuck," he continued.

"And...?"

"And we should be going in heavier numbers and with more firepower, don't you think?"

"Just another day in paradise, Martin," I said. "But anyway, those aren't our choices to make, and you know that."

"You're right, ours is not to reason why..." he said with a Gallic shrug.

Martin unwrapped a piece of chewing gum then offered me a piece, which I took.

"Martin, do you have to wear those shades when we go out in the field? You know, some of the people here think you can see their women naked with them."

"Well, they think right and I can; it's great! You can borrow them today if you want...!"

"I don't know why I like you, Martin; you can be a real prick some times."

"You like *me*, Sebastián, because I like *you*. That's how life works."

I carried on charging the magazine of my weapon with twenty-nine rounds of ammunition. It could take thirty but that would mean a full magazine, therefore increasing the chances of my rifle jamming had I the need to fire it on automatic.

Slapping me hard on the shoulder, Martin turned to walk away.

"See you later."

I watched Martin take a few steps towards the truck he would be travelling in, then went to call after him. Something stopped me - I can't say what - but instead I carried on loading the rounds into my magazine, as he clambered into the back of the vehicle that was to take him to our rendezvous with the enemy.

Setting off in a convoy of twenty vehicles shortly after our chat, we drove out of the base in the mid-morning. Travelling in a north easterly direction, we passed through ramshackle villages along the way, where local Afghan eyes met ours with a mixture of insolence and apathy.

One thing that had often intrigued me when encountering the Afghan people was the prevalence of individuals amongst them with green and often blue eyes - even completely blonde-haired people.

It was actually Duriuex who enlightened me as to the reason behind this observation one day, as we chatted in the compound over a smoke. At the time we had been in the country for six weeks or so.

"These people you see here, Alvarez, the ones with blonde hair and blue eyes," he said, after sucking hard on a Marlboro, "they are the great-grandchildren of Alexander the Great."

I was intrigued.

"Alexander the Great came all the way here on horseback from Greece with his army?" I asked.

Wiping the sweat from his eyes and blinking in the sunlight before replacing his sunglasses, Duriuex continued his history lesson.

"Yes, of course - he got all the way from Greece to here on horseback a thousand years ago. He extended his empire to the boundaries of the known world. In fact he went even further east than here, all the way to Kashmir in northwest India."

I took a swig of water from my bottle.

"So his descendants are..."

"Still here!" Duriuex interrupted. "That's who a lot of these people are; descendants of Alexander's conquering army. Respect them." Duriuex's face sank.

"Adjutant Alvarez; these people have a pedigree and a long and proud tradition of fighting. It is vital that you impart that understanding to the men also."

For some reason, as we set off in the convoy that day, Duriuex's words kept coming back to me as I sat with Taylor and Clasen in a jeep directly behind the lead personnel carrier.

Taking the opportunity to relax in the relative safety of our jeep, we passed chocolate around between us before the convoy entered the badlands of Sorubi. Martin was in a vehicle somewhere in the middle of the convoy.

After clearing the inhabited areas surrounding our main base, we struck out across the countryside in order to reduce the chances of a vehicle striking a hidden mine. Upon reaching higher ground, it became necessary to use the stone-strewn roads that would eventually become mountain passes.

At around three pm, after a few hours driving, the convoy stopped to check for mines in the road ahead, the left of which rose steeply to a rocky peak and fell away to the right down a ravine. Engineers from the rear of the convoy dismounted and began the process of sweeping the ground in front of us.

After some time, and having covered a considerable distance, they returned and gave us the all-clear to continue. Restarting the vehicle's engines, the convoy pulled forward and continued its journey.

The engineers had missed a mine.

Chapter Eight

Around two hundred yards along the road, at the point where it began to curve around the hillside, the personnel carrier in front of us hit an improvised explosive devise buried in the ground, coming to a sudden stop as rocks and stones rained down on it in the aftermath of the explosion.

Reacting immediately with the others in the convoy, Taylor, Clasen and I leapt from the back of our vehicle and ran for the safety of the ravine's edge, as a large number of Taliban fighters fired at us from the rocks above. Once there, Taylor rolled onto his side, looking down at his right leg.

"They got me, the bastards!" he growled through gritted teeth. A Taliban bullet had cut clean through his calf. Pulling a field dressing from his equipment, Clasen crawled over and slid in close to the wounded Australian.

"I'll dress it!" he said.

Taylor snatched the dressing from Clasen's hand.

"Fuck off! I'll do it myself, -just fight back, for fuck's sake!"

Peeping over the lip of the ravine I tried to identify the Taliban's positions and firing points, to no avail. The bullets cracking through the air around us were too close for comfort, and I slunk back under cover.

With the convoy now static, the Taliban began firing rocket-propelled grenades at the abandoned vehicles. Fear and alarm began to grip me as the seriousness of our situation quickly dawned on me. Looking left along the slope, I searched in vain for Martin amongst my colleagues cowering in the rocks. I couldn't see him anywhere.

"Get some heavy fire back up there!" I shouted

along the length of the ravine.

Our Ecuadorian machine-gunner, Hernandez, got himself into a kneeling position fifty yards from us to our left, and began raking the rocks above with machine-gun fire as others fought back with rockets of our own. Amongst the din, Pashtu voices shouted from the rocks above us.

Aware of the risk of being outflanked by our attackers, I decided to move over to Hernandez and bring him back with the machine-gun to protect our right flank. Leaving Clasen and Taylor, I got up and began running towards Hernandez.

Stooping as low as I could, I headed left just below the ridge line. Almost at once I saw a blinding flash coupled with the awareness of a bang, but no pain. Then there was nothing.

When I finally came around I found myself lying on a stretcher amongst the rocks at the bottom of the slope where the ground flattened out. I was amongst other wounded Legionnaires on the hard cold ground,.

Gathering my senses, I heard voices around me on the ground. They called out for water. Just feet from where I lay, someone was screaming in pain. Turning my head to look around, I found that my left eye was full of blood. Struggling to focus with my right eye, I saw several medics hunched over casualties. They were doing what they were trained to do, as the sounds of battle echoed all around. Bloodstained bandages, bits of blue paper, and cellophane wrappers lay strewn across the ground where we lay. Now I felt the pain, and a frightening thirst.

Through the cries of fear and desperation came the medic's voices of calm professionalism.

"I know it hurts; turn on your side... turn on your side..."

"Bear with me; his veins have contracted."

"He's cold, slap his arm; bring it to the surface," from another.

"Get him on his side."

"I'm cutting your trousers open so I can help you, okay? Lie back." And so on.

I had been triaged. No-one attended to me. I knew the system. Either I was considered to be too far gone to be helped, or I was in a fit enough state to wait for treatment.

I realised then that I was shivering. My whole body shook. Every part of me shook, except my left leg from the hip down. Raising my right hand in front of my face, I counted the fingers on it out loud.

"*Uno, dos, tres, quatro, cinco…*"

Just to make sure, I then did the same with the fingers on my left hand as well.

"*Uno, dos, tres, quatro, cinco… vale, vale; tranquillo Sébastian, todo bien*," I told myself.

But now I was cold; so very, very cold.

With the fire-fight continuing high above our position, I looked around for my weapon. It was nowhere to be seen, and I felt completely naked without it.

Pulling my water bottle from the equipment pouch on my hip, I found it shattered by shrapnel, and empty. Slumping back on the ground, I covered my face with my hands, as if that would some how block out reality, and I urinated.

In time, I heard the sound of a helicopter coming into land.

At first it was the sound that most people would instantly recognise as that of a helicopter; a loud and distinct *chukka chukka chukka, chukka chukka chukka*. Then, as the chopper swooped in close and low over our desperate group, the sound produced by its whirling blades changed from an ear-splitting clattering racket to a familiar and reassuring *whoop whoop whoop whoop*.

Almost immediately, several pairs of hands picked me up off the ground. Shouting over me on the stretcher, they struggled to make themselves heard above the noise of the helicopter.

"*C'est bon, tu l'a?*"

"*Tu l'a, on y va!*"

"Okay - *aller, aller, aller, court!*"

As I was carried past the cockpit of the helicopter, I looked up at the pilot. He sat facing me under the spinning rotor-blades of the aircraft, doing the job I should have done, in the seat I should have sat in. A bullet had passed through the top right-hand corner of his windscreen, leaving the impression of a magnified snowflake with a black hole in its centre.

Looking down at me on the stretcher as I passed beneath him, the pilot chewed gum with all the nonchalance of a Parisian taxi driver picking up a fare.

The helicopter's load master helped the medics to load me into the back of the chopper. I caught the scent of his aftershave and registered his clean uniform and smoothly-shaved chin.

Once inside the crew compartment in the rear of the helicopter, and feeling relieved that the responsibility for others had been lifted from me, I basked in the illusion of security. Watching from my stretcher on the floor, I saw the Loadmaster helping to bring other wounded men on board, before giving a thumbs-up to the medics and sliding the door shut.

With that, the pilot eased back on the joystick and eased the helicopter off the ground. Dipping its nose, he skimmed fast and low over the stony ground towards Kabul with his damaged and bleeding cargo.

After arrival at the French military facility there, shrapnel was removed from my left hip. Something, also presumably shrapnel, had cracked the orbital bone around my left eye-socket. Waking up after the operation, I found the pretty young army doctor from Paris standing by my bedside.

Chapter Nine

Val-de- Grace Hospital, Paris, Winter 2004

During the revolution of 1776, Benedictine Nuns treated wounded revolutionaries within the walls of the Val-de-Grace hospital in Paris. Because of this, the building was spared the vandalism and damage meted out to many of the city's other grand buildings. It stands today as one of the finest examples of French pre-revolution Baroque architecture, and has done so since 1667.

The original hospital, now used for administrative purposes, is beside the Museum of French Army Medicine, which is housed in the Abbey next door. The modern hospital building that I was taken to upon my return to France was completed next to the original during the 1970s.

Sitting in a wheel chair and dressed in a green tracksuit in the hospital corridor, I used the pay-phone to call Carole in Nîmes. Her answer machine clicked on. Being eleven am on a Tuesday morning, I knew she would be at work. She would also know that elements of the Second Foreign Regiment were presently deployed in Afghanistan.

With my comrades still there, and feeling vulnerable, I had no-one else to reach out to in France. I didn't want to take the risk of Carole putting the phone down on me, but I wanted some one who might care, to know that I was wounded and back in the country.

From the phone's handset, a detached electronic voice coming down the line invited me to leave a message.

"Carole; its Sebastián," I said. "I'm back in France; I've been wounded but I'm okay. It's just some shrapnel. I'm at the Val-de-Grace in Paris. Hope you're okay. Perhaps you could get in touch? The numbers' 1140-514-000. Just ask for the post operative ward, Extension fifty-six... Adjutant Alvarez."

She didn't call. I knew she wouldn't when a week had gone by. As the cold wind buffeted the window of my room, I had to work hard at not feeling sorry for myself.

Soon after my arrival at Val-de-Grace, the doctors had reconnected the shattered orbit of my left eye-socket, holding the pieces together with small metal plates secured with wire. The surgeon came to see me the day after my operation.

"Well, Alvarez. You were lucky - there's no lasting damage to your left eye and your vision won't be affected. You were wearing a Helmet, I presume?"

"Yes, I was."

"Mmm, that bit of shrapnel got in just under the rim, I think. But without a helmet..."

"How long will it take me to start walking again?"

"A few weeks with physiotherapy and rehabilitation; I don't suppose you will even have a limp," he said. "You suffered a deep puncture wound to the *gluteus medius* muscle; it controls rotation of the hip."

"So I'm not going to be a cripple, then?" I smiled.

"You will feel considerable pain for a period because of the tissue damage, but the shard of shrapnel was relatively small, so no, you won't be a cripple; just a little work to get better, that's all," he said.

Leaving a session of physiotherapy one day, I bumped into Turan on his way in. "Turan!" I smiled.

"*Mon Adjutant?*"

"Yes, I copped a packet near the Uzbin valley a couple of weeks ago; I'm on the mend though. You?"

"Well, *mon Adjutant*, I'm finished in the Legion.

They say I won't use my arm again properly."

"Sorry to hear that, Turan," I said. "I won't forget how you stuck by me on the way into that wood; you were very brave."

Later that day we shared a tasteless lunch of fishcakes and green beans.

"What will you do, Turan?" I asked as we ate.

"I always intended on staying on in France, but…"

"But what? They have good health care here."

"I don't know what I would do for work now with this arm. I want to go back to Istanbul and live with my family. I'm sure I can find a wife and settle down."

"That sounds like a plan. You've had your adventures now, right?"

"Right." The smile on Turan's face didn't reach his eyes.

Before he left I went to see Turan, giving him a pack of smokes and a watch I had bought from the hospital's gift shop to say goodbye, telling him again that I would remember his bravery always.

Being in peak physical condition, I healed as quickly as anyone could, and after three weeks I was transferred to the university hospital in Nîmes. There, amongst other Afghan "returnees", I continued with a programme of physiotherapy.

Shortly before my arrival in Nimes in February 2005, the Regiment returned to France.

Lying in my bed one Tuesday morning, I watched a middle-aged Algerian lady polishing the floor of the corridor outside my door. It was one of those moments when one's senses are switched to autopilot. We see, we hear and we smell, but nothing really registers, as our brains tick over like the idling engine of a car waiting for its driver. As I stared, the figure of a man appeared in the doorway.

"So! Sebastián, they are giving you a medal!" he said breezily. My brain clicked back into manual.

"Martin!"

Striding into the room with a smile, Martin stretched out his hand. I shook it in my own. "A nice going away present after fifteen years, eh? You look ugly as fuck, by the way," he said.

Martin sat on the edge of the bed. Dropping my guard for a moment in the excitement and relief of seeing my friend alive, I said, "Martin, I didn't know if you'd..."

"Didn't know if I'd what?" Martin asked, as if he didn't know what I was talking about. Remembering again that we were soldiers, I immediately steered a course away from sentiment. "How was the rest of the tour?" I asked.

"Same old, same old; never did find a decent brothel in Kabul though!" he joked.

"Don't make me laugh, Martin, it still hurts," I grimaced.

Picking up the grey metal walking stick by my bed and waving it around like a sword, he laughed.

"Bet you're fighting the nurses off with this, aren't you?"

I smiled.

"Talk about me being ugly; have you seen the nurses here?" I said.

"Yeah, well, beggars can't be choosers, Sebastián. Has Carole been to see you?"

"No," I said, my smile fading. Picking up on my disappointment, Martin put the walking stick down, shifted gear, and changed pace. "Last time I saw you, you'd pissed your pants."

"No; it was blood, Martin."

"No, mate, it was piss."

Looking over Martin's shoulder, I noticed the lady

in the corridor had stopped polishing the floor and was looking into the room at us with the look of some one's disapproving mother on her face.

Noticing my distraction, Martin looked behind him and decided to behave himself. "There's an Argentine *asado* restaurant opened in town since we've been away," he said. "I could get a vehicle from the pool and take us there for some grub, if you like. Looks like you've lost weight."

"Yeah, Martin, just get me out of here."

Two nights later he took me into town and I limped from the car using crutches to La Parilla Restaurant, where we ate steaks and drank beer. Martin was in an upbeat mood as usual. "Remember the night we met Carole and her friend in that place around the corner from here?" he said as we sat down.

"Yeah, we had veal and got them pissed, I remember."

"I knew we were on to a winner when they spoke to each other in English." He laughed.

"They were good times." I smiled.

"No regrets, eh, Sebastián?"

"No, of course not. I was nineteen when I came here, Martin. I had a thirty-two inch waist then; nearly fifteen years later I'm a thirty-four. I don't think I'm doing too badly."

"Going a little grey around the temples though, mate!" He laughed. "I take it you're over Carole?"

"Who?"

"You can't lie to me, Sebastián."

"Really?"

"Look," said Martin. "Life's about survival. You can't afford to go around loving people. *Let them love you.* Life doesn't give, you have to take."

"I get the picture, Martin; let's change the subject, yes?"

"So, when are you leaving?" he asked.

"I'm staying on until next year for physio and light duties. I need some after-care then..."

I wanted to tell Martin all about my grandmother's farmhouse and my plans to leave France and start again in Spain, but something wouldn't let me.

Martin had never revealed his past life in Québec to me. To some extent, just as in life, each Legionnaire is a man alone. Keeping my past to myself was all part of my life in its ranks as far as I was concerned; why change anything now?

"Then what?" said Martin.

"I really don't know. I get a pension and I've saved a bit - who knows? I'm not making any decisions yet."

After eating, we talked until late. Guyana, Afghanistan and Djibouti all came into it. We covered the lot.

Back in my room at the hospital, and realising that my excursion with Martin into town had taken more out of me than I had expected, I quickly allowed myself to fall into a deep sleep.

Chapter Ten
Nimes 2005

Sometime during the night, as the late Nîmes traffic swept over the dark wet tarmac outside the hospital, I found myself back in Afghanistan.

Instead of lying safe in my bed in France, I stood out in the cold on the dirt-track where the Taliban had attacked us outside the village, on the day Turan was wounded. Standing silently at my side in the middle of the track was Major Duriuex.

All was quiet; eerily quiet. The wood, the village nearby, and the irrigation ditch that had provided cover for the section when we had come under attack. To my horror, standing alone 100 yards away in the middle of the track, I saw my mother with a yard-brush in her hands. She was busily sweeping up the spent shell-cases of the rounds we had expended in the fire fight with the Taliban.

"Tut tut tut tut," she muttered away to herself as she swept.

Again, she wore the beautiful white dress covered in the blooming red rose pattern that she had worn in previous dreams I'd had. Confused, I turned to look at Duriuex. He spoke angrily and impatiently, his voice, slow and heavy, the words taking an age to pour from his mouth, like thick viscous porridge in the cold winter air. "What the hell's *she* doing over there...?" he demanded to know. How could I have known? Without answering I turned back to my right, looking up the track to where my mother stood, still sweeping up the spent cartridge cases.

"Mamma!" I shouted over to her; the soles of my boots were glued to the ground underneath where I stood, anchoring me to the hard grey earth. Hearing me call, my mother stopped sweeping and looked over to me, wagging her finger accusingly in my direction.

"Why don't you boys clean up after yourselves when you've finished playing?" she scolded, in the half hearted way mothers do when they accept that boys will be boys.

Before I could answer, I saw a group of ten or so Taliban fighters emerging slowly from the trees to her right, creeping up on her from behind. My feet wouldn't move. Looking down at my hands in agonising slow motion, I found that I had lost my weapon.

Returning to her work, my mother carried on sweeping up the brass shell-cases as the Taliban got closer. I tried crying out to warn her of the danger once again, but the words wouldn't come. In desperation, I took in a huge breath and screamed out to her as loudly as I could.

"*Mama!*" I cried, my voice ringing out like the single peal of a church bell struck by lightning on a stormy night.

Disappearing from my dream as painfully as she had disappeared from my life, my mother was gone and I woke alone in the darkness of the university hospital in Nîmes. Panting with fear and anxiety, I was relieved when the nurse on duty arrived at my bedside to reassure and calm me. In the absence of my own mother, I allowed the nurse to take me in her arms and shield me from the overpowering presence and power of the night.

It is often hard for a man to admit to feeling scared and alone, especially to a woman, but at that moment I didn't have to; my free-flowing tears said it all.

This was the first time I had cried since sitting alone on the beach in Montevideo so many years before. So long, in fact, that I thought I'd forgotten how to.

Shortly afterwards, I was released from hospital and returned to my room at St Nicholas.

No longer carrying out full duties, I had plenty of time to go into town and have coffee and lunch. Mostly, though, I stayed in camp and recuperated.

For the next year I regained my strength and worked on my fitness. I worked behind a desk most of the time unless giving lessons on map reading and First Aid.

The scar on my temple turned from vivid scarlet to a softer pink and in time I walked without a limp, no longer needing physiotherapy. Eventually I returned to my full duties and began participating in training exercises again, and slowly but surely, the time for my departure from the Legion drew closer.

Chapter Eleven

A couple of weeks before I left for good, Martin came to see me in my room one evening. "Hey, Sebastián!" He smiled as he let himself in. I put down my book.

"Hi, Martin, what's up?"

"Look Sebastián, I have to go up to Castel Naudary in the morning. I'm there for a month to help out the training team; someone broke a leg or something."

"Oh," I said. "Tomorrow; well, I'm..."

"Yes, I know," said Martin. "You won't be here when I get back, so..."

As Martin paused mid-sentence, a sudden heat in my chest and a tightening in the back of my throat caught me off-guard. Getting off the bed, I walked towards him, my hand stretched out. Gripping it firmly, Martin spoke quietly for once.

"Sebastián, it's been a pleasure knowing you, and I wish you all the best, wherever you go." Tightening my grip on his hand, I reached out to hold him by the elbow with my free hand.

"Martin, I want to thank you for your friendship, mate. So many times you've made my life here easier."

"You too, Sebastián; good luck," he replied, the poignant smile on his face bringing to mind a setting sun on the last day of a fantastic holiday. We had been through a lot together; heat, cold, fear, hunger and pride. In a rush of sentiment I hugged my friend, and he hugged me back. Nostalgia hung in the air as he left the room.

As soon as I was alone I began the process of sorting through my uniforms and gear, ready for my departure from Nîmes and the Legion. Another passenger had left the train, but my own journey would continue.

For the next fortnight, I existed in a vacuum. Surrounded by familiar faces, yet removed from them at the same time, one foot in the past and one in the future.

I was now thirty-five.

Chapter Twelve

Nîmes, early Spring, 2005

It was time to go. Fifteen years and a bit since walking through the gates of Fort Nugent in Paris, I was leaving the Legion.

Comrades and colleagues held a dinner in my honour at St Nicolas, and I took one last stroll around Nîmes. Passing under the balcony of Carole's apartment overlooking the Place aux Herbs, I noticed the living room light was on and the suggestion of movement behind the drawn curtains.

Now at this point in my tale, and if this was a movie, feeling drawn by some sixth sense, Carole would have opened the curtains and seen me standing below in my uniform. Then, realising that we needed to be together, she would call me upstairs with tears of love running down her cheeks. We would then tumble into bed in a union of flesh and destiny, living happily ever after, together in the south of France.

But this wasn't a movie. This was life, and I had to get real, bite the bullet, and move on. That being the case, and remembering a quote from a book I'd read - *Its fine to look back, but never stare* - I resisted the temptation to call on her.

Having bought an old Saab 900 from one of the Officers wives on the Base, I drove myself down to Aubagne to formalise the end of my service.

Keeping my beret and my medals as keepsakes, I handed over the rest of my kit and uniforms. I was given a certificate of service and a small plaque with the Legion cap badge in the middle. Below this, embossed in gold, was the Legion's Motto: *Legio Patria Nostra*. Or, *The Legion is our Country*.

I no longer believed in that. No, that belief was floating in the dirty water of an irrigation ditch somewhere in Afghanistan.

Driving out of the First Regiment's main entrance, I didn't look back as I turned west on the highway and pointed the car towards Spain and a new beginning.

In the boot I had a holdall full of civilian clothes, a tent, camping gear and some books, including the book of poems by Federico Garcia Lorca, which I had taken from Esteban's locker and kept all these years.

With plenty of time to become accustomed to my newfound freedom and to get where I was going, I spent April meandering the minor roads of southern France, as the countryside around me came to life in the first flush of spring. I told myself I that I was on holiday and that I deserved a break.

I was lying to myself. I meandered the back roads of Languedoc because I was scared to leave France. Like a child in the deep end of a swimming pool, I was scared to let go of the side. I felt safe in France, even though there was nothing there for me any more. Spain was an alien place on the other side of the Pyrenees; what lay beyond those glittering snow capped mountains was unknown to me, and I was scared to go there alone.

As April turned into May, I tentatively nudged myself closer and closer to the Franco-Spanish border.

I decided on impulse in late May to spend some time relaxing in the medieval town of Pau, about sixty kilometres from Spain. Arriving in the afternoon, I found a campsite outside town.

Chapter Thirteen

Pau, Pyrenees-Atlantiques, France, 2005

Marie Antoinette tended a small garden in the grounds of the Chateau in Pau during summer holidays with Napoleon the First, whilst he used the place as a summer retreat. By the time of France's *Belle Epoch*, Napoleon the Third was restoring the chateau and rebuilding the surrounding streets in the architectural style of the Golden Age.

Seeing as Napoleon himself liked Pau enough to keep a holiday home there, I thought I might take the opportunity to find a place to camp and relax there myself before crossing the mountains and leaving France.

Covering a couple acres of ground, the site I found lay to the southwest of the city beyond the River Gave. I arrived to find Rhododendron bushes dotted around, exploding in pink and hunched in the shade of Scots pines and silver birch trees. Citril finches and firecrests fluttered and dipped amongst their branches, whilst hedge sparrows and dunnocks hopped and foraged on the ground between the campers tents.

Parking the car, I went into the reception office attached to the small bungalow just inside the site entrance. Outside the front door, a large scent-dripping magnolia tree gave relief from the spring sun.

As I walked inside, a middle-aged man holding a mug of black coffee emerged from the living quarters through a curtain of beads covering the door behind the desk.

"Hello," I said.

"You want a pitch?"

"Yes, thanks; there's just me."

Opening the register laid across the counter in front

of him, the man flicked through its pages. Over his shoulder in the living room I spied a clutch of toffee-coloured puppies tumbling about under the gaze of their mother, who was curled up in a basket in the corner. The man noticed my interest.

"Rhodesian Ridgebacks," he said. "Seven weeks old."

"Yes, I know, I've seen them before in Africa." The man took a closer look at me.

"Oh? Whereabouts in Africa?" he said. I looked past him, at the puppies.

"Djibouti; the whites like to keep a couple in the yard for security."

The man took a swig of coffee; then, pretending to be stern, he turned and called to the pups, "Play nicely now." Watching the puppies scrambling in and out of their mother's basket in the corner of the room, I remembered a time years before when I had laid down to sleep next to a lonely Swedish boy amongst the chestnut trees of Languedoc on the first night of the Raid march outside Perpignan. Thinking of Roland from Gothenburg, and his puppy, I said,

"I would like one of them, if you have any for sale." The man ignored my question, asking me one instead.

"The army, was it?"

"Sorry?"

"Were you in Djibouti with the army?" He asked affably.

"Yes, with the Foreign Legion."

Regarding me a little more closely for a moment, he focused on my scarred temple.

"I have two dogs and a bitch still available, but none of them will be ready to leave their mother for at least another week."

Being in no particular rush to get to the Spanish frontier, I said, "No problem. I don't mind hanging around for a week or so." The campsite looked like a nice place to relax for a while.

"I'm Jean," he went on. "Why don't you come out the back and watch them play around. You can choose one of them."

We went into the garden at the back of his bungalow together, where he offered me a beer as I watched the three puppies he had available playing on the grass under an enormous weeping willow tree.

After only a minute or so, one of the boy dogs broke away from his siblings and gambolled through the dandelions at me, before undoing the laces of my desert shoes with his needle-sharp teeth. "Take off your shoes and come and play with us," he seemed to be saying.

Jean laughed.

"Well, that's your choice made for you I suppose!"

"Yes, I think you're right." Picking up the wriggling pup, I turned his face to mine. "Hey, pup. Do you want to come and live with me?" Licking the end of my nose and nibbling at my ear, the puppy left a thin coating of dew in its creases.

"What will you call him?" asked Jean.

"I'll think of something."

Jean and I had another beer together and watched the puppies play for a while. Afterwards I took the car over to a quiet space in a far corner of the site, and set up my camp.

My pitch was on a level patch of grass surrounded by dense conifer trees with cowslips growing amongst their bases. A blanket of daisies covered the site. In no time, my poncho was stretched from the car's side, and over my ground-mat and sleeping bag. I dug a circular fire-pit in the middle of the pitch, and filled its shallow bottom with stones.

After buying food and wine from the camp shop, I went for a swim in the open air pool next to it. Besides me in the water, a pair of teenagers stood French-kissing in the shallow end. I didn't stay for long.

On my way out, a young woman passed me on her way in. She was around thirty-five years old and wore a tie-dyed sarong around her waist and a sky-blue bikini top. A pair of sunglasses held her tousled black hair back from her face. In one hand she carried a towel, in the other, a pack of smokes.

"How's the water?" She smiled as we drew level.

Nodding back over my shoulder at the water babies, I smiled back. "Alright for some."

The woman giggled and carried on walking. I went back to my pitch, where I ate bread and cheese and began to read *Of Mice and Men*.

As I opened the book, a postcard fell out. It was the one which Anya had sent me from Caesars' Palace in Las Vegas, eleven years before. Turning the card over and reading the message on the reverse side, I smiled at the memory of our time in La Rochelle. I thought of Tony and Veronique and days spent on the beach at Mineimes, and felt glad that all our paths had crossed.

Chapter Fourteen

The following morning, after a short steady run around Pau, I returned to the site and had another swim before going over to Jean's to play with the puppy for a while.

"He likes you," said Jean, as I let the little dog chase me through the branches of the weeping willow tree brushing the grass. "Have you thought of a name for him yet?"

"Yes, I have; I'm going to call him Caesar."

"Caesar; why?"

"Just reminds me of a friend, that's all."

A couple of times that day, I saw the black-haired girl around the site in her sarong and bikini. We didn't speak, though I thought she was quite beautiful. Then, I bumped into her the next day as we both bought bread in the camp shop.

"Hi, swimmer!" she said with a bright smile.

"Hello, blue eyes," I replied.

Bright, confident and warm, she didn't hang about with conversation-warmers or anything like that.

"Are you here on your own?" she asked.

"Yeah, all alone. I'm waiting for a puppy from Jean, the owner. It's ready to leave its mother soon. I just have to hang out here for a few more days."

Sucking the bubblegum she'd been blowing back into her mouth, she smiled.

"I've seen those puppies - they're gorgeous."

"Yes, they are. I think perhaps a man needs a dog."

"Especially if he doesn't have a woman, right?" she giggled.

"I suppose so…" I laughed back.

I felt relaxed with her. "Are you here by yourself?" I said.

"Yep." She smiled again.

"Would you like to have something to eat tonight? It

would be nice to hang out with someone while I'm waiting for my puppy."

Popping another bubble, she smiled again.

"Okay, nice; thanks. Where were you thinking of eating - in town?"

"I was just going to cook a bit of something over the fire at my pitch on the other side of the camp. I'm at..."

"Oh yes, I've seen your pitch. You're sleeping outside next to your car, aren't you?"

"I like the fresh air," I said.

"So, I'll come over later then and let you feed me," she replied.

"Okay, see you this evening."

"I'm Monica, by the way," she said, holding out her hand.

"Sebastián; pleased to meet you."

With that, she skipped off, and I went to the pool for another swim. On the way back to my pitch on the far side of the camp I pulled some wild fennel from beside the footpath. Once there I soon fell asleep reading Steinbeck on the warm grass under the sun.

By the time I woke it was much later and cooler. Sitting up on the grass, I brushed myself down. As I did, a Jenny wren with a beak full of insects cut through the still air above me on her way to feed her chicks in the bushes near by. In the tranquil interlude between day and night cicadas called out to each other through the trees, as two small bats took to the sky above me.

The air was much softer now, the grass still warm from the heat of the day. I didn't bother putting my shoes and socks on, just a light sweater. After pouring white wine into two paper cups, I began preparing a meal.

Soon enough, as I chopped a garlic clove on a small wooden board on the ground, Monica arrived barefoot in the grass. She was smiling again.

"Hi! I bought these," she said. Holding a brown paper bag of peaches and a bottle of spiced rum, she sat close to me on the grass. That's when I noticed the tiny pink flowers and green leaves tattooed around the edges of her feet.

"Something to drink, and fruit for dessert," she said.

"Thanks; I have wine here as well," I replied.

Laying the bag down next to her on the grass, Monica asked, "Would you like me to help you with anything?" I passed her a green pepper.

"Cut this up, if you like."

Chopped onion and garlic sizzled with shock as I tossed them into the hot oil of the pan before nudging them around with a wooden spoon. With my sleeves rolled up, Monica noticed the tattoo on my arm. "You were a soldier?"

"Yes, a soldier."

Looking closely at the scar on my temple, she frowned slightly before taking a knife to the pepper. "I'm not sure I like soldiers."

"I'm not sure people are supposed to *like* them..." I said, before a silence fell between us.

Monica finished chopping the pepper then reached for a cigarette from my pack on the ground, before leaning forward and lighting it from the fire in front of us.

"Sometimes people think I'm a gypsy," she said. Now it was my turn to look more closely.

"And are you?" I asked.

Monica didn't answer. Instead, tilting her chin up to the evening air, she blew a long stream of white smoke into the gently gathering gloom. As she did so, I noticed the soft skin of her neck and the feminine definition of her collarbone and jaw line.

"Oh look, bats!" She smiled.

"Yes - pipistrelles, I think," I said as I followed her gaze.

Then, gathering together several pieces of pink rabbit meat, I added them to the pan. Monica picked up her wine and drank as the bats caught moths in the pine-scented air above us.

"Cheers!" I said as I picked up my own cup.

"Cheers! I take it from your accent, which I can't quite place, that you have been a soldier with the *Legion Etranger*."

"You're right. I'm Argentine; I've been speaking French every day for a long time now. Sometimes I feel more French than a Frenchman. The Legion holds on to tradition while the rest of France moves on, I think."

"What happened to your face?" she asked. I kept my eyes on the meat.

"Afghanistan."

"Oh."

"It's alright. I was lucky."

Now the rabbit was browning nicely and I covered the tender pieces with cream and stirred them slowly around the pan. "Could you drop a spoonful of mustard into this and a half-handful of that fennel?" I said.

"Don't forget this!" Monica perked up. Reaching out with her wine, she tipped half a cupful into the mix before adding the chopped pepper, fennel and mustard. Minutes later, we settled down to eat and talk.

"So, where are *you* from?" I asked.

"Laval. It's up in the Pays de La Loire. I left there a year ago, after my husband died."

"Oh?"

"Before you ask, he was a furniture maker. He killed himself and I don't know why."

"Oh. I'm sorry."

"Don't be. I'm not; I see things differently lately."

"How so?"

277

"I've been travelling around Southern France in my camper van for almost a year now. I paint pictures and sell them in the markets. I'm parked on the other side of the site, under a silver birch. It's nice, the leaves are like emeralds at this time of year. You see, my husband didn't want to live anymore, but I do, and that's all."

"Fair enough," I said.

"After he was gone, I realised that I hadn't actually been living either anyway, so..."

"So what?"

"So I quit my job as a teacher's assistant, rented out our apartment, grabbed some paints and hit the road."

It was dark now, and the burning birch on the fire threw a rich orange light on both our faces, crackling and hissing as above us a sprinkling of stars hung silently in space.

Remembering Carole and another outdoor meal in the lagoons of the Camargue, I finished the sauce off around my plate with a chunk of bread. Then, tossing it to one side, I poured out two cups of spiced rum before lighting a cigarette.

"Isn't the Legion full of murderers and thieves, by the way?" said Monica, before taking a swig of rum.

"It's full of all sorts," I said.

"And what sort are you?"

"The *I'm a civilian now* sort."

"Fair enough," she shrugged.

After we had eaten the peaches and drank most of the rum, Monica thanked me for the food, said goodnight, and headed back to her camper.

Somewhere in the darkness, I heard her drunkenly tripping over the guide ropes of someone's tent.

"*Hey! Il montre!*" I heard a man shout from inside a flimsy collapsing structure.

"*Desolee... je... suis... ivre...*" came Monica's slurred reply. I slept alone by the fire.

For the next three days Monica and I explored Pau, or sat talking and relaxing by the campsite pool. In the evenings we ate in town, as an unacknowledged sexual tension built up between us. On our last night together we found a small restaurant in the crooked lanes surrounding the Châteaux, and ate late.

Both the waiter and chef were Spanish. We ordered lava beans, chives and Serrano ham cooked in sherry and dappled with parmesan. The food and the origins of the chef all hinted at our proximity to Spain. As we ate, Monica told me that she was heading east to Saint Laurent du Var, close to Italy, the next day, to paint and sell her work on the coast. Without being specific regarding whereabouts or what I had planned, I told her that I was heading south to Spain.

After a desert of spiced apple cake and cream, we headed back to the campsite.

Walking through the narrow streets towards the edge of town, Monica tried to hold my hand. But I couldn't. I couldn't hold her hand. Instead, I lit and smoked cigarettes, adjusted my watch, and stopped for a piss behind some garbage bins in an Alley beside a small hair salon.

Despite me recoiling from intimacy on the walk back to the campsite, once there, soaked in the light of a silver moon and serenaded by crickets, my baser instincts took over.

We didn't bother closing the sliding door of her camper. Inside, on the fold-down double bed, we tugged at each others clothes to get at the flesh beneath. Monica wore a short denim skirt and it was easy for me to remove her plain white cotton panties.

As the night air filled the camper van with the scents of warm grass and rhododendron flowers, Monica held my head, kissing my scarred and wounded face in the shadowy light. Frustrated at my inability to undo the clasp on her bra, she relieved me of the task.

"Pull it off... just break it... rip it..." she panted. The scent of red wine and spiced apple cake infused her warm breath.

Ripping the flimsy material of her bra from her round and ready boobs with one hand, a primeval thrill ran through my body as my tongue experienced the contrast between the smooth skin of her breasts and the rubbery texture of her exited nipples.

Excluding the world outside the confines of the camper, I tugged my jeans down around my thighs. Monica opened her mouth, pulled my face back to hers, and let her tongue meet mine. In time, I eased myself inside her, whilst she moaned and clawed at the skin on my back.

When she was about to come, I felt her reaching down between our bodies. With the hand she used to paint beautiful pictures, she massaged my balls, softly milking me into her as we joined.

In the bright new light of the next day, we made coffee on a gas stove under the silver birch branches before saying our farewells.

"Do you have an email address, Sebastián?"

"No email; don't need one."

"Okay, here's my mobile number. Text me if you want, I'll text back. Promise..."

I gave Monica my own mobile number, and we kissed on both cheeks. I was still in no rush, and she left the site before me. Later, I picked up Caesar and a bag of puppy food from Jean; then left the little campground, turned my car south, and headed for the mountains.

Chapter Fifteen

Franco-Spanish Frontier

The Col du Somport is the tunnel that connects France with Spain through the Pyrenees Mountain range. Just before arriving there I pulled over by the side of the road, put Caesar inside my sleeping bag, then into the boot of the car. Once on the Spanish side I pulled over, got him out, and put him on the grass by the side of the road for a pee and a leg-stretcher. It was time to look back.

They say home's the place they can't turn you away from. Well, France had been a home of a kind. I had arrived there, a stranger with a past, and she had taken me in.

For the last fifteen years I had spoken in her tongue, taken her money, defended her interests and saluted her flag. Now I was leaving.

Standing by the side of the road, breathing in the fresh mountain air of Spain whilst looking back at France, images from the previous fifteen years floated like phantoms in my mind.

That first cold day at the Gare du Nord in Paris so long ago, when I couldn't speak French; memories of the monkeys and birds taunting us from the jungle canopy in Guyana; fighting the sailors together with Cresus in Marseille; lying on the ground scared and in pain in Afghanistan. It all came back to me.

And of course there was Esteban and Hans, Cua, Quang, and Carole; Wilson, La Roche, Turan, and the others too. But it was over now.

I had reached another milestone and a new beginning. Looking down at my feet, I smiled at my new friend. My only friend. Caesar was busily chewing the grass on the verge. I bent down and picked him up.

"Come on, little fellow, let's go and find a place to live, eh?"

After driving southwest to Pamplona and staying at a campsite there for the night, we turned to the northwest and struck out for the Atlantic Ocean, about 150 kilometres away.

Our first port of call along the coast was the Basque town of San Sebastián. The destination names on the buses heading for town and the road signs confused me for a while.

The Basque name for San Sebastián is Donostia and as my map was French, I had never heard of it. Once in town, I noticed Basque nationalist signs displayed in shops and bars, reminding those of us who were outsiders that we were in neither France nor Spain, but the Basque Country.

Leaving *Donostia*, our route took us west along the country roads of Cantabria then Asturias, squeezed between the mountains and the coast.

To our left rose granite peaks that would have no reason to feel shy in Alaska. To our right, happy coves of marzipan sand refreshed by easy waves tumbled playfully ashore from the Bay of Lions.

We were heading for the compact and pretty seaside town of Ribidesella, roughly four kilometres north of our new home.

Now empty winding roads led gently through a land of vivid rural splendour, decked out in every shade of green. Mottled chickens scratched about on grass verges outside rustic houses and under the hedgerows on the edge of hamlets. Airborne thrushes and blue-winged jays kept up with the car for moments at a time, like dolphins escorting an oceangoing liner.

A world of beech and chestnut forests, rushing rivers and spritely laughing streams unfolded all around us. Caesar, his eyes bright and alert, put his front paws up on the dashboard, his ears pricked as he jerked his head inquisitively from side to side. I turned on the car's radio.

Voices spoke with the Asturian accent of my parents. Thinking fondly of them both, I drew my shoulders in and hunched over the steering wheel to take in every aspect of the land they had known as home.

Driving on, steep-sided valleys offered tantalising glimpses of waterfalls suspended from high wooded valleys, like crystal chandeliers hanging in the landscape. Copper-coloured cows chewed the cud on either side of the road as a large bird of prey followed our progress, effortlessly riding the thermals high above the meadows and foothills.

Every house or farmstead we passed seemed to be growing their own food on their own piece of land. Pumpkins looked like a favourite, with every other house having three or four stacked outside the front door. Corn, drying on the cob, hung from washing lines drooping under the weight, while family dogs at the end of driveways sniffed the air as we passed.

Pulling off the road later in the day I drove into the pretty sea side town of Ribidesella, squeezed tightly between the Mountains and the coast. Leaving Caesar asleep in the car I went and found a place to eat in the centre.

The bar owner seemed friendly, pulling out a chair and offering me a seat. I ordered red bell peppers stuffed with cod cheeks and shrimp, and a mineral water.

"On holiday or just passing through...?" the man said as he brought the food to my table.

"On my way do a little business in Oviedo. Can you tell me how long it would take to get there by car from here?"

"On the highway? About two hours." He was a friendly fellow, and obviously liked to chat.

"Have you been to Asturias before?"

"No, never."

"This is the real Spain, you know, not the Spain of paella, palm trees and siestas."

"Yes, I can see that. I'd heard it was green, but I didn't think it could be *so* green." On the television in the corner of the restaurant, a news article showed footage of Spanish soldiers operating in Afghanistan. We were both momentarily distracted by the pictures. After a while, the man turned to me,

"Asturias was never Muslim, you know."

"Oh?" I said.

"No, they never conquered us; and when the Christians reconquered Spain, they started out from here!"

"Interesting..." I said.

"Enjoy your meal,"

And with that, the man threw his hand towel over his shoulder and left me to eat alone. Looking back to the images of Afghanistan on the television screen in the corner, I found myself thinking of Sorubi province, Hadia, and her doll, Elaha.

I finished my food and paid the bill. Back at the car Caesar had woken up and bounced between the front seats in his excitement at my return. I opened the door and picked him up.

Thinking about Afghanistan and the way I had felt in the back of the truck with Taylor and Clasen as we left Hadia with her chocolate bar, I headed on foot with Caesar to the beach on the edge of town. Once there, I put him on the sand, before removing my shoes and socks.

Walking silently across the sand into the clear waters until the ocean covered my ankles, I stood alone and faced north across the Bay of Biscay. Behind me, Caesar sniffed and circled on the beach as the sea kissed my feet, cooling them down as the water ebbed and flowed around them.

Whispering gently on the sand, the ocean seemed to talk to me; the part of me that had yearned for peace. "Hush...hush..." it whispered at my feet.

Closing my eyes, I breathed in through my nose, filling my lungs with the fresh saline air sweeping inland from the bay to the mountains behind me. Opening my eyes again, I exhaled slowly.

Staring out across at the blue water, I felt peace; peace, at last, for me.

Back on the road, I wound down the car's windows, letting in the wind as we motored westward.

As it rushed into and out of the car again, I pressed on the accelerator and allowed it to blow everything away; all the dirt, all the dust, the boot polish the cordite and gun oil.

All the sweat mud, blood and filth that I had waded through over the years. Everything, except the memories.

However low I could have pushed the accelerator, however fast and however far I could have driven, I was never going to get away from the memories.

Chapter Sixteen

Arriving in Oviedo that afternoon, I booked into a *pension* where I stayed in my room and read. By eleven o'clock the next day, my business with my grandmother's lawyer was completed. Now, furnished with her keys, I started on the road back the way I had come, in search of the farmhouse.

It was mid-morning when I found the place, partway down a winding country lane of deep hedgerows snaking between the cordilleras and the ocean. Guarded by two ancient willow trees at the head of its gently curving driveway, the two-storey property was set back from the narrow road.

Built of stone and oak timbers in the early 1700s, local folklore has it that the house was built by an Irish mercenary at the end of the Spanish war of succession, having fallen in love with the landowners daughter.

Enclosed by a roadside fence, a large unkempt lawn stretched towards the house. The fence itself was nearly collapsing beneath the weight of a glorious bougainvillaea, busily celebrating itself in full bloom.

The soothing sound of the car's tyres rolling over the warm gravel on the drive seemed to assure me in welcoming tones that I could make this place home.

Pheasant berry bushes grew either side of the wooden front door. To the right of that was a shuttered kitchen window, partially covered by a large orange-blossom bush reaching across to the corner of the house and softening its edge.

Caesar jumped from the car as I got out, scampering around my heels while I put the key in the door.

Inside, ancient beams of holm oak, wise as the years, looked down contentedly on spacious rooms and open fireplaces. My grandmother's furniture was covered with dust sheets, and stone floors lay patiently in wait for homecoming feet.

Framed pictures of the Virgin Mary hung on the kitchen wall and at the top of the stairs. The staircase itself was oak wood and led from the far side of the living room up to four bedrooms; two at the front and two at the rear.

Once upstairs I flung open the shutters of the back bedroom windows.

As I did so, the fragrance of the sparkling Cantabrian Sea, laced with blossom from the orchards dotted across several miles of green rolling pasture swept into the house.

Before exploring further, I leaned out over the window, crossed my arms on the sill and took a moment to watch the sunlight hitting the distant water and shattering into a million shards of silver on the gentle swell.

To the side of the property, the grand peaks of the Cordilleras beyond the orchard seemed close enough to touch from the bathroom window; even though separated from it by numerous Grassy meadows criss-crossed with thick hedgerows. The whole place smelt of wood, and time.

After throwing the windows open to all the rooms, I spent a couple of days clearing spider webs from corners and cleaning dead flies from the windowsills. Once I had removed the dust covers from the furniture and cooked a few simple meals in the kitchen, the house slowly came back to life.

Chapter Seventeen

Stretching for a couple of hundred yards, the overgrown back garden of the farmhouse was separated from a sloping grass meadow by a swiftly-flowing stream that ran parallel along the width of the garden. The field beyond this rose gradually to a dense copse of oak and birch trees at the top of the rise.

To the left of the garden, an old post and rail fence line separated it from the apple orchard next door. Six soaring poplar trees grew along its length. Both the orchard and the meadow belonged to the farm.

For the next fortnight I set about the business of tidying and clearing dead grass and overgrown brambles from the vegetable patch in the back garden. There was so much to clear that I had a bonfire most days.

Soon after arriving at the farmhouse, I found an old colour photograph amongst some papers in the bottom draw of the dresser in my grandmother's room. In the picture, my mother held me in her arms one sunny day long ago.

Standing at the back of a tourist boat on the Lake of the All Saints near Bariloche, with the wind in her beautiful black hair, she wore the same white dress with the red rose pattern that she had worn in my dreams so many times before.

That's when I understood; that she had always been there with me, throughout the years of longing for home and family. Right then, a sensation of heat rose swiftly behind my eyes. I felt my bottom lip constrict, then wobble uncontrollably as I held the picture in my hands.

From the photo's fading paper my mother radiated love and pride, hugging me affectionately as we both smiled for the camera. This was the first time I had seen her image in fifteen years, and it made me weep.

Wiping the tears that ran down my cheeks with the sleeve of my shirt, I remembered a time when I was twelve years old, being reprimanded by my father for breaking a neighbour's window.

"Why do you do these things, Sebastián?" he shouted in frustration. "They were good friends of your mothers - what do you think she would say?"

"Well she shouldn't have died then, should she!?" I howled back.

Whilst at the time I had begun to accept that she was gone, there were many painful moments when I wished she could come back again; just for five minutes, just once. If only I could have had one more hug, one last kiss, even just to smell her one more time, I would have let her go again.

Composing myself, I put the picture of my mother and I on the wall of my room, where I could see it from my bed. I wanted her to be the last thing I saw each night and the first thing I saw in the morning.

That evening in bed before falling asleep, I remembered the time back in 1979 when, shortly after my mother's death, my grandmother visited us in Argentina for the first and only time.

She was already sixty years old then and had never met Raul and I before. Arriving at the front door of our house after an internal flight to Bariloche from Buenos Aires, she scooped my bewildered brother and I up in her arms and cried, "You poor poor babies! I'm going to look after you all for a while; everything's going to be alright."

I recall her smelling of apples, and both Raul and I finding her strong Asturian accent fairly peculiar. Later that same night as I lay awake in bed, I heard my father crying out his pain to his mother in the living room.

It frightened me, as it was the only time I had ever

heard him cry.

For the next month of her visit, our grandmother did all she could to help and support us; cooking empanadas, maize cakes filled with minced meat, and comforting rice puddings with cinnamon and lemon; love on a plate.

She played in the garden with us and took us for picnics on the shores of Lake Nauhel Huapi.

After my father told her that I had refused to attend my mother's funeral, she offered to take me to visit her grave to take flowers. Again, I refused.

"What's bothering you, Sebastián?" she asked as she sat on my bed one night. "There's nothing to be frightened of; I will come with you."

"I'm not going!" I said stubbornly, my arms folded across my front with my chin on my chest. "She's not there, and I'm not ever going."

It is one of the defining elements of the human condition, I feel, that in moments of undiluted emotional pain we experience it individually and in isolation. I meant what I said, and I never went to my mother's grave.

One evening over dinner, my grandmother implored my father to return to Europe.

"Why don't you come home to Spain?" she said. "Franco's gone; things are changing."

"It's too late, Mamma. The boys were born here; this is their home. I have my work and this house," he said.

My grandmother looked sad as we finished our meal in silence.

When the time came for her to return to Spain we had become fond of her, just not fond enough to miss her after she'd gone. Thirty-one years later her house was mine, and I had decided to make it my home.

The days at the farm were long and hot. I worked hard and had only Caesar for company. I had chosen a bedroom at the front of the house with a large brass bed and a view of the Bougainvillaea and the lane beyond. Caesar slept downstairs on a rug in front of the old kitchen range.

With my dog as a companion and so much work to be done I didn't have time to be either lonely, or contemplate my newfound solitude.

Having no lawnmower and a rapidly-growing front lawn, I bought a grey billy goat from a local farmer, named him 'Belcourt', and put him out the grass to get on with it.

After finding an old small bore-rifle under a bed in one of the rooms upstairs, I often spent hours at a time exploring the surrounding countryside and hunting small game amongst the forests and over the meadows.

With both France and the Legion now behind me, I began to feel that I had finally severed my links with all that had gone before. As far as I was concerned, what mattered now was focusing on this opportunity to truly begin afresh.

Chapter Eighteen

As May turned into June, much to my surprise I received a text message from Monica.

Sebastián. I'm in Barcelona, where are you? Monica. (From Pau)

I phoned her back. She was upset.

"Sebastián, I was in Marseilles and I got robbed. They broke into my camper and took everything; all my paints and paintings, everything."

"Were you hurt?"

"No, I wasn't there."

"It's okay," I said. "What are you going to do?"

"I don't know; where are you?"

"I'm in Asturias, up on the north coast."

"Where abouts?"

"I'm at a farmhouse near Ribidesella; you can come here if you like. There's just me and the dog."

"Thank you, Sebastián. I am going to come, if that's okay."

"That's fine - call me from Ribidesella and I'll direct you from there."

She arrived late in the morning four days later, after taking directions from me over the phone in town. Taking her into the kitchen, I made us coffee before sitting down to talk.

"So," she asked, "whose is this place?"

"It was my grandmother's. I was born in Argentina, but my family came from here. She died two years ago. I own the place now."

"What will you do for a living?" she asked.

"I get a pension from the Legion and a bit from the sale of cider apples in the orchard at the side. I don't need much. What about you; what are you going to do?"

"I don't know, really. I just don't know. All I know

292

is that I don't want to go back to Laval. There's nothing there for me anymore; there never really was."

"You can stay here if you want. As long as you like. Some company would be nice."

"Thank you, Sebastián. I think I'd like that."

"We can go into town and get you some more paints when you're ready," I said.

That evening I prepared a meal for us and we sat down to cold garlic soup with grapes and bread. Perhaps it was my cooking, but Monica didn't leave. We got along well together and over time we set about making the farmhouse our home, tending the garden and planting vegetables out back.

As spring became summer the meadow behind the house transformed itself into a carpet of wild flowers. Caraway and sulphur clover covered the slope from the stream all the way up to the copse at the top of the rise.

Caesar spent his afternoons chasing Green Hair Streak butterflies and swallowtails amongst the dog-violets and grass vetchlings, before stretching out to doze amongst the wild onions and blue columbines.

By the time a year had passed, tomatoes grew along the front wall of the house and we hung pink and white fuchsias from baskets around the place. We trimmed the orange blossom and grew parsley and mint in the kitchen's window box.

With Monica's help, I turned the vegetable patch into a cornucopia of silver chard, pumpkins, Welsh onions, parsnips and radishes. There were lettuces and potatoes too.

I bought a clutch of Asturian painted hens from the local farmers market and gave them free rein of the front lawn with Belcourt the Goat. They provided us with fresh eggs each day, whilst together, Monica and I settled into a life of quiet simplicity.

In time, we found ourselves living quite happily

together in a world of our own.

Caesar grew into a fine strong dog. He often accompanied me on my frequent hikes into the countryside to hunt and fish. Gradually, Monica started to paint again, selling her work at the local market. Slowly, we made some casual friends in town, and Monica learned Spanish.

One balmy afternoon in the summer of 2007, whilst Caesar tried his best to wrestle a stick from my hand in the front garden, Monica called down to me from our bedroom window.

"Hey, Sebastián," she said. "I've been thinking. We've been here for two years now, and this place doesn't have a name; a farm needs a name."

"What were you thinking of?"

"I don't know. We'll think of something," she said with a smile.

Later that evening, after supper, whilst I read Monica the poem *"The Ballad of the little square"* from Esteban's book of poems by Lorca she suddenly interrupted me. "That's it!" she said. *"Lost Bells."*

I looked up from the book, "That's what?"

"Lost Bells Farm." She smiled. "The name for this place; and what a beautiful poem."

"Yes, it is."

I soon made a wooden plaque with the new name inscribed across it, and nailed it to one of the willow trees at the entrance to the drive.

We now lived at Lost Bells Farm.

Chapter Nineteen

As the seasons came and went, we settled into the rhythms of country life. There were picnics on the beach with langoustines and whelks, the annual apple harvest, and lots of work around the farm. Periodically, we attended the local festivals.

Monica had a softening affect on me as a man, and around the farm in general. She filled the kitchen and living room with fresh flowers, and planted cyclamen and Star of Bethlehem around the bases of the poplar trees between the garden and orchard. In this way, she made her feminine presence felt.

One day, I walked into the bedroom to find her hanging a loop of entwined willow twigs, with bird feathers hanging from its bottom, in the window.

"It's an American Indian dream catcher," she said.

"How does that work, then?"

"The good dreams know how to pass through the willow twigs; they slide down the feathers and into the room."

"And the bad dreams...?"

Stepping down from a small stool, Monica smiled. "Well, they get caught up in the pattern and die in the first light of dawn."

It wasn't something that I necessarily believed in, but I liked the fact that she did.

The following year Monica became pregnant, and we began turning one of the bedrooms at the back of the house into a nursery as we made plans for our new family.

One sunny sunday morning in April when Monica was fourteen weeks pregnant, I sat behind her in the bath, washing her hair with honey and olive oil. A bumblebee hovered in circles above the sink in the corner, and outside the open window a blackbird sang in the apple-blossom.

The spring sunlight reflecting off the snow capped Cordilleras beyond the orchard struck Monica's wet shoulders, and as I massaged her temples, I couldn't help feeling like life was on its way to being somewhere near perfect.

Without warning, Monica tensed and reached up to grip my hands tightly in hers. "Oh, Sebastián," she cried.

"What is it?"

She didn't need to answer. Looking down over her shoulder as she sobbed, I saw the life we had made passing into the warm water and honey as the blackbird sang on.

That night as we lay in bed, even though I held Monica in my arms, I felt far away. Selfishly, I found it hard to reconcile the reality and sadness of my own loss with the fact that, somewhere out in the world, I knew mothers still cried for the sons I had killed.

Then there was the child I'd left behind in Argentina so long ago. Monica wasn't quite so selfish. Turning her face to mine in the dark, she stroked my cheek. "Are you alright, Sebastián?"

Still selfishly thinking of me and my life, I turned my face to the bedroom window before answering, "We hung the dream catcher in the wrong window."

Monica was bereft for some months, and returned to painting with a newfound intensity. Eventually, we picked ourselves up and carried on.

At the end of that summer I cut down five trees in the far corner of the orchard and installed some beehives, the blossom honey from which we sold at the local farmer's market.

By the autumn of 2010 I had passed my fortieth

birthday and put a good twenty years between myself and everything that had happened in Argentina. In that regard, I felt safe.

I shouldn't have.

Chapter Twenty

Autumn, 2010

It was early in November that I rose at dawn one day. Feeling fidgety for some reason, I dressed and decided to take Caesar on a long walk through the fields, leaving Monica sleeping soundly in bed, before heading back to the house for coffee and eggs.

Turning my collar up against the sharp air, we jumped the stream at the end of the garden before striking out across the meadow, our feet slicing swathes of dark green through the mist covering the crisp frosted grass of autumn.

We walked for miles and I lost track of time. At around eleven o'clock in morning we returned, to find Monica in the kitchen drinking tea.

"Someone came here asking about you this morning while you were out."

"Oh?"

"Yes, a young girl. She didn't say what she wanted; just asked if Sebastián Alvarez lived here, that's all."

I took off my coat and hung it on the hook behind the door.

"Is that all? What did you say?"

"Nothing, just that you'd be back later; then she left. She was on a bicycle. She said she'd be back. That's it."

Sitting down at the table with Monica, I poured myself some tea.

"Who do you think she was, Sebastián?"

"I don't know."

We left it at that, but I felt uneasy. After breakfast I drove into town to buy some new boots, then spent the afternoon back at the house chopping logs in the cold at the side of the house.

Later in the evening, as I carried an armful of wood from the side of the house around to the front door at dusk, Monica appeared in the doorway with a mug of coffee. As she passed me the warm drink, a woodcock flew low over the house heading for the copse beyond the dew-strewn meadow.

The kitchen window beside Monica reflected a spectacular mackerel sky, hanging like a silver and red tapestry in the air behind me. Just then, Monica looked over my shoulder and up the drive.

"Oh, she's back."

Turning around, I saw a girl cycling down the drive on a mountain-bike, wrapped up against the cold in a dark fleece and gloves. She wore blue jeans and had a green scarf wrapped several times around her neck.

Slim and pretty with long black hair, her cheeks were pink and flushed against the chill breeze. I put down the logs.

"Hello?" I said, as she drew to a stop in front of me.

"Sebastián Alvarez?"

"Yes... Who...?"

"Sebastián Gonzalo Alvarez from San Carlos de Bariloche?" The girl's breath hung like candyfloss in the air as she spoke.

"Who are you?" I asked.

"My name is Zulima Bauman, and I'm your daughter."

Now there was a silence as we both regarded each other without saying a word. I suddenly felt shocked, vulnerable and exposed; I couldn't think of anything to say. Monica spoke to the girl from the doorway behind me.

"Do you want to come in?"

"Yes; I want to talk."

Still unable to think of anything to say, I stepped to one side as Zulima propped her bike against the house, then I followed her inside with Monica and shut the door on the darkness behind us.

Inside, the warm kitchen smelt of the apple and eucalyptus wood burning in the hearth. Caesar looked up from his place in front of the fire, and wagged his tail. Before we sat down at the kitchen table, Monica spoke.

"Would you two like to be alone?"

"No," I said. "What about you, Zulima?" I asked.

"No, it's fine. Are you his wife?" she asked Monica.

"No; we live together, it's been nearly five years. I'll make some more coffee - would you like anything to eat?"

"No, really."

When we were all seated, I ventured the obvious question.

"Who told you where I was?"

"My Uncle Raul; he doesn't want to know you, but things have happened back home and I pressed him to tell me. I have a right to find you."

"It's okay; I understand," I said, looking down at the table.

Monica poured coffee for all of us, then sat back calmly.

"Where are you staying?" I asked.

"I'm in a *pension* in town, its fine. I just flew into Madrid three days ago."

"Oh, okay," I said.

Wrapping both hands around her mug, Zulima took a sip of coffee, then looked at me across the table.

"Mama died."

My heart constricted. Closing my eyes, I sank a little in my chair; images returned of Tania, laughing and galloping beside me in the sunshine years ago.

"What happened?"

"It was a brain haemorrhage, she didn't suffer. It

was in June."

"I'm sorry," I said. "I loved her."

Glancing to one side, Zulima gave a weak shrug and I felt ashamed. Monica reached over and covered my hand with hers. I tried to drink some coffee, but it wouldn't go down. Shifting in my chair, I looked straight at Zulima.

"I suppose you know what happened before you were born, then?"

Before she even answered, I felt the blood begin to throb in my palms wrapped around my mug, and through the scar at my temple.

"Yes," she said.

"You killed my Uncle Ignacio, and ran away."

Chapter Twenty-One

Monica looked up at me with a start, her mouth falling open. "Sebastián?"

What could I say?

"It's true, Monica. I did something terrible, but I'm not a murderer, there's more to it than that. I…"

Monica looked at Zulima. "What did he do?"

"I'm not sure; it was before I was born. Let him tell us himself."

I had nothing else to hide, nowhere else to run. The past had followed me 7,000 miles and landed right at my table.

In the aftermath of my actions my name had become mud in Bariloche, and the Bauman's never spoke of me again, although they nurtured and cherished my daughter their whole lives. It was time to talk.

I rubbed my temples and forehead with the tips of my fingers. It was time to get it all out. Whilst I wanted to know what had become of my father and what efforts had been made by the authorities to hunt me down, now wasn't the time for being selfish.

As the Bauman's never spoke of me since it all happened, back home in Bariloche rumours had contradicted rumours over the years, and Zulima wanted answers. It was only fair that I should tell her and Monica the whole sorry tale; and besides, I'd told enough lies to last a lifetime.

Chapter Twenty-Two

Argentine Patagonia, Christmas 1989

My family had been invited over to the Bauman's ranch for Christmas day. My father, brother and his girlfriend Ruth had all made the drive from town and down the long track to Tania's place for a festive lunch in the valley.

We all sat together around the old pine table on the wide veranda. Tania's father cooked half a lamb over hot coals in an open pit. Her mother roasted eight small chickens wrapped in bacon and filled with butter, and herbs from her garden.

There were bowls of fresh salad with crushed pistachio nuts and orange slices, sweet potatoes with melted marshmallows, and plenty of cold Quilmes lager and white wine mixed with fruit juice. For dessert, Tania and Ruth made flan *panqueques* with caramel, cream and rum.

This was Christmas as it's supposed to be; a time for family and friends, food and conversation. During lunch, Tania's mother smiled as she poured me a beer.

"How are you getting along with your studies, Sebastián?"

"It's a lot of hard work, but I've finished my essay on the Argentine constitution, so I have until the end of the first week in January to relax."

"Not too relaxing, though," said Ignacio. "Remember we are heading into the Sierras to fish in a few days!"

"Don't worry," I said. "We're going to have a good time. It's definitely going to be more interesting than the amendments to the constitution of 1853 and the division of Political power since 1860, and..."

"Yes, yes," he laughed. "We get the picture - now

where are those *panqueques* and rum?"

We had planned on heading into the mountains on horseback together with a friend of Ignacio's, Ricardo - who I didn't know - to catch landlocked Atlantic salmon. The trip should have lasted around four to five days.

We would be sleeping on roll-mats under the stars. My intention was to return from the trip and, along with Tania, inform both our families of the news that we wanted to be married and move to Buenos Aires by the end of that summer. It wasn't going to work out that way.

Around a fortnight before going on Christmas leave, my class at the Academy had been on a military exercise with the army on the pampas outside Buenos Aires. We learned some rudimentary infantry skills such as basic patrolling and navigating at night, and broadened our knowledge of the different weapons that we might have at our disposal during our careers in the Gendarmeria.

One of the weapons we were introduced to was the grenade. In order to learn how to use these effectively and safely, students were taken individually by an instructor along an L-shaped reinforced concrete trench around six feet high. The leading edge of the trench that constituted the bottom of the L-shape faced a long wide pit of sand that would catch the grenades and allow them to explode in a static position, without them rolling around.

When my turn to throw my two allocated bombs came, the army Sergeant emerged from the trench, then led me along its length and around the corner to its leading edge.

"When you're ready, Alvarez."

I took a grenade from my equipment pouch with my right hand and held it at chest height.

My knees began to shake as I pulled the pin with my left hand, leaving a live bomb in my right. As per instructions I looked the sergeant in the face and then, as calmly as I could, looked firstly towards my right hand then my left, before issuing the standard declaration.

"PIN! GRENADE!"

"CARRY ON!" ordered the instructor.

The reason for delivering this declaration is that it has been known in the past for inexperienced recruits to panic immediately on pulling the pin on a grenade, and actually throw the pin and keep the bomb.

Spreading my legs, I threw the weapon as hard as I could over the lip of the trench, then watched as it took a wide arc through the pale sky. Instinctively I went to duck, but the Sergeant grabbed me by my equipment straps, forced me up onto my tiptoes, and snarled, "WATCH!"

I registered the place in the pit where the grenade landed, and screamed, "SEEN!"

This procedure is necessary in case a particular grenade fails to detonate and is buried in the sand. In this event, the student who has thrown the device has the task of walking out into the sandpit with a bomb disposal expert to show him exactly where it has landed. The sergeant let me go and we ducked, the grenade went bang, and I went on to throw another bomb and left the trench.

That was in the morning. The beginning of the end of my life in Argentina began after lunch.

Myself and another student named Rodriguez had gone in a Jeep with another sergeant, back to the armoury to pick up more grenades for the afternoon training session of another group.

As officer candidates we were trusted and expected to take responsibility on board early in our careers.

That being the case, Rodriguez and I were left to look after the Jeep behind the weapons range and check all the grenades back in that were left over after training.

We were responsible for the entire paper inventory for all the grenades assigned to that vehicle. What did we do with that responsibility? We abused it.

I took two grenades for myself, and altered the figures on the paperwork so that they wouldn't be missed. By saying nothing, Rodriguez colluded. What was I thinking of ? Looking back, I simply don't know or can't remember. I must just assume that I wasn't thinking at all.

What I did know was that Christmas leave was approaching, I was heading home to Patagonia, and I was going to have some fun with those grenades.

Chapter Twenty-Three

That's how I came to be carrying two small bombs amongst the supplies in my saddlebags as I set out on the New Year's fishing trip with Ignacio and Ricardo.

Christmas came and went. Our families socialised, enjoyed meals together, and went to church.

On New Years Eve, together with the Bauman's, my family and I stood on the lawn of the ranch house and watched the last sun of the 1980s take a graceful bow behind the mighty peaks of the Andes mountain range. We drank a toast to all our futures and wished each other well.

At midnight, Ignacio and I set fireworks off on the lawn, standing back as brocades of red, gold, silver and blue burst in the night sky above us.

When the last rocket had been spent, Tania and I decided to share our news with our families early.

Every one seemed happy as we retreated to the warmth of the ranch house. At its steps, señor Bauman held me back.

"Let's take a walk down to the river, Sebastián."

Once at the water's edge, I began to shiver in the darkness. Below the freezing water the sound of large rocks bumping over each other on the riverbed seemed to grumble disapprovingly. Señor Bauman lit a Montecristo cigar, then offered me one.

"Thank you." I said.

"You've grown up a lot, Sebastián."

"Thank you; I think so too."

Señor Bauman looked up at the moon. I noticed its light sparkle in his eyes, before he turned his head to face me.

"I'm only going to say this once," he said menacingly. "If you ever hurt my daughter, or fail to look after her properly, I will kill you, boy." Suddenly the smoke from my cigar caught in the back of my throat and I was overcome by a coughing fit.

Helpfully, Señor Bauman slapped me hard on the back several times. I got the message. The 1990s announced themselves at dawn the following day.

At first light, we saddled up to go fishing. Above us in the valley virgin white clouds, seized by a blaze of crimsons and pinks, blushed and then turned angry; shot through with vivid streaks of bloody vermillion, bursting and glowing across an impossibly wide sky.

Looking up at the natural canvas daubed with the paintbrush of creation, it was easy to believe in a brighter future and that all was well with the world.

None of us could have foreseen that the new decade would give rise to the conflicts about to erupt in Iraq, Europe and the Balkans, or what was about to come because of me.

Those things were, however, on their way and I was to be part of them, even though I could never have imagined the tangent my life was about to take as I mounted my horse and headed into the wild that early morning with Ignacio and Ricardo.

Heading west that first day, the sun rose through the trees behind us, sending beams of amber light streaking past our little group and up the valley as if to light the way ahead.

Taking things steadily we ambled through the landscape, passing around cigarettes and engaging in easy throwaway chat. There was no hurry and it was good to break the horses in gently.

We rode at a steady pace, before stopping by a lake in the afternoon. We had a swim and ate bread and cheese. Later, amongst a tiny natural clearing deeper in the forest we made a camp.

Ricardo found a small snake in a rotting log and we spent time teasing it with a stick, before getting bored and opening some beers and frying bacon on the fire. That evening, Ignacio talked of his plans for the future.

"I think when I take over the ranch, I'm going to try and get more land to the east of here and raise sheep and do less of the fruit."

"What about the horses?" I asked.

"Oh, we will always breed Criollos, but I have never been interested in the fruit."

"You're so lucky, Ignacio. You're gonna inherit that ranch house and all that land - most of the valley," said Ricardo.

I chipped in.

"When I get my helicopter pilot's licence I'm gonna fly down here, Ignacio, pick up your sister, fly her up to Mendoza, and buy her dinner," I joked.

"Yes and you can fly me around my land so I can keep an eye on my flocks, ha ha..."

For breakfast the next day we made porridge and fried eggs, before moving on. We were heading for a clear shallow river in a wide valley with only a scattering of trees higher into the Sierras. I didn't know the place, although Ignacio and Ricardo had been there before.

At around two o'clock that afternoon we struck the valley and followed the course of the river up stream for about a mile or so.

"There's some very low rapids a little further on from here," Ricardo said. "It's past this bend a way. The plunge pool is pretty deep and there's always trout in there."

Happy and relaxed, Ignacio and Ricardo smiled as we rode, their faces flushed, radiating youth and health in the clean southern air.

"Okay, great. It'll be good to have a little practice here before we get to the salmon higher up." I said. "If we catch a couple, we can have them for lunch."

I had already decided how the fish were to be caught. I was going to show off, impress the hell out of my two companions and use the stolen grenades to bomb the plunge pool and kill all the fish in it.

They would see that I hadn't totally sold out to the system. I would show them that I could still be a loose cannon and a free spirit.

We arrived at the pool under the rapids, dismounted, and unpacked the rods and tackle. I refilled my water canteen at the water's edge.

"Look over there!" said Ricardo, pointing at some brown shapes loping around the scrub to the north across the width of the valley. "There are some hares running around up here!" he said.

"You two start fishing," I said. "I want to go and see if I can shoot one."

Leaving my saddle-bags, sleeping-roll, blanket and fishing rod on the ground, I got on my horse and pulled my 22 rifle from its holder below the saddle's cantle.

Setting off north at a gentle trot, I held my reins high over the saddle's horn in my left hand, gripping the rifle with my right by my hip.

There were several large hares in the distance, all of which quickly took flight and disappeared into the distance, kicking up little puffs of light grey dust as soon as their huge ears and large brown eyes alerted them to my approach.

Having quickly given up on the idea that I might get a shot at one of the animals I decided, just for fun, to try and outrun them.

Flaying my mount's flanks with the soft leather reins, by flicking my left wrist rapidly from side to side, I let him feel the firm presence of my spurs at his sides.

I remember the musky smell of horse sweat filling my nostrils, and his hooves making the sound of ten more like him on the hard ground beneath us.

I didn't have to be in class. I didn't have to report for duty, and my assignments were up to date. Tania was having my baby; I was in love and still in my teens, if only just.

For one brief moment and for the last time, as I chased those hares across the Patagonian scrub with the wind in my hair, I felt free.

Then I heard the bang.

Chapter Twenty-Four

Racing back to the river as fast as I could, I met Ricardo and Ignacio's horses galloping past me the other way at speed; Ignacio's mount, Chuchi, was streaked with blood. Panic and fear rose inside me.

Arriving at the water's edge, I found Ricardo on his knees, bleeding badly. Pulling my horse up beside him with a firm yank on the reins, I looked down into his eyes, wide and glassy with shock.

"We were just playing!" he pleaded.

Lying face-up at the water's edge, Ignacio's broken body lay crumpled and lifeless. He was gone.

The two of them had found my grenades and decided to have some fun with them.

Unable to take in the scene before me and unable to cope with what I had done, without saying a word I dropped my rifle, turned my horse around, and bolted.

First my horse lost a shoe in flight, and then at some point it started to rain, which slowed me down even further. It took the rest of the day to reach the highway, and my rendezvous with Juan Cruz and his truck.

Chapter Twenty-Five

So that was it. In stealing the grenades I had committed a federal crime, my actions led to the death of my girlfriend's innocent brother and badly wounded his equally innocent friend.

That grenade blew our families apart and changed all our lives forever, the consequences spreading like ripples on a lake after a stones been thrown in.

It was late when I had finished talking, and we were all tired. Monica said nothing. What could she say? I felt drained.

Zulima looked at me across the table. I spoke before she could.

"It was an accident, you understand…"

"Was it? Nobody made you steal those grenades; that wasn't an accident!"

I didn't know what to say. But Zulima did.

"Accidents don't happen, they are *caused*."

I couldn't disagree, and rubbed my eyes with the full palms of both my hands. Perhaps now Zulima felt I was backed into a corner and that the dialogue had no where else to go.

"Mama married a good man; they raised me together on the ranch until Grandpapa couldn't carry on. He lives in town now with Grandmama; they know I'm here."

"Your mother; was she happy?" I asked.

"She told me once, when I was younger and asked her about it all, that she had cried a river of tears, then built a bridge over them."

Monica looked into the coffee mug cradled in her hands and smiled a slow sad smile

"What became of my father?" I asked.

"He was ashamed. He moved away to Puerto Madryn on the coast."

"Is he…"

"He's still alive. He married a widow; they live in a bungalow behind the dunes. He retired. I have never had much contact with him."

The fire in the hearth was dying out. Caesar got up off his rug, turned around in a circle a couple of times, then settled back down to sleep. Now Monica spoke.

"I think that's enough talking for tonight. We should all get some sleep. You'll stay, of course, Zulima?"

Perhaps somewhat rudely, I raised my hand, showing Monica its palm as if to stop her talking.

"Wait…"

Getting up from the table, I left the kitchen and went into the sitting room. Once there, I retrieved the medals I had been awarded in the Legion from the bottom drawer of a chest, and then returned to the kitchen to sit back down. Placing the bits of ribbon and tin on the table in front of me, I pushed them slowly towards Zulima.

"Here; they're all I've got, all I've got to show for myself. Not much I know, but… take them."

"I don't want them."

"Well… I am your father when all's said and done, and I *have* earned them. Like I say, it's not much, but at least you know that I have done something."

"I won't take your medals, Señor Alvarez."

"Señor Alvarez; it sounds so formal. You could…"

She cut me off.

"Señor Alvarez, I don't want your medals, I want something else."

"Well, yes, okay… what is it? What can I do?"

"Señor Alvarez, I want you to come with me."

"Go with you; where? Go when? I…"

She didn't answer. Instead, she unzipped her fleece a couple of inches, fixed her eyes on mine, and reached inside to pull out a gold chain. As I watched, a metal badge attached to the end of the chain began to emerge.

In the middle of the badge was a cockerel, pictured sideways on. Standing erect, the bird displayed a crest running along the crown of its head, from front to back. Behind the cockerel was a raised map in the shape of the Federal district of Buenos Aires.

I can't remember now what I did at that exact moment; I suppose I just looked at the badge. I do know that I didn't say anything. I remember Monica pushing her chair back, then slowly and silently placing her hands on the table, palms down in front of her with her coffee mug between them.

I remember her slowly dropping her head like a flower wilting in the heat, until her forehead rested on the table-top next to the mug between her hands. 'Zulima' spoke again. This time into the sleeve of her fleece, which was now raised to her mouth.

"He's ready; so am I..." she said.

Reality began to sink in. I recognised the discipline, pitch and tone of a radio procedure voice, as 'Zulima' spoke calmly and succinctly into the microphone concealed in her sleeve. She then turned to me coldly.

"Sebastián Gonzalo Alvarez; I am Officer Spalter of the Argentine Federal Police, and I have a warrant for your arrest and extradition to Argentina."

My hand tightened around my medals, as if they could somehow save me; as if holding on to them tightly enough would somehow stop me from being taken away.

"Senor, I have two colleagues waiting to meet you outside, together with members of the Spanish Civil Guard."

Now the soldier inside me kicked in, and my mind switched on. Sensing this, the police officer in Spalter did the same.

"You have a stream at the end of your garden, Senor

315

Alvarez; there are guards posted there, and others in the meadow beyond also..."

At that moment, the front door opened and two guards of the Guarda Civil walked into the kitchen's open doorway. With them were two men in suits. Around their necks on gold chains they wore the badge of the Argentine Federal Police. The younger of the two had blonde hair; the older one had his silver grey hair cut short in a close crop. As the soldier in me finally gave up, so too did the fugitive.

I was going home.

Epilogue

Federal Penal Institute,
Campo de Mayo, Buenos Aires province, Argentina.

They gave me seven years. Most of my days are spent at Lost bells farm; but only in my mind you understand. They can't lock that up.

During a cold case review into my crime and disappearance, the police had called at Raul's home in Buenos Aires. During a search of his study, they had found the letter I had sent him from France in 1990, and had taken things from there.

Given the choice of telling the police what he knew and being taken to a downtown police station for questioning, my brother had quite rightly put his family first and told them where he presumed I would be.

Once back in Argentina, I pleaded guilty to the theft of the grenades and involuntary manslaughter. What was the point in lying? Officer Spalter had done her job well. Using one of the oldest tricks in the book, she had lied by telling the truth and recorded my whole confession.

Zulima had been born at the Bauman's ranch six months after I fled the country. Tania had brought her up with her parents and later her husband, until her death in 2010.

Several weeks prior to Spalter's arrival at the farm I was stopped in my car by a Guarda civil patrol in the lane that runs past Lost Bells Farm. The officer asked to see my papers and ID. I told him my address and that I was a French citizen.

"And your accent?" he asked.

"Oh, I was born in Argentina."

The next day I drove into Ribidesella and presented

my vehicle's paperwork and my passport at the station. They took my fingerprints and told me that it was just standard procedure as I wasn't a Spanish national. Of course, they were providing confirmation of my identity to Argentine law enforcement.

Some of the things that catch you out in this life are so obvious that you tend to miss them easily. So many years had passed that I had gotten comfortable.

In an attempt at making life here more bearable, once in prison I asked my father to send me a couple of books a month to read, which he does regularly. He also writes fortnightly. In his last letter he described beautifully how he had been watching hump-backed whales breaching in the ocean from his balcony overlooking the dunes to the sea beyond.

One of the warders here, who for reasons of his own took an instant dislike to me, decided to rip out the last page of every book my father sent. This way he ensured I never knew how a story ended.

Finding this behaviour reminiscent of Corporal Amars years before, and feeling powerless, I quickly became enraged. Kicking and punching the walls, I would curse the warder through the observation hatch of my cell door, a reaction he found most satisfying.

In some respects, life in the Legion prepared me well for being where I am now. Routine, discipline and rules are all part of life in an institution. After leading such an active life I found it hard at first, being locked in a cell for the greater part of each day. In the end, I've had no choice.

My father has committed to making the long journey from his home in Puerto Madryn twice a year to visit me. My beautiful daughter Zulima visits once a month from her home in Lujan outside Buenos Aires. Raul stays away, and I accept that. Monica still lives at Lost Bells Farm with Caesar, and no doubt in time she will meet someone. If that happens, I will have to accept that too.

After everything I've been through and seen, I didn't think that there was much to be gained or learned from being locked up in here; but I was wrong.

Whilst shaving alone in the shower-block one day, my eye was caught by a single drop of quivering water hanging from the ceiling.

Out of nothing but sheer boredom, I stopped shaving and watched the droplet as it slowly but surely lost its tenuous grip on the ceiling. In the instant before falling, I observed that it suddenly became totally calm and still.

As it fell through the air on its journey to the floor there was a moment, just a brief moment, about a third of the way down, when a rainbow struck the drop, filling it with a kaleidoscope of colour.

As it hit the floor, the rainbow was gone. The water was still there, but the colours were gone. And that's when I realised a truth about life; and that is this.

The moment we are born, we are as a droplet separating from the ceiling. The inevitable journey to the floor amounts to the sum of our life. Some people fall from high ceilings and others from low ones, but we all fall and we all hit the floor. It is the space in the middle that counts, because that's where the colours are; and therein lays the magic.

The colours are always there. We just have to catch them and let them fill us up while we can. Everything else is a waste of precious time. Each of us is on a journey.

We all laugh, cry, hurt and heal. We find love and we lose it again; but if we can be the best that we can be, give the best we have to give, love and be loved, then I believe we have made our journey worthwhile.

This is the only approach with value and meaning I now believe.

There comes a point in everyone's journey, I think, when we realise that we are very much closer to the floor than the ceiling. That's the time when the laughter comes from the throat and not the stomach. The smile, whilst still there, no longer parts the lips.

This can be the result of fatigue and regret, or if one is lucky, it is the result of contentment. The giveaway is in the eyes.

It is not how we begin, or how we end up that counts, as we all begin and end in the same way. What matters is the experience.

Back in my cell, I continued reading one of my father's books. As usual, the warder had ripped out the last page. That's when I realised another truth. I realised that I wasn't the only one locked up.

The warder was locked in a cell far smaller than anything the system could throw a man into. He was locked inside the cell of his bitter little mind, and with very little chance of ever escaping.

I began to make up the endings to my books for myself; expanding stories and having them end how I wanted them to. In this way I found a new freedom, and from there I began to write for myself.

Everything's relative; life tends to give with one hand and take with the other. My Legion pension is accumulating in a Spanish bank, and I'm free of the lies I once lived by.

I now understand that prison, like the Legion, is just part of my own personal journey. I did what I did, I made mistakes, and I'm paying the price. That's life; and whilst I'm obviously not going anywhere anytime soon, I do have hope.

Because if I can find a rainbow inside a prison, I can find enough hope inside myself to hold on until the day that I return to Lost Bells Farm...

French translations for Lost Bells Farm by Dr Aurelian pommier of Clermont Ferrand - France.

Lightning Source UK Ltd.
Milton Keynes UK
UKOW03f1244260814

237591UK00005B/510/P